VERITY VANISHES

A B MORGAN

This edition produced in Great Britain in 2022

by Hobeck Books Limited, Unit 14, Sugnall Business Centre, Sugnall, Stafford, Staffordshire, ST21 6NF

www.hobeck.net

A CIP catalogue for this book is available from the British Library.

ISBN 978-1-913-793-79-1 (pbk)

ISBN 978-1-913-793-78-4 (ebook)

Cover design by Jayne Mapp Design

Printed and bound in Great Britain

❀ Created with Vellum

VERITY VANISHES

ARE YOU A THRILLER SEEKER?

Hobeck Books is an independent publisher of crime, thrillers and suspense fiction and we have one aim – to bring you the books you want to read.

For more details about our books, our authors and our plans, plus the chance to download free novellas, sign up for our newsletter at **www.hobeck.net**.

You can also find us on Twitter **@hobeckbooks** or on Facebook **www.facebook.com/hobeckbooks10**.

FOREWORD

The story told in these pages is a work of fiction inspired by some true events that occurred during the first 2020 lockdown and which fired my imagination. The need for discretion prevents me from giving away the finer details. Suffice to say that a friendship borne out of adversity gave rise to some outrageous WhatsApp exchanges and the plotline for this story.

This book also makes reference to Fairfield Hospital, somewhere I had close connections to and visited on a number of memorable occasions, although I never worked there in my time as a registered mental health nurse.

The history of the place is fascinating and is captured in *A Place in the Country: Three Counties Asylum 1860–1999* by Judith Pettigrew, Rory W. Reynolds and Sandra Rouse (Hertfordshire Publications, 2017).

To Yasmin, whose inquisitive nature and sense of humour inspired this story. Good neighbours are a gift not to be taken for granted.

FINDING HERSELF

*H*er name was on the headstone, but her body did not lie in the grave. In the light summer drizzle, Cara Laidlaw closed her eyes for a moment and swallowed down the wave of despondency that arose as she read the words carved in the granite: *Taken by the angels to do the Lord's bidding.* The dates were in days rather than years because the baby born to Gregor and Muriel Laidlaw had lived for less than three weeks; a fact Cara knew nothing about. Her father, who had succumbed to cancer two months previously, had taken her hand two days before he died and declared how much he loved her. Even then he didn't reveal the secret held tightly for so long. Instead, it fell to the family solicitor and executor-nominate of his will to hand deliver an envelope to Cara.

The first lines of her father's letter were etched in her mind: *'Our darling daughter, there is something you must know...'* The end paragraph of that heart-rending disclosure was the catalyst to Cara's compulsion to turn her back on the present and unravel the mystery of what her own life could have been.

'Given your enquiring mind and thirst for knowledge, no doubt you will choose to seek out your birth family. A word of warning;

prepare yourself to uncover a harrowing truth. However, always know in your heart that our overwhelming love for you remains as enduring in death as it did in life. Choose your friends wisely, keep that wonderful zest for life burning bright in your eyes and be true to yourself. We will always be with you.'

Tucked safely away to be read dozens of times over, Cara was now left to grieve the painful loss of both parents and wonder at their deception. Believing she was an only child, a much-loved daughter who was doted upon and encouraged all her life, with their parting she learned that she was a replacement. Cara mark two. Adopted to fill the void left by the death of their real child and named after her. She didn't doubt that she had been loved, but that fact hurt deep inside somehow.

It hadn't taken her long to find the grave; it was in the cemetery where her parents were buried side by side as they had stipulated, and she had followed those wishes without question. They had chosen to be buried in the land of their birth, because for her parents it was a homecoming. The grave of baby Cara Louise Laidlaw was to be found near a small coppice at the edge of the cemetery, outside the town of Paisley, miles away from the small North Yorkshire village where Cara had been brought up.

Apart from the constant hum of the M8 close by, the graveyard itself was a peaceful place, somewhere she had chosen to visit each year and lay flowers at her mother's grave on her birthday; the place her father was laid now to rest, a place for contemplation but not somewhere Cara wandered around noting names of the dearly departed, until today.

Interred together, her parents were a mere fifty feet from where their only real offspring was buried. A family reunited in death.

Cara Laidlaw stared again at her name, wrapping the lightweight raincoat around herself for comfort. 'Well, wee baby Cara, I hope I've made a good job of living your life for you.

Make no mistake, your mum and dad were the best you could have wished for.' She glanced across at the graves nearby before smiling down weakly at the small ivy-clad headstone. 'They were the kindest, most hardworking, and generous people I've ever known. You could not have done better. Thanks for lending them to me. I'm off now. Time to find my real parents because I can't stay being you forever. As soon as I do, you can have your name back. Lovely though it is, it doesn't belong to me.' She sniffed and rummaged for a tissue in her pocket. 'Look after them for me.'

NO PLACE LIKE HOME

*T*he ringing sound in her telephone headset distracted Cara and she was forced to refocus her attention on her computer screen where she immediately identified the caller and adjusted the mouthpiece.

'Cara Laidlaw. How can I help you, Brian?' The managing director for Archer Home Care Solutions had become more demanding than usual since her upgrade of their website. It was hard to drag her eyes away from her personal emails, but she had work to do, so she picked up a pen ready to scribble notes and instructions.

'The hit rate on the care packages has gone through the roof,' Brian said, and she could hear the smile in his voice as he thanked her for her efforts.

'Glad to hear that. It's one of the many things you pay me for,' she replied, forcing herself to sound chipper. Indeed, website management was only one of the many tasks she carried out in the course of a working day. Although not exactly scintillating, being a virtual administrator paid the bills and was proving to be helpful for Cara as far as flexibility was concerned. Wherever she went now, she could take her work with her.

Ending the call to Brian, relieved he hadn't wanted anything more than to compliment her, she settled back at her desk where her eyes fell on a large envelope containing another contract awaiting her signature. She tore at the envelope to release the contents.

Her main income stream came in the form of freelance research, mostly signposted her way by Channel 7 documentaries. They were in the throes of producing a new series with TV personality, journalist, and presenter Konrad Neale. Expecting her participation, some time ago she had been sent an outline of the episodes and a schedule. The format had been decided upon a year in advance and was yet another remake of *This is Your Life*, once fronted many decades previously by Eamon Andrews, then Michael Aspel, newscaster Trevor McDonald and now they were trundling out the same show making use of Konrad Neale's magnetic charm. Cara couldn't recall ever having seen it but quickly accessed archive footage on YouTube.

'Oh well, in for a penny,' she said ruefully. 'Even if it means having to cope with your excessive demands, Mr Neale.'

One hand on the computer mouse, the other idly fingering the pages, she read through the final lines of the most recent contract before reaching for her pen. A shrill but sweet chirping sound made her turn before she added the date to her swirling signature.

'Give yourself a break there, Jimmy, if you wouldn't mind. I have thinking to do. And I'll thank you both to remember that you are on borrowed time, so pipe down.' She hated the fact that if compelled to do so, she would have to find new homes for her father's two budgies – Jimmy and Rab McTartan. Purchased to keep him company after Cara's mother had died, they were now in her care and wheedling their way into her affections. They hopped about on their perches as she talked to them, bobbing their heads in syncopated rhythm.

Her new landlord had been unequivocal: 'Any noise complaints and they are out. The tenancy agreement is clear enough; no pets... but I'm making an exception for goldfish, stick insects and for your budgerigars. Just this once.' Cara had given the sob story, ladling it on thick, and vowed to be a responsible pet owner, promising never to allow the birds to fly free in the property. She had her fingers crossed at the time.

The phone rang again, this time a personal number.

'How are you doing, Bev?' Cara asked, checking her watch.

'Never mind me. More to the point... how are you?' Since her move to Bosworth Bishops, her old friend Beverley Brown had taken to calling daily, usually during her office lunch break. 'Have you decided to come home for Christmas? You will come, won't you? We've plenty of room, you'll be no bother.'

The knot that had formed in Cara's gut the day she found out she was adopted, tightened slightly. The last few years had been spent living in Essex with her boyfriend Matt. From their home in Rayleigh, she had frequently commuted into London for work because, since leaving university, that was the direction her career had taken her. With a busy life and irregular demands, her visits home to Yorkshire had become infrequent, even during her father's protracted illness. 'I'm not sure where home is anymore,' she confessed. 'I'm not even a Northerner.'

'Anyone hearing you talk right now would argue that with you. So will I. You grew up here, you're a lass just like me. A Tyke. Anyhow, the new flat... taking shape, is it?'

Cara looked around her at the lack of furniture and bare walls. 'Not really, if I'm honest. The office space is just grand, but as for the rest of it... I'll get there.'

'Started those tablets yet? You should... they could do you good.'

'Tablets aren't the answer and no matter what that doctor

said, there is no way I'm taking antidepressants. I've just had a shite time of it lately.'

There was a mocking laugh from her old pal. 'Shite is the word. Lost both parents, Matty chickens out and pisses back off to his wife, you find out you're adopted, and a soft Southerner… why you had to up sticks and move to Bosworth Bishops makes no sense to me. You should have moved back here with your friends…' Bev let out a sigh of resignation and added, 'Still, it could be worse. You could have been a Wankastrian.'

The laugh from Cara was instinctive though edged with sadness. She missed Bev with an ache in her chest. Bev was her rock and Bev always spoke her mind. She now said firmly, 'It don't matter to me where you were born. You were made in Yorkshire. Any sign of a neighbour yet?'

'No. All quiet so far, but the streak o'piss from the letting agent tells me there's one moving into the flat next door in about three weeks. He's right useless so I'll double the estimate.'

'And have you spoken to *her* yet?'

Cara knew exactly who Bev was referring to. She shook her head. 'No. As I said yesterday, I've seen her once from a distance so far. I've made friends with her cat though… Look, Bev… I have to be certain before I make any overtures. I'm biding my time, keeping a low profile. As your gran would have said, "a nail sticking up gets hammered".'

'I'm still in shock,' Bev said.

'About what? That I'm adopted?'

'Aye, that too. But I meant about what you're up to now. What on earth possessed you?'

3

A LINK

*D*espite her best efforts, the search for her birth parents had taken far longer than Cara had imagined possible and had resulted in minimal information and frustrations aplenty. According to her father's letter, Cara's birth mother was called Verity Anne Hudson and with that information she had been able to apply for her original birth certificate. While she waited for it to arrive, she had trawled the electoral register, social media, registers of births, deaths, and marriages, and contacted the official organisations for adoptees, but with limited luck.

When her birth certificate came in the post, it brought with it a shocking discovery. As she had hoped, it bore the name of the baby girl; her name – Caroline: Caroline Hudson. Other than that, the record was a puzzle. The female child born to Verity Anne Hudson, widow, aged thirty-one, maiden name Thorn, had been given no middle name. No father's name was recorded either, just the word "unknown" in the space where that should have appeared. Place of birth: Fairfield Hospital, Arlesey, Bedfordshire.

At first glance, Cara had smiled briefly at the sight of her real name; Caroline. 'Not too bad,' she said. It was a name not too dissimilar to the one she had been called all her life. Then the questions began to form in her mind. *Why not name the father? She's already a widow but...* Nervily, she scanned the precious document in her shaking hands as if answers would somehow reveal themselves if she willed them to. 'That may explain the adoption, I suppose. Mr Hudson ups and dies, and she can't cope with a baby...' This was one of several possible scenarios, Cara conceded.

Her subsequent internet searches into Fairfield Hospital revealed an appalling fact. 'Christ-al-bloody-mighty!' she blurted out as the truth about where she was born revealed itself on her computer screen. The hospital had closed in the late 1990s because it was a psychiatric facility, not a General Hospital as Cara had assumed, thus revealing an alarming possibility. Battling with the rising fears, she recalled the carefully chosen words in her father's letter to her. 'Prepare yourself to uncover a harrowing truth'. The mystery was a galling one. *Had her mother worked at Fairfield hospital or was she a patient when she gave birth? How long had she been there? Was she a victim of rape?* Cara's insides churned with every awful thought that occurred to her.

As legally required, Social Services held the details of her adoption on file, so she was left to make a Subject's Records Request hoping to find answers. With endless forms to complete it was a protracted exercise and the wait could be months. Even then, she was told, there was no guarantee she would be allowed full access.

She had already found the marriage records for Verity Anne Hudson which confirmed that Verity had married Raymond Charles Hudson when she was only twenty years old, he a much older man in his forties. Ray died when Verity was pregnant, because the birth certificate for Caroline Hudson confirmed the birth as taking place less than six months after Ray Hudson's death. If this was the case, then why hadn't he been named as the father? The mysteries had begun to pile up.

Thwarted by bureaucracy, out of desperation Cara made a rash decision. With a promise to 'find new branches of your family tree' and 'discover new relatives' she bought a DNA testing kit and set about finding whether she had any other family members out there in the world. Family who could lead her to her mother.

* * *

*W*hen she was informed by Ancestors Reunited of the astounding news that there was a highly likely match, Cara had danced around the budgie cage until she could no longer catch her breath. There was a cousin on her mother's side and a glimmer of hope on the horizon. 'I have a tribe,' she shouted. 'I belong to someone!'

In no time at all, both parties were put in touch anonymously, each corresponding through the dedicated email provided by Ancestors Reunited. Cara's cousin, calling themselves "Only Child 125", revealed much in the frequent correspondence that ensued. "Only Child 125" was male, in his late thirties, married, two children, privately educated, trying hard to please a high-achieving father who had lofty expectations of his only son. Little by little the clues came and were slotted together by Cara who, in sharp contrast, held back. Careful not to let slip anything significant about her personal circumstances, she gave herself the pseudonym "Timid Mouse" – a name designed to give the impression of someone unlikely to be gutsy enough to meet face-to-face and she consistently declined offers to speak over the phone. All in all, Cara had reservations about the wisdom of direct contact, and rightly so. All her careful research led to the conclusion that she was related to the Harkness family. She didn't know how this was possible, but if the facts and the genetics were correct then nothing else seemed to fit.

* * *

*S*he looked again at the list containing the names of the celebrities timetabled to make an appearance on *This is Your Life*; an Olympic rower, a renowned scientist, an author, a musician, a newscaster, and an entrepreneur made up the six episodes scheduled for filming in back-to-back live shows.

The entrepreneur businessman was the mysterious Austin Harkness; Cara was certain his son was "Only Child 125". So certain that she had immediately forwarded the suggestion of Austin Harkness for the show and now she emailed the programme producer to tell him of a missing relative, a long-lost sister to the man. The story she spun was not far from the truth, but she failed to mention her connection to the family. 'He was adopted, and his name changed from Thorn to Harkness. That's how I found the existence of a sister. It's marvellous stuff. So, I'll crack on and see if we can persuade her to give her side of the story.' She typed with care. Anything in writing would be subject to a great deal of scrutiny should the truth of her blood relationship to Austin Harkness ever be revealed. Konrad Neale would be all over that juicy snippet like a vulture on a carcass.

'If I can track Verity Hudson down, the episode will have the surprise ending to outdo any other in the whole series,' she wrote.

It was time for "Timid Mouse" to bow out, and to enlist the help of her cousin indirectly and through devious means.

Dear Only Child 125,

It has been good to chat with you over email and you have been very friendly and welcoming. Thank you for offering to help with my search. Taking advice, I am seeking counselling to help prepare me for the day I track down my real mother, who we assume would be your aunt. However, until then, I hope your own family can shed some light on where she might be found.

Good luck and please keep me informed of any progress, no matter how small.

Kind regards,

Timid Mouse

Channel 7 was about to give her legitimate grounds for what she had in mind. The lies she had already told had paid dividends and thanks to "Only Child 125", subterfuge, and a suspension of honesty, here she was staring out of the window of her newly rented flat at the bright October day and across a car park in Browns Court, Bosworth Bishops.

4

TEA WITH AUNTY

*I*saac stared at an important email as he waited impatiently for his mother to answer the phone.

'Olivia Harkness.' His mother sounded flustered.

'Mother, I thought I should let you know, I've found her,' Isaac said, holding unexpected nerves in check. 'She wasn't dead. I've been in touch with her and, if everything goes well, Father will be in for one hell of a surprise if we can pull this off without him finding out.' There was a long pause from his mother who eventually drew a steadying breath before giving her response.

'Good God… really? Are you sure about this, Zacky?'

'Yes. It's her. She checks out. I can't wait to see the look on his face if I can get her to agree.' He gave a short laugh and waved a free hand around in the air, flicking his eyes from the laptop screen to the bottle of wine on the kitchen worktop. Despite the hour, he had already downed half of it, convinced that Dutch courage was required. Invariably this was the case when he had need to speak to either of his parents.

'I'd be very cautious if I were you. Have you talked with her yet?'

'Calm down, Mother. All in good time.' Isaac lifted the

bulbous wine glass to his lips, taking another gulp before continuing. 'I couldn't confirm anything before now because she took time to respond to my letter. It wasn't easy to trace her, but one of the researchers for the show got in touch when we discovered we were both looking at the identical part of the Harkness family tree. Amazing, isn't it?' He smiled to himself in satisfaction at the lie. 'After that we put some adverts on social media, local press, that sort of thing.'

'He must have been very thorough, this research fellow,' Olivia Harkness said, her manner starchy.

'Her name is Cara, and she *is* very thorough. Cara Laidlaw. Nice woman. Think she's based up North somewhere.'

Without the fortuitous link to a cousin, facilitated through Ancestors Reunited, Isaac doubted he would ever have stumbled on the sister his father rarely mentioned, other than to say she had probably died years ago. The fact that a television company were keen to pick up on the story was icing on the cake. His father would be impressed at the lengths he had gone to, and with any luck the new-found cousin would be persuaded to join in the emotional reunion on the latest version of *This is Your Life*.

Deliberately, Isaac had kept the secret of a cousin to himself. Something he could personally reveal to his father. Something he could take all the credit for. As far as Channel 7 were concerned, the finding of a long-lost sister would be the biggest surprise of all, and the TV company wanted to reserve the stunning twist in the tale until the end of the scheduled live broadcast, after that the glory would be his. Although he felt he could trust his mother's discretion, Isaac's wife was not party to anything involving his father's surprise; he'd made sure of that. She would like nothing better than to ruin everything out of spite. He looked at the clock on the wall. Another two hours and Natalie would be home, badgering him about a holiday to the Maldives or buying another pony for one of their daughters.

They already had one each and rarely bothered with them when they were home for school holidays.

Cara Laidlaw, the researcher at Channel 7, was assigned to the episode he and his family were to appear in. She had mentioned that reconnecting someone as well-known as Austin Harkness with his estranged sister would make for a fascinating story and a spike in viewer ratings. However, she also conceded that without help from the public, Verity Hudson would be extremely difficult to locate, which was often the way when families were torn apart by tragic circumstances.

Her prediction was correct, and some weeks dragged by before Verity Hudson's most recent whereabouts were finally disclosed by an internet-savvy member of a local Neighbourhood Watch Scheme who had no qualms about sharing information over the phone but preferred to remain anonymous.

'Have you seen her?' Isaac's mother asked, nervously.

'She's sound, honestly. I've never met her in the flesh, we just phone or email but she seems really professional.'

'Not her... Not the research woman... Austin's sister, have you seen *her* yet?'

'Once, yesterday. We agreed to meet on neutral ground, nothing fancy. A little cafe, somewhere she could easily get to on the train. I took an extra day off.'

'And?'

Isaac thought carefully before replying to his mother's open-ended question. He was far from confident about telling her. 'Oh, you know, Mother. Middle-aged, frumpy, hair cropped short. Ex-smoker by the looks of things. Tattoos on her arms.'

'Tattoos?' His mother was sounding unimpressed by the description but appeared to let it slide. 'Does she remember him?'

* * *

*I*saac had expected Verity Hudson to bear a family likeness, to have the same confident manner and intellect as his father did. It came as a shock to meet someone whose lemon-sharp bitterness was worn so blatantly. When the slab-sided woman with backward bending knees approached the table, he thought it was someone about to insist he move to another seat until she introduced herself. 'I'm Verity Hudson. You must be Isaac.' The woman didn't offer a hand to shake, instead, she pulled out the chair opposite and sat heavily into it, a frown fixed in place on her mottled, bloated face. 'Vera. Call me Vera.'

Isaac couldn't help noticing that Verity Hudson's clothes were supermarket brands worn with little attention to style or fit. Practical enough but not meant to attract the eye. They appeared brand new, as if bought especially for the occasion.

As he told his mother about it, the nervous and forced conversation held in the airy Bridge Street Tearooms filtered back into Isaac's head.

'I can't stay long,' the woman had said in a wheezy voice as she settled into the seat. 'I have to get back to feed me cat.' From the way she spoke, all dropped aitches and no Ts, it was clear that Vera, as she insisted on being called, was not privileged to have had the education her own brother received. The edge to the woman's voice was borne of harsh times and social struggles.

'Yes, of course. I'm sure this won't take too long. No *Mr* Hudson to dash home to?' asked Isaac. Cara Laidlaw had said he should be careful to check that Verity Hudson was who they believed her to be. Records had indicated that Verity was a widow, so this seemed to be as good a way as any to check credentials. However, at that question, the woman shuffled uncomfortably in her seat, eyes moving briefly back toward the exit. She picked up her small rucksack from where she had just placed it on the floor, sitting it in her lap. She eyed Isaac with overt suspicion. 'I thought you said you looked into my family background.'

Isaac tapped his mobile phone which lay to his left on the tabletop. 'I have, and I know that your husband died some years ago. It can't have been an easy time for you.' Isaac had to think quickly. In an attempt to clarify Vera Hudson's validity, he had earned nothing but distrust. 'I'm sorry. I didn't mean to be rude,' he said, pulling the slim menu from its stand. 'I wanted to be certain... you know.'

'No, I don't know,' Vera replied with a rasp. 'You send me a letter out of the blue claiming to be my nephew. You ask me to contact you. I did. You asked me to meet you and here I am. Now, what do you want? Because if you want to pay me hush money, you shouldn't have bothered coming to find me in the first place. Or have the press got to you?'

Isaac cringed inwardly. This hadn't gone as he had rehearsed it in his mind. Nothing was going to plan. 'The press? No, nothing like that, I'm pleased to say,' he replied, trying to force a smile to appear. It wouldn't come. 'Did you turn up here expecting money?' he asked, suddenly dubious about the pot-bellied woman purporting to be his aunt.

'I'll take it if you've got it,' the woman replied, flatly.

A silence descended as Isaac was stared out. First to blink, he looked at the menu once more. 'Shall we order something, and start again?' he suggested, in the hope that bribery with food and drink may help to calm the storm brewing rapidly on Vera Hudson's face. 'My shout.'

While they waited for the drinks and cake to be delivered, Isaac posed a few more delicate questions, intent on teasing out what Vera could remember of her childhood, wanting to know more about his father's hidden past. In response, the woman had been evasive, again challenging Isaac's motives rather than replying to enquiries.

'Why now after all these years? What's the real reason?' the gruff woman asked.

Isaac hesitated, taking time to unfold a paper serviette and place it in his lap. 'My father's birthday is coming up. He has everything he could wish for, as you probably guessed...'

'Guessed?' Vera huffed. 'Difficult to miss. His face has been in the papers on and off for decades. Rolling in it he is.' Tutting, she screwed up her eyes. 'I'm to be the surprise present at his birthday party, am I? Harrods run out of gold-plated bellybutton brushes then?'

The delay was painful. Isaac couldn't find the right words, and in the time he took weighing up which ones to use and in what order, Vera Hudson filled the gap.

'Hasn't it struck you that I could have got in touch at any time? Why I never wished to?' She snarled at Isaac, curling a lip. Making as if to leave, she said, 'I shouldn't be here. It was a bad idea. Stupid.'

Isaac raised a hand. 'No, please. It's not what you think...'

The challenges kept coming as Vera took a firm grip on her bag. 'Look, kid, I didn't come up on the down boat. If I had wanted to see my brother again I could. You want to know what happened when we was kids, then you can pay me for it. You came digging, I have the dirt... but I'm not going to be no birthday present. Not unless you can give me very good reason.'

Taken aback at the simmering rage, Isaac pressed his lips together and tried again. 'Aren't you the least bit curious?'

The uncomfortable vacuum of silence descended again as the strangers weighed up each other. 'Like I said when we spoke on the phone... when me and him went into care we were split up,' Vera volunteered. 'For years I didn't even know that our parents had killed themselves. Suicide pact. Sick ain't it?'

The shocking revelation resulted in Isaac drawing away from her, leaning back in his chair. 'I didn't know...'

'There you go, sweetness. You can have that one for free.'

'Is there more I should know?' Eyes widening, Isaac tried to make sense of what he was learning. 'Look, Verity... Vera... my father hardly mentions you. Actually, he never talks about you. I only found out that you still existed when my wife bought me one of those genetic tests as a present. I think she wanted me to be descended from the Vikings...' He trailed off, realising he had wandered off topic. Unwittingly, his wife Natalie had set the wheels in motion to unravel the Harkness family secret about an estranged sister, the aunt Isaac had hardly heard of. In reality, he knew no more than he had been told by Cara Laidlaw who had meticulously researched the Harkness family tree and unearthed a mysterious past.

'I still don't understand why you and my father were separated as children.' He braced for the answer but soon realised that the conversation had moved on too swiftly. Vera Hudson stood, abandoning an untouched teacake.

'No. No more questions,' she snapped. 'You ask your father. Let him tell you his side of the story if he can bear to. My bet is, he will deny anything you throw at him and paint me as a monster.'

Isaac held out a manicured hand, expensive watch jangling gently. 'Please, sit down. I've been thoughtless. Why don't we get to know one another and have a chat about our lives, then we can build some bridges.'

'Stick your bridges up your arse!' Vera barked, dragging the chair backwards. Turning before she reached the door, she hurled more spiteful words across the room. 'He can do one, for all I care.' Stumbling to the doorway, Vera continued to rant, spitting out the words, pointing a threatening finger at Isaac. 'But I tell you something, unless you want to slap him in the face with his own shit on his birthday then leave me well alone. You want my side of the story? You pay for it! And if you do want the truth, the whole truth, and nothing but the truth, then the price just went up.'

Stunned, Isaac sat immobilised by the sudden show of venom, and he watched speechless as a stony-faced Vera stormed past the window, heading back the way she had come from the station. The lull in the chatter from the other tables was short-lived as people tried to cover the embarrassment of the moment, in the way the British do, returning to stilted conversations… pretending they had heard and seen nothing.

Even as he recounted this to his mother the following day, Isaac realised he was a long way off making any sort of reunion happen. Money he could supply; luck and some leverage was what he needed to be in a position to impress his father.

5

NEW NEIGHBOUR

*L*ois had to admit that she hadn't chosen the best time to move home, but the Brookside flats at Browns Court were a new build and came on the rental market at the time she had made the difficult but necessary decision to move closer to the primary school where she had started teaching in the September. Cornered by life, she had been left with two choices: stay with a man who threatened her sanity or start again. She chose the latter.

Two weeks after signing the lease and there she was carting boxes and furniture up to the third floor, the smell of new carpet and paint assaulting the nostrils every time she opened the front door to 29 Brookside. Why the developers had chosen the name Brookside was a matter of poetic license; the rubbish-strewn stream at the rear of the flats was hardly a babbling example of nature's wonder.

A row of unappealing 1980s maisonette flats took up most of Browns Court with the numbers nine to eighteen being directly opposite Brookside. At first sight, Browns Court didn't appear too bad; in the cul-de-sac most cars were parked rather than abandoned, with one notable exception. Residents seemed to keep to themselves, or so Lois had assumed when they failed to acknowledge her polite hellos. Initially she took no offence, brushing the snubs off as poor social skills or shyness.

On the day she took possession of the keys, the place was eerily quiet and the car park for Brookside residents contained only one other car. She had been told by the insipid Wayne Mayhew, the letting agent, that she had an immediate neighbour across the landing at number thirty. 'The other flats are empty for now,' he said looking up from his computer screen. 'But as I told you, this is such a popular development, the rest of the properties will be filling up fast before Christmas. You were lucky.'

She was, because in a serendipitous moment, two days later, Lois opened her door and there was Cara Laidlaw. What a relief to meet her neighbour; a relief she was female, a relief she was immediately friendly. A relief not to feel so alone. A slender woman slightly older than Lois, Cara exuded the type of confidence she could only dream of achieving. They swapped numbers and after that began a regular chat on the compact landing of the top floor, mostly about how long Cara's sofa was taking to arrive.

The top floor landing of the left-hand block of the Brookside flats was theirs and theirs alone.

'The inflatable chairs are not doing it, if I'm honest,' Cara said, in a fabulous accent Lois couldn't place precisely other than to note that it was northern. Very northern. 'A reet sweaty arse and bad back weren't in Amazon's product description. The only saving grace is the wipe-clean feature, and the fact I can deflate them for use at the beach when the bloody sofa does arrive.'

Cara's turn of phrase was a delight to Lois, although she often had need for a translation. She had no idea that a 'reet gradley brew' was a nice cup of tea. Cara's WhatsApp updates about the goings on at Brookside, and in Browns Court as a whole, kept Lois smiling during many a dull day that winter.

The third arrival at Brookside rocked up in a Silver VW Polo. According to Cara, who had her eyes set to scan any activity in the close, the young man who drove the Polo was the first to move into the next block, Brookside's right wing, which Lois couldn't see from her flat without sticking a head out of the full-length windows.

Most newly constructed blocks of flats seemed to have the same features including French windows which opened inwards, with a metal balcony to prevent a disastrous fall and allow for maximum benefit of fresh air in the summer months. Brookside was no exception. Because of the way the flats were configured, Cara's side of the building was angled and had triple aspects, making it easy for her to see into the flats of the next block, as well as across the car park, the full length of the cul-de-sac and, like Lois, she had a view into the fields and railway track at the rear.

'What's he like? Mr VW Polo?' Lois asked her when she returned home that day.

'A scrawny lad, nowt to him,' Cara replied. 'I'm guessing at mid-twenties, but you know what some blokes are like, they don't seem to grow up until they're at least forty. Silver VW is a puppy and thought I'd fall for his stupid exaggerations. Reckons he's an accountant. There's more chance of me winning the lottery than that being true.' She shook her head at the thought. 'And there he was next to his tatty car wearing jogging bottoms and a hoodie. Accountant, my arse.'

The time Cara had taken off work to accommodate a pre-Christmas sofa delivery and a trip to the GP surgery had really cemented their fledgling friendship and kick-started the top floor committee scoreboard. It began with a text message:

Met neighbour on bottom right taking out his bin, but his flat did smell of bins. I think, as the original "Brooksiders", we should be able to score all the other residents. I will give him a 1/10 as he was also wearing flip-flops. Cara.

Fortunately, for Lois she only checked her phone during breaks or in the staff room because she laughed out loud at that one. The score was quite harsh, so later that dark and drizzly day she questioned Cara. She needed cheering up. Work had been hard and not helped by the exhaustion of flat pack furniture instructions and the dreaded "To Do" list. Cara was just the tonic she needed.

'Why only one out of ten?' Lois asked whilst leaning in the doorway to her flat. Cara had seen her arrive and park her car beneath the trees and they waved to each other before Lois approached the door entry system, fully laden with house-warming gifts from well-meaning colleagues. Having buzzed open the main door for her, Cara followed Lois inside her flat and headed for the kettle. They had reached that friendship level quite rapidly. Unburdened, Lois sank into the settee and gladly let her new friend make her a coffee, chatting away merrily as she stirred in the milk.

'He didn't deserve any more than a one.'

'Just because he smelt of bins and wore flip-flops?' Lois patted her damp winter-chilled hair and ran a fingertip under her eyes in case mascara had smudged. Not that it mattered.

'No, that would be petty. It's because he had hairy toes and I don't want to be seeing that.' Cara was serious. 'And because he's the bloke who wanted this flat. The guy Woody didn't like. Thank God. Imagine... I could have had Hairy-Toes as a neighbour and not you.'

Woody was the simple nickname they had awarded Gary Wood the landlord, an obvious *Toy Story* choice given his status as a cowboy builder, with his lank hair, country and western shirts, and rolling gait. In addition to this, he had an unnerving ability to stand too close if you happened to be female. Woody was a bizarre throwback.

'Oh, him,' she said to Cara, recalling the story of how she had jumped the queue to get the flat she wanted, purely because the landlord preferred her application to that of a man who wore flip-flops.

The coffee smelt delicious, and Lois inhaled deeply before daring to ask how the day had gone. 'Did it come? Your sofa?'

'Did it heck as like!' Cara replied. 'They rang this morning to say the delivery should never have been confirmed because the sofa hasn't even arrived in the warehouse. I knew it was too good to be true. Should never have paid a deposit. They've given me a date back end of January.' She walked towards the window and parted the vertical blinds to look out over the car park. 'There's the bloke,' she said. Standing beside her, Lois followed the direction of her neighbour's gaze and accidentally banged her head on the glass, making Cara laugh.

'The walking tree, that's Hairy Toes,' Cara said.

'Is that his car? What is it, a Fiat 500… how the hell does he fit inside it?' They watched in fascination as an extremely tall man, not slim by any means, folded himself into the little red car and reversed out of the parking bay. 'Definitely a one,' Lois conceded. 'Crappy car and hairy toes. One out of ten.'

'What score did we give to Single Dad below me?' Cara asked with a frown.

'The Liverpool football supporter with the blue car was awarded a three but only because he has been quiet so far and doesn't rev his car before he drives off, unlike the tosser opposite.' The man who lived in the maisonette above number eighteen, rode an uncared-for motorbike in all weathers and had little regard for the amount of noise he made.

'If we are going to extend this to all twelve flats at Brookside, should we set guidelines for scoring?' Cara asked. They looked at each other and 'ummed' for a second or two.

'We need to know who we are living with,' Lois said. 'None of us know each other, and... should we include the Browns Court neighbours?' She sucked air through her teeth. 'There are some odd characters to be accounted for.'

'You say odd, but I would go so far as to say downright weird.' Cara too made a face to express her mistrust. 'Agreed then, but remember, these scores are general, judgemental ratings for neighbours. So, we shouldn't be too scientific about this. The ratings should not be based on qualifying criteria, just hunches and first impressions.'

Looking towards the pile of gifts from Lois's workmates, Cara heaved a sigh. 'Any wine?'

A small chuckle left Lois's lips. 'I suspect amongst that lot will be a vase or a plant pot, a tea cosy from Jill because she's knitting obsessed, a set of mugs that I won't like and some jam. But no wine.'

'Something to add to your charity shop box then,' Cara replied in sympathy. 'Of course, what we really need is a blackboard or some flip chart paper to record our scores. You'd think being teachers they would have known that. I'll set up a spread sheet. Nothing fancy.'

6

PILATES

*B*efore moving into Brookside, Cara Laidlaw had devised a cunning plan to help improve a dire social life and avoid long nights by the telly. She vowed to join some evening classes: Pilates, Yoga, Zumba, anything to give her some semblance of a life to replace the one she would be permanently leaving behind. So far, she and Lois had found one class for Pilates which ran on a Tuesday and Thursday evening at the Wigmore Memorial Hall, a draughty 1950's building with few endearing features. In its favour was the fact that it was within walking distance of Browns Court and the instructor was one of life's eternal optimists, a cheerful soul by the name of Hazel Nutt, who – given her first name – had made an unfortunate choice of husband. For Lois, a Pilates class was something to look forward to after a trying day at work herding unruly infants and battling Ofsted bureaucracy. For Cara it would be an escape from the uninspiring walls of her flat.

When she and Lois had turned up at the hall for their first lesson, they made camp, side by side, at the back of the hall, hoping to be less obvious as total novices that way – a hope quickly dashed by Hazel the instructor. 'New members this evening, everyone. Please welcome Lois and Cara who have just moved to the town and live in the new flats in Browns Court.'

The murmurs around the room preceded scrutinising glances from several people pretending to busy themselves aligning yoga mats; none more so than the lady who had taken up the space next to Cara. She made no effort to hide her displeasure, increasing the gap between her personal yoga mat and the borrowed one being used by Cara. Nike leggings under strain and in danger of ripping at the seams, not a hair on her coiffured head out of place, she rounded on the newcomers. 'You'll have to move if Lisa turns up. She usually takes that corner.' The words were sharp, the manner dismissive, the accent pretentious.

Cara was having none of it. 'Oh, aye, is that right?' she whispered brightly. 'Hazel never mentioned pre-booking floor space. Don't you worry yourself, if Lisa needs the extra space, then we can all shuffle up and get cosy.'

As if the hall wasn't chilly enough, the atmosphere within it had turned decidedly frosty at the mention of Browns Court. Something not missed by Cara.

However, and quite unwittingly, Hazel provided some reassurance with her next comments to the class. 'Lois is a new teacher at the Lower School, and Cara is a freelance journalist.' She wasn't entirely accurate with this information, but her announcement settled the disgruntled mutterings. Some of the attendees smiled apologetically towards the back of the room, not quite making eye contact with either of the two fresh faces.

The man one row in front, laying out his Pilates resistance band next to his mat, turned. 'And I'd keep your fleeces on if I were you. It doesn't get much warmer than this in here. It's positively Antarctic in the winter.' He shot a look at the lady next to them who had been so blatant in her snobbery. 'But we've been assured the council have approved an upgrade. Isn't that right, Mrs Fowler? Oh, and don't let Christine there talk you into joining the Neighbourhood Watch Scheme. Spying on *your* neighbours could result in hospitalisation.'

Lois shrugged at Cara. 'Something we should know about?' she asked.

'Plenty—' came the reply, but forthcoming details were cut short by Hazel who stood tall on the wooden stage and began the initial warm up by expelling myths about Pilates and demonstrating the correct posture and lateral thoracic breathing techniques 'for the benefit of the newbies'.

Almost an hour later, backside in the air for a final downward-facing dog and Cara's nose was still cold. She risked a peek at Lois and tried not to laugh. Coordination was not her new friend's strong point and several times that evening had resulted in Hazel dashing over to give hands-on instruction and untangle limbs. Cara returned the smile from Lois. 'Arse-end to ceiling, chuck,' she said with a grin.

Pleased with their efforts, the two neighbours chatted animatedly as they returned the mats to the front of the hall and thanked Hazel for accepting them into the established class. On their way to the doors, they were stopped by Christine Fowler who had changed her attitude towards them completely, or so it seemed. 'I do hope we didn't get off on the wrong foot,' she said, wrapping a pashmina around her neck.

'I always do,' Lois replied with a cheerful grin. 'Can't tell my left from my right.' She held the door open for Christine. 'Apology accepted.'

Cara was less forgiving and more suspicious, remembering the words of warning from the man at the beginning of the class. 'What exactly is so wrong with Browns Court, anyway?' she asked.

The expression from Christine was one of pity. 'You come back to me when you've worked it out and we will have a serious chat. In the meantime, my advice to you both is to remain vigilant, check out the Bosworth Community Facebook page for details. The crime rate in that part of town is somewhat higher than the national average. Good night.' With that she turned and walked to her car, a four-by-four, gleaming under the car park lighting.

The two ladies looked on and waved as Christine drove past, after which they hurried along the empty pavements, arms linked against the late Autumn chill. 'How's your new man working out?' Cara asked as they rounded the corner heading onto Station Road.

'I daren't say in case I jinx it,' Lois said with a sigh. 'When I landed this new job, I was determined not to be stabbed in the heart anymore and had pretty much resigned myself to being single. It's safer that way.'

'Agreed. The palpitations, thrills and warm glow of romance are all very well, but the ever-present fears of rejection, abandonment, and betrayal, have a tendency to hover menacingly in the background, don't they?'

Lois nodded. 'I hate those feelings. The ones that threaten to turn me into a needy limpet. Needy limpets get dumped because they are unattractive. Fact,' she added emphatically.

Cara had to agree. It had taken her the vast majority of her adult life so far to work out that being a perfect girlfriend usually resulted in total capitulation, loss of independence, and emotional pain. 'I seem to attract the wrong type and the pattern repeats. Joy, lust, tears, pain. Joy, lust, tears, pain. An inevitable loop. Either that or I play it safe with a drippy, boring, lame twat who I end up hating and *he* has to go through the pain instead. Joy, boredom, dump, guilt.' She released a hollow laugh and Lois joined in, gently teasing her.

'So true. I'm the same and I still managed to fall for Dan. You never know... he may be Mr Right.'

After the last debacle with Matt, Cara had vowed to put up some solid psychological walls and let men bounce off them. 'I'm done with the lot them. Best check he's not already married.

That's what happened to me. Matty wormed his way in and kept me dangling for three years.'

'Bloody typical,' Lois said as they marched along, heading home to Brookside. 'With Dan it was a spectacular cliché. When I least expected it, I meet someone worth spending weekends with.'

'And just how did you two meet? You've never got round to telling me the whole story.'

Recounting the events of her first meeting with Dan, Lois let out a long sigh. The breath formed a cloud in the cold night air.

'Back in September, my car developed a flat tyre. I was on my way home from a late meeting, so I pulled off the road and when a vehicle drew up behind me in a dark lay-by, warning lights blinking, I panicked,' Lois said. 'Like something out of a horror film, it was. Can you imagine the state I was in when a man got out, flashing a torch? The bloke was huge, a good six foot two and beefy enough to fill a doorway.'

'Yes, I did notice,' Cara said with a laugh. 'And I expect your imagination had you hog-tied and murdered before he even opened his mouth to offer help.'

'Too bloody right it did. And with that accent of his, to my shame, when he did speak, I assumed... you know... all the bad things. I was shitting myself, so he passed me his phone to talk to his boss, of all people. "Our Dan is as honest as the day is long", the woman said. "You'll be safe with him".' Lois went on to explain to Cara that she had been reassured enough to accept help from Dan but not confident enough to sit in his car to keep warm while he changed the tyre for her. 'That would have been a foolhardy move,' she conceded. 'Instead, I phoned Mum to let someone know my whereabouts, just in case...' The two ladies laughed, appreciating the dramatics and then Lois continued her story.

'It was inevitable: the lovely Dan had stopped to help a damsel in distress and when he happened to mention he was single through no fault of his own, bam! All my good intentions departed with one involuntary twitch from overexcited pelvic floor muscles.' At this the giggles began again, and she nudged Cara gently with an elbow. 'Ergo, winter weekends accounted for, sex life restored, and the emotional seesaw begins again. Dan has arrived and I'm already infatuated. So far, he hasn't put a foot wrong, he's even from a posh part of Glasgow, but stand by for emotional wreckage at some point.'

Cara hadn't shared too much in the way of her personal life, least of all told Lois the real reason she had moved to Bosworth Bishops, but she was warming to her neighbour. A sincere friendship was in the offing.

7

UNKNOWN QUANTITIES

*W*hen January had arrived, Lois and Cara came to a pause in their neighbour-scoring, waiting for the next Brooksider to move in. Their natural curiosity had drifted to the homes opposite where the behaviour of one or two inhabitants had already become a source of morbid interest.

'Have you seen Vera lately?'

'Who the hell is Vera?' Lois asked, thinking that Cara had changed the subject completely.

'The miserable looking woman at number eighteen,' Cara said staring out of the window once more. 'The cat is still prowling around, trying to pick a fight, but I haven't seen her for days. Think I should knock on the door and see if she's alright?'

Lois shook her head. 'I'm not sure… maybe. She could just be visiting relatives.'

With a frown, Cara glanced across at the laptop computer on the desk by the window. 'Aye, 'appen she could. Or a friend maybe.'

'Or perhaps she's poorly. Got the flu.'

'Or... she went to borrow a cup of sugar from number thirteen and couldn't find her way out again.'

Lois chuckled at the reference and recalled the events with a grin.

a few evenings previously, she had been snuggled down with a hot drink and a mindless television programme, trying to switch off from a difficult working day. Hours of rounding up small children had then been followed by a Pilates class in temperatures usually found within a walk-in freezer, which resulted in her final stretches being somewhat lacklustre. Her energy had been drained.

All these weeks after their first meeting, Dan was very much a part of Lois's life and she had been on the phone to him, making plans for the weekend ahead, chatting about the day. 'Do you know something?' she said. 'When I undertook teacher training, there was no module on changing a child's wet knickers or how to deal with exploding bowels. Today I've had the dubious pleasure of both scenarios and I can definitely still detect the faintest whiff of poo lingering in my nostrils despite scrubbing my hands raw.' A nasty case of Norovirus had been sweeping the school since the start of term, felling pupils and staff in rapid succession, a fact causing much anxiety for Lois. 'I'm bound to catch it sooner or later,' she added, making a face that Dan couldn't see.

Mid-chat, her mobile had vibrated with a message from Cara.

Without making it obvious, take a look across the road to the upstairs flat to the left of the alleyway. Number 13. What do you see?

'Dan, I'm going to hop in the shower... See you tomorrow evening. Can't wait.' Groaning from the weariness of a stressful day, she had dragged herself to the smaller window in the lounge, placed her mug on the sill and poked a finger between the vertical panels of the blind. The scene was intriguing and a conversation with Cara was required. Phone to her ear she had stared beyond the orange glow of the streetlamp and focussed in on the light from the largest window of 13 Browns Court.

'What's all that stuff behind him?' she had asked.

'God knows. Bags, clothes, boxes, mess,' Cara replied. 'Piled high, everywhere.'

'What on earth is he wearing?'

'Oh, hang on… He's getting up. Is it a he? … Not sure, he maybe a she.' It was hard to be certain, because the person at number thirteen was dressed in a two-piece high-vis pyjama set and when they moved, they were hidden amongst a five-foot-high cliff of rubbish. 'I thought the mess in the pokey front garden was a sign of laziness, but it looks like we have ourselves a hoarder,' Cara had said. 'How fascinating.'

8

VERA IS MISSING

*W*hen the intercom rang on the Friday evening that same week, Lois grabbed a tea towel to wipe her hands. She looked across the breakfast bar at Dan who was in the lounge hanging a cluster of framed photographs. 'I'm not expecting anyone,' she said. Making her way to the front door of the flat she was puzzled. She had no friends who would call without prior notice and her mum and stepdad were not expected until the following weekend.

'Who is it?' she asked into the mouthpiece. With the reply came uncertainty. 'Hang on a second.' She returned to the lounge to seek advice. 'There's a private investigator downstairs with his wife, or so he says, and they're looking for help with a missing person. What should I do?'

Dan sent her an encouraging grin from his full-bearded face. 'Let him in, we can check out his credentials when he comes to the door. Don't look so worried, I'm here, I'll protect you.' He folded up the step ladder as Lois returned to the intercom.

'Come on up.'

She stood in the doorway to her flat, Dan looming over her

shoulder, and watched the man as he climbed the stairs. She wasn't sure what a private detective was supposed to look like, but this one seemed to be lacking the prerequisite deer-stalker hat, although he was wearing a belted wax jacket with a scarf at his neck keeping out the winter chill. Making use of the bannister, he appeared to be favouring his left leg. His wife, Lois assumed, was the petite Oriental lady trotting up the stairs in front of him, a spring in her delicate step and the bobble of her woolly hat bouncing with each stride. Both were, at a guess, somewhere in the region of her parent's generation. The spritely lady smiled warmly when she caught sight of Lois and Dan.

'Thank you so much for agreeing to speak to us. We weren't having much luck with your neighbours across the way.'

'Aye, I think most of them are out at the pub,' Dan piped up. 'Friday night and all that…' He leaned past Lois and shook hands with the lady who made the relevant introductions as her husband arrived on the landing. Unexpectedly, he wasn't out of breath, and neither was she. Somewhat shorter in stature than Dan, the man was of equal presence, broad and confident. His missing hat was in one hand, a flat cap, a la *Peaky Blinders*.

'I'm Connie Quirk and this is my husband Peddyr. We are from P.Q. Investigations,' the cheery Chinese lady said, removing her knitted gloves and producing a business card from a neat leather bag, the long strap of which was slung diagonally across her chest. She handed the card to Lois.

'Peddyr is an unusual name. Not one I've heard before,' Lois commented. 'Gaelic or Celtic I would imagine.' She was rewarded with a genuine smile of appreciation from Peddyr.

'Right first time, I'm impressed… Mrs?'

'Finnegan. Miss Finnegan… please call me Lois. And this is Dan, Dan Radford.' On the card were details of the agency and an address in Bosworth Bishops laid out in a neat font. 'Dyer street. That's a nice part of town. Are you near the park?' Lois asked. She would have liked a flat in that area, but nothing had become available at the time she had begun her search for somewhere to live in the town. The brand-new flats where she had ended up had been a practical compromise. Head over heart.

'Yes, that's us. Above Lily Fields the florist,' Connie replied. 'We've been there for years.'

Peddyr pulled off his leather gloves and unzipped his coat to reveal a cream Arran jumper worn over jeans. He slid a colour print-out of a photograph from an inside pocket. 'We wondered whether you had seen anything of your neighbour in Browns Court. The lady at number eighteen,' he enquired.

Dan took a backward step. 'Over to you, hon. I don't actually live here,' he explained. 'Lois is the tenant, I'm the "not yet live-in lover". But you never know...' Lois's heart gave a little jolt at the thought. He really was keen, more than she had dared to imagine. With an embarrassed giggle she too stepped back from the door.

'Why don't you both come in for a few minutes. It's not very nice standing on the landing.' The truth was that this was unlikely to be a long visit. Lois didn't have much to contribute. 'I think her name is Vera,' she offered, feeling ashamed that she was ignorant of the surname. 'I only moved in a couple of months ago. Actually, some of the flats in the next block are still empty which is probably why you couldn't get much of a response to the intercoms,' she added, justifying why she knew so little of the people who surrounded her. 'Vera has a cat.' It sounded as unhelpful as it was, but Lois hadn't gone out of her way to befriend any of the neighbours and certainly not those who lived in the maisonettes opposite.

Both Connie and Peddyr stood on the doormat until Lois insisted that they join her and Dan in the lounge. Both stepped out of their boots smiling at each other, sharing a joke. 'I told you...' Peddyr said to his wife. 'The older we get the more use of elastic is required. Elastic and slip-on footwear.' Something about the way they interacted with each other, as they tucked hats and gloves into jackets and hung them on the pegs in the hall, put Lois at her ease.

'Do you recall the last time you saw Mrs Hudson?'

Peddyr Quirk looked directly into her soul with his kindly puffin-shaped eyes, which made the embarrassment so much worse.

'Oh, that's her name... I didn't know. I think I've only actually spoken to her once or twice. Although sometimes I've spotted her out with her shopping trolley, and she was at her door the night before Christmas Eve, when the Rotary Club Santa did the rounds on a flatbed lorry. They didn't stay long. Nobody hangs around here if they can help it.'

Working at a lower school in town had been useful when she began her search for a flat but was no substitute for solid local knowledge. If Lois had done her homework and taken time to research Browns Court with more thought and less rush, she may well have made a different decision when it came to signing a rental agreement.

Browns Court was home to a cast of unedifying characters, some of whom were very unsavoury indeed, if first impressions were to count for anything. 'She always has a light on,' Lois added in the hope that she would come across as more caring than she felt towards the Browns Court neighbours she so deliberately went out of her way to avoid.

'What about the other tenants in this building, would they have seen more of Mrs Hudson?' Connie Quirk asked, looking around at Lois's furnishings and smiling. 'Gosh, haven't you got unpacked and organised in record time. How many weeks have you lived here did you say?'

'Coming up ten weeks,' Lois replied. 'I can't bear to live in a mess.' She thought about the question Connie had asked her and noted how Mr Quirk was also taking an interest in the contents of her flat. He scanned around as he strolled to the French windows where he gently parted the vertical blind to look out onto the maisonettes and an uninspiring parking area in the cul-de-sac below.

'We noticed the light on at number eighteen too. Unfortunately, light or no light, there is no sign of Mrs Hudson. Her nephew has been unable to get hold of her and was worried, which is why you may have seen the police call by with someone from the housing association in the last day or so. Although there were signs of occupation, they found the property to be empty, with the exception of the cat, which still comes and goes through the cat flap.' He rubbed at his chin. 'Somebody must be feeding it... When the police spoke to neighbours, nobody seemed to know anything about Mrs Hudson's whereabouts.'

Unable to help herself, Lois gave a short derisive laugh. 'None of that lot will speak to the police. They shouldn't have bothered asking. Scratch the surface and this area isn't the nicest.'

Connie joined in with a brief chortle and nodded at Dan who sat quietly on a high stool at the breakfast bar, absorbing the diplomatic scene being played out in the open-plan lounge. 'There's no getting away from the fact that this part of town has a history of being uncooperative with the law, it's why we are here together,' Connie explained. 'Peddyr looks too much like a policeman because he used to be one, but we get away with more nosing about as a couple. We can ask questions the police can't.' She let out a short sigh. 'Mrs Hudson's family is understandably concerned. She's quite a lonely soul by all accounts.'

Lois felt at a loss. She had nothing more to contribute other than to suggest they speak to Cara. 'My neighbour across the landing at number thirty,' she explained. 'She was the first to move in here. She must have spoken to Vera to know her name.'

Peddyr was peering out of the window again. 'Your neighbour has an all-round view,' he noted. 'Is Cara local?'

'No. She's originally from up north but moved here for her job. She's some sort of freelance journalist. Works from home a lot. I could give her your contact details. She would know more than me.' The offer was a gesture of her willingness to help, because Lois had nothing else to give the couple who had braved the cold winter evening in the search for a missing woman.

'Shame she's not about this evening,' Peddyr remarked, noting the darkened windows of flat number thirty. 'Do you know Cara's surname or is that still something you have yet to find out?'

At last, Lois felt of some use. 'Actually, we seem to have hit it off as neighbours. Her last name is Laidlaw. She and I are trying to get to know the area together. If we hear of anything we can always call you.'

Dan left his position on the bar stool and headed to the window to stand beside Peddyr. 'The top floor committee, that's Lois and Cara, have amused themselves by identifying their new neighbours, giving them nicknames, the wee dafties. They also give them a score.'

'How brilliant,' announced Connie, grinning at Lois and clapping her hands. 'I love that idea.'

'It's only a bit of fun,' Lois replied, a bashful grin spreading wider. 'Some of them aren't very sociable, so we have to find a way of working out whether they are trustworthy or to be avoided. Sounds awful when I put it like that, but you get my drift.'

Peddyr nodded, facing Dan, looking up at him. 'Very sensible. Two young ladies, living alone, new to the area, strangers moving in around them, an unknown quantity on each occasion.' He turned away from the window. 'How far have you got with this list of yours?' he asked.

'We've only just started really. Everyone is hibernating.' Lois was apologetic once more. 'It seems you've had a wasted journey.'

'Not at all,' Connie said, leading the way back into the hall to retrieve coats. 'You have been the most helpful person we've spoken to this evening. We shall be back to knock on doors in daylight hours and see who else we can find who may know Mrs Hudson better. You have our card.'

9

THINKING TIME

*T*he walk back to Dyer Street was brisk through necessity; any dawdling could have resulted in hypothermia. Along the way Peddyr and Connie chatted about their unsuccessful foray to Browns Court.

'It was doomed to failure from the start,' Peddyr commented, striding out. 'A bitterly cold Friday night and the only other people out in that part of town were the local drug dealers and that interesting couple on their way to the station.'

Connie giggled at the mention of the two extremely attractive individuals who had almost bumped into them as she and Peddyr walked down Station Road, heading for Browns Court, earlier that evening. Scantily dressed in miniskirts with faux fur jackets, berets at a jaunty angle and ludicrously high heels clipping along the pavement, the two could have been glamorous twins heading for a night out. And that is what Peddyr had assumed when he had said good evening to them. He even turned his head as they passed by, their long hair swishing down their backs. When his wife informed him they were in fact of the male gender, he took another much longer look, shaking his head.

'I still can't believe it,' he said as he and Connie recalled the event.

'Believe what you like, Lao Gong. I'm telling you they are not female… Check the Bosworth Facebook gossipmongers and you will find I'm right. Christine Fowler is appalled,' she said, giving her best impersonation of Mrs Fowler: local busy-body, chair of every committee, elected member of the town council, staunch churchgoer and Neighbourhood Watch coordinator.

'Well, if the formidable Fowl-Mouth says so, it must be gospel, but you could have fooled me.'

'They did fool you,' his wife replied, barely keeping the laughter at bay.

'Come on, give me a break it was dark at the time.'

Peddyr and Connie could easily have scheduled their first visit to Browns Court for the following day, which in hindsight would have been a more sensible option, were it not for Bernard Kershaw.

'I promised Bernie we would make a start straight away, and that's what we've done. A quick and dirty recce of the immediate vicinity and nothing to report, other than the cat is still alive and a light remains on at number eighteen.'

Bernard Kershaw, solicitor and friend of the Quirks, had been approached by Vera Hudson's brother, a certain Austin Harkness who said the family had been unable to contact his sister for several days. According to Bernard, Mrs Hudson had only recently been found after decades apart from her family. Mr Harkness's son had made considerable efforts to trace the lost sister and finally come up trumps in good time for Mr Harkness's sixty-fifth birthday celebrations due to take place in the spring. There had been no communication between the two estranged siblings as yet, but the son had met with her and arranged another phone call for New Year's Day when they were to make plans to meet up again. That call was answered but at some point between then and the third week in January, the cat-loving, lonely widow Vera had mysteriously vanished. When she failed to show up at the agreed time and place on Tuesday, Isaac Harkness called the police to report his concerns.

'The picture of Vera Hudson's life doesn't seem exactly thrilling, does it?' Connie acknowledged, trotting to keep up with Peddyr who had maintained a steady marching pace for the journey home. 'And could you slow down a bit please, Lao Gong. I'm out of puff.'

'All that Christmas grub slowing you down, is it?' He wasn't being serious. No matter how much food his wife tucked away, she never put on so much as a pound in weight. Her natural effervescence and boundless energy saw to that. He was the one keen to shed the fat accumulated during the festive fortnight of gorging and enforced captivity.

'If Vera Hudson rarely ventured further than the local convenience store, then she has to be here somewhere, dead or alive,' he said. 'She was not seen at the railway station nor the bus station, as far as the police have determined, although it isn't known exactly when she upped and disappeared. If what we are told is correct, no local taxi firm picked her up either. The Knit and Natter group has restarted but nobody, apart from Pamela Whats'er-name from the church, raised concerns with the police. She did so before Vera Hudson's own family, which surprises me. We are led to believe that Vera has no friends elsewhere who she visits on a regular basis, so where the hell is she?' he questioned, pulling keys from his pocket.

The front door to P.Q. Investigations tended to be reserved for clients and visitors because Connie and Peddyr made everyday use of the back entrance to their flat. Their comfortable home covered two floors above a florist shop for which they owned the freehold. The rent from the shop below was a safety net, a handy source of income and a pension plan in addition to the one Peddyr received from his years in the police service. The flat itself was spacious and with a balcony overlooking the park had all the benefits of a house, without the burden of a garden to care for.

'Doesn't it seem quiet now the children have gone back home?' Connie said as they stepped into the kitchen, stripping off their coats and hats.

'Bloody blissful,' Peddyr remarked, quickly correcting himself. 'Sorry, blinkin' blissful.' He had struggled with the no swearing rule introduced because of their grandson and had quickly reverted to the vernacular as soon as the young family had returned home after a short stay over the festive season.

Euan was seventeen months old and had caused chaos when he arrived for a visit with his parents from Glasgow to spend the Christmas period. 'Don't get me wrong, Lao Po,' Peddyr said to his wife, using the Mandarin term of endearment as he so frequently did. 'It was fantastic to have our boys back home; both together, both so happy, but there were times when I couldn't hear myself think. You and Joe chatting about weddings, Hannah talking babies, Marshall and Alleyn bickering just like they did when they were young kids and as for Euan and his passion for bashing everything that made a noise... Thank goodness I could shut myself away in my office.' He strode over to the kettle and filled it at the sink. 'Tea? Or do you fancy a hot chocolate?'

When there was no reply forthcoming, he turned in his socks to find an empty kitchen.

'Pedd! Come here... you're never going to believe this.' Connie's excited request had come from the direction of the lounge. Holding a plant pot with outstretched arms she beamed at her husband as he entered the room. 'Look. There's a flower on my amaryllis.' Her eyes were bright with astonishment. 'I nearly threw the blessed thing away three days ago because all it produced was a long green stem. Take a picture with your phone, I have to send this to Kathy. She'll need to see proof. I bent down to light the fire when I noticed it. A miracle,' she said, reverentially replacing the plant next to the hearth. The gas fire was already flickering and giving a warm glow to the room.

'I think we should send this to everyone we know,' Peddyr said checking the photograph on his phone and grinning. 'Famous plant killer turns over new leaf.'

'Very funny.'

For the previous five years, Kathy the florist who rented their shop, had set a challenge in the belief that anyone can grow an amaryllis for Christmas. Connie had defied that belief until now. In all those years, this was the first and only amaryllis to have survived and to have produced a flower, albeit several weeks later than hoped. Peddyr didn't have the heart to tell her that he had been taking special care of her plant, knowing she would forget to water it.

'When you have finished sending messages, could we have a chat about the ne'er-do-wells of Browns Court. If Vera Hudson didn't leave, then someone must have removed her, and somebody there must have seen something.' Peddyr headed back to the kitchen to finish making a hot drink for them both.

'Kidnap? A penniless widow?' Connie shouted as she followed on some seconds later.

'Or she's still there somewhere. Lumpy patio... Smell from under the floorboards...' Flicking a teabag into the open bin he released the foot pedal and the lid dropped with a clang. 'Tea for me. I've made you a hot chocolate,' he added with pride. Perfecting the art of the hot chocolate had required seeking out the right brand. Disliking the watery affairs most readily available, he had reverted to a more expensive but superior option to which he added condensed milk. The result was a decadent treat for Connie who rewarded him with a hug.

'Oh, how lovely. Just what I needed. Shall we sit by the fire and admire my amaryllis?'

'Kinky... but I'm game if you are.'

Connie ignored this remark with a dismissive wave of her

free hand. 'Talking of hiding dead bodies, did you notice the smell of bleach at number twenty-nine? For a new flat, I wouldn't have thought it necessary unless Lois Finnegan is a touch cleaning obsessed.'

This had also occurred to Peddyr who thought his wife was probably correct in her assumptions about Lois. The flat was neat, tidy, clean, and orderly, rather like the girl herself. 'I think we may have interrupted a romantic evening for two,' he said. 'You could feel the thrill of young love in the air.' Lowering himself into his favourite chair, he picked up the TV remote control. 'I think we'll give programmes about debt collectors and drug dealers a miss tonight. There'll be enough of that in real life now we've landed a job in Bosworth Bishops' answer to the Chatsworth Housing Estate in that TV series.' The name eluded him. 'Err... You know the one.'

Lifting the mug of hot chocolate to her lips Connie grinned, her eyes teasing him. 'Ah, the razor-sharp mind of Grandad the detective,' she purred.

10

KNOCKERS

On Saturday morning, Lois put the milk back in the fridge while Dan cleared the plates. 'What did you make of the private investigator people?' she asked him. Despite the unscheduled visit from the Quirks looking for Vera Hudson, their Friday night dinner for two had been a resounding success and Dan had been in no rush to leave the next morning. Lois took this to be a good sign, although she remained sensitive to any indicators that he was tucking his feet under her table for opportunistic reasons. Because of her track record with men, she had at last become cynical about their motives for wanting to spend time with her. So far Dan hadn't done anything wrong, which in itself was of concern.

'Aye, I liked them,' he replied, wiping down the breakfast bar with a damp cloth. He had made the breakfast. Another tick in the box. Another reason for Lois to be wary. This couldn't last, she told herself. 'Solid,' he said. 'But a wee bit more switched on than your average. Why do you ask?'

'Because they are back knocking on doors,' Lois replied, checking her watch. 'Mind you, ten-thirty may still be too early for the good folks of Browns Court.' With Dan at her side, she sat down to watch from their elevated position, as Peddyr and Connie Quirk knocked on the door of number sixteen. Through the full-length French windows and the safety of the vertical blinds, the Quirks were seen to take rapid steps in reverse when the occupant stepped out to confront them.

'Quick, open the window a crack so we can hear what's going on,' Dan said. 'He's proper shady,' he added as the sounds of an irate man and the accompanying profanities reached the third floor of Brookside.

Lois had only rarely caught sight of the people who lived there – exchanging nods was as far as communication had progressed to date. They were never about when she went to work in the mornings, and she was now alarmed at how aggressive this man in particular could be. 'They are the reason social housing should be called anti-social housing,' she remarked.

Connie and Peddyr were seen backing off slowly, hands raised in apology. Dan and Lois remained at their observation post as the Quirks tried at number fourteen, but with no answer to the door moved their interest to the contents of a wheelie bin. After this they crossed the alleyway between the two blocks of maisonettes, heading for numbers twelve and ten.

'We really must get our act together,' Lois announced. 'The ogre over there is clearly someone to avoid,' she said, pointing a finger at 16 Browns Court. 'I'll catch up with Cara, see if we can't help out the Quirks somehow.'

* * *

The Housing Association had provided P.Q. Investigations with a list of residents and length of tenancy in each case because they were asked to do so by solicitor Bernard Kershaw who had the backing of the police – at least that's what he told the housing officer responsible for Browns Court. Peddyr's decision to begin door-to-door inquiries halfway through the morning had been arrived at by simple logic. 'It gives me plenty of time for a morning swim and besides, arriving any time before ten o'clock on a Saturday will be pointless. The vast majority of this lot will be in bed until closer to lunchtime,' Peddyr said running a finger down the column of names before they set off on foot.

'A little judgemental, don't you think?' Connie replied.

'Not when you see who is on this list. A delightful soul by the name of Jed. Real name Jethro Dart. A man who is renowned for involvement in drugs and banned from most social clubs and pubs for a radius of twenty miles at the very least. Another one or two in the same vein and...' He glanced at Connie. 'Would you bloody believe it? Nora Evans the clapped-out call girl who works part-time at Clouds. I only spoke to her an hour ago on the off chance an unclaimed body was lurking in their mortuary again.'

A few doors down from Lily Fields, the florist shop below the Quirks' flat, nestled a funeral service by the name of Clouds – in reference to heaven, Peddyr assumed. Work had come his way from several funeral directors in town, mostly seeking to track down relatives in the hope they would contribute to costs when it came to local authority funeral arrangements for unclaimed bodies. He had come across Nora on one such occasion. There was no actual evidence that she earned her living by selling what was left of her desiccated body, but Peddyr had determined this through sound observation. A chapel of rest was no place for the likes of the tawdry Nora Evans or her taste-less attire and yet Trevor Shaw, the managing director of Clouds, had kept her on as his 'Saturday girl' for well over a year now. Peddyr suspected there was more than a back scratching arrangement in place, in Trevor's favour and without the knowledge of Mrs Shaw. He squirmed inwardly at the very thought.

'There's our first possible suspect then,' he announced. 'She has the means to dispose of a body. Not that she would have the strength to move it. One heave of a dead weight and she'd snap in two.'

Connie baulked at the idea. 'Stereotyping isn't necessarily helpful, Pedd. I was expecting us to take several angles of approach. One being the residents of Browns Court, another being Vera and her long-lost family, and thirdly the great and good of Bosworth Bishops.' Reaching for her coat she then slipped it on and zipped it up, taking the gloves from the pockets.

'Are you suggesting we involve Christine Fowl-Mouth?' He considered this for a second or two as he too prepared for the morning walk across town towards the station. Exploring the Vera Hudson family connections would be standard practice, as would knocking on doors, but making use of the likes of Christine Fowler was fraught with unpredictability. Maybe such a risk was needed, he conceded. Not only would it widen their search across the right demographic, but it was a well-known fact that Christine Fowler could be relied upon to create one hell of a stir on social media which could garner some unexpected responses. It had to be more effective than ringing door bells, only to be met with sealed lips and cold shoulders.

'What have you got on Austin Harkness and his son so far?' he asked, ramming his peaked cap onto his head, then taking it off and replacing it with a woolly beanie hat to avoid frost bite of the ears. 'Could we be looking at a smoke screen? A member of the family had their nose put out because a sister could strip them of the inheritance they were expecting to benefit from?'

'It's always a possibility,' his wife agreed. 'The process of elimination will be the way forward. At least we can discount some of the residents in the new flats.'

'Apart from Lois Finnegan and Cara Laidlaw, both of whom moved into the left-hand block well before Christmas. Who else moved into Brookside before Vera Hudson mysteriously vanished, I wonder?' He pulled his hat more firmly into place. 'Remind me to account for more recent arrivals.' Closing and locking the back door, Peddyr laughed as he turned the key. 'Of course, it could be our first case of spontaneous human combustion, which will render all the leg work completely useless.'

The agenda for the day was to discover who was feeding Vera's cat. The good deed would indicate a level of compassion and hopefully lead to some information on her whereabouts. They were not expecting anything helpful from Jethro Dart and his wife Tracey. In fact, Peddyr had pre-warned Connie to beat a hasty retreat if the man answered the door. 'The bloke is a psycho,' he told her. 'He'd punch you soon as look at you. But we have to try.' Which is what they did and soon enough Peddyr's words proved to be accurate. Having peered through the kitchen and lounge window of Vera's home, they approached 16 Browns Court with Peddyr hoping there would be no reaction to his firm pounding on the cracked double glazing of the grubby UPVC door.

Unfortunately for them both, the man of the house appeared within seconds, wrenching the door open and letting fly a string of expletives at being disturbed. 'Well? What the fuck do you want?' he challenged. He reminded Peddyr of a fearsome bulldog about to enter a pit at an illegal dog fight. Teeth bared, blood-shot eyes fixed on Peddyr, he widened his stance in the doorway.

'Just wondered if you could say when you last saw your neighbour,' Peddyr stated with a nod aimed at Vera Hudson's front door to his left.

'The fucking council, the rozzers and now you,' Jed seethed. 'I ain't seen 'er, Tracey ain't seen 'er, nobody gives a flying fuck whether she's alive or dead. The bitch is gone. Now fuck right off and don't bother me again or I'll rip off your head and shit down your neck. Got it?' The door slammed, rattling in its frame.

Connie was ruffled by the experience. 'I wouldn't want to live next door to that cretin,' she said vehemently. 'Even the poor dog looked petrified. Did you see the thing cowering behind him? Awful.'

Having moved on, the evidence they were seeking was to be found in the form of a pet food bowl outside the door to number fourteen. Dried smears of cat food coated one side of the double feeder; a small amount of frozen water remained in the other. As they waited for someone to come to the door, Peddyr risked a quick look inside the wheelie bin abandoned beside the crumbling concrete pathway. Empty cat food tins were tossed in loosely, other rubbish tied up in black refuse sacks.

'For a minute there I thought the cat was dead,' he said lifting something up using a short length of bamboo stick. On closer inspection it was a wig. A shining asymmetrical fringe and wavy chestnut hair emerged, crusted in places with what looked like bolognaise sauce. 'Now then, what do we make of that?' Having released the hairpiece back into the depths of the odorous bin, he checked the names on the housing list to remind himself of the tenants. 'Jody Oakden and Timothy Taylor,' he grinned fleetingly. 'Thought that was the name of a brewery.' Apparently, the pair weren't early risers and there was no sign of life other than steam coming from a vent above the kitchen window.

Connie was already heading back along the path, her sights on the properties either side of an alleyway, which provided a short cut through to Station Road and to the doors of the upstairs flats. She turned and looked up. 'Curtains have just twitched,' she commented. 'Once we've tried twelve and ten, we should head for the odd numbers on the Station Road side before we try the next block.'

Peddyr caught up with her as she tapped at the door of number twelve, home to a Marie Delgado. The door was opened only wide enough for the occupant to scrutinise the Quirks, a snuffling noise and Marie's awkward pose was explained when she spoke to her dog. 'Now then, Petunia. No need to get over-excited.' There was a rhythmical sound coming from the shadowy outline of the stocky dog as it wagged its tail, hitting the paper-thin wall of the entrance hall. 'If you're Jehovah's Witnesses you can piss off.'

With a laugh Peddyr assured her they were no such thing. 'Looking for Mrs Vera Hudson. The lady at number eighteen.'

'Lady? That's a laugh.' The door opened wider to reveal a middle-aged woman and a cloud of cigarette smoke. Despite being wrapped up in an oversized jumper, her fragile frame was about as well disguised as her smoking habit. 'What's the old witch done now, poisoned another dog?' Stopping herself from saying anything further, Marie ran her suspicious eyes over Peddyr. 'You a copper?'

Once satisfied that neither were officers of the law, Marie was at pains to make good her allegations against Vera Hudson.

'We all know she did it, but we can't prove it. The wicked cow used to throw things at Petunia, over my garden gate and all because she reckons her cat is being targeted by dog owners. She's unhinged that woman. Her poxy cat roams where it wants to; our dogs are in the garden or on a lead – apart from that one time when Kyle chased it onto the road, but that was a one-off. I'm telling you, Vera is barking bloody mad. If you so much as look at her cat wrong, she goes off on one.' Marie took a drag at the ever-present cigarette and blew smoke out the side of her mouth. 'Should be locked up if you ask me. And she's light fingered into the bargain.'

'She's gone missing,' Peddyr informed her.

'Good. It'll be a pleasure not seeing her ugly mug.'

'And you think *she* poisoned Petunia?' Connie asked.

'Not just Petunia, she did it to Bonzo, and Gordon, and Kyle.'

Peddyr made a note of the names. 'All dogs, I take it.'

Marie nodded, sucking in a lungful of smoke. 'She laced

chicken legs with poison coz Tracey at number sixteen found the bones. We had to take all four of them to the Blue Cross. It was touch and go for Petunia, wasn't it my petal?'

She reached out with stained fingers and smoothed the fur on the dog's muscular back. Petunia wagged in reply. 'The police said it wasn't worth pursuing because we had no real evidence, but the vet said it was rat poison.'

Waving two scrawny, tawny forefingers like a handgun, Marie screwed up her face and said, 'She comes near my Petunia once more and I'll 'ave her.' She didn't say how but, given the zeal with which the sentiment was delivered, Peddyr didn't doubt Vera would need to keep her shopping trolley at the ready to duck behind – if she did ever show up again. Perhaps there was a simple explanation as to why the old lady hadn't been seen for a while. Maybe she was in hiding from irate neighbours.

11

INSIDE

*D*uring an unexpected phone call at midday, Peddyr made arrangements to meet up with a Sergeant Kevin Spratt. Preferring to work in conjunction with the local missing persons unit, rather than strike out on his own in the search for Vera Hudson, Kevin was one of the first people he had spoken to before setting out to Browns Court the previous evening. Glad of the help from an ex-policeman, Kevin informed him that within the hour there was to be a wider police search of the area to include nearby allotments, outbuildings, abandoned vehicles and anywhere a body could potentially be found. As part of a small missing persons unit which covered the east of the county, Kevin was thoughtful enough to give him a heads-up. 'I'm leading the search. Thought you might want chance to access number eighteen. I'll be there in thirty minutes.'

He was as good as his word and met with Peddyr by the entrance to the railway station, not wanting to draw attention to their acquaintance, should anyone be looking.

'I like to be extra thorough. We've been embarrassed before,' Kevin announced as he outlined the plan of action for the afternoon. 'Four years ago, a woman's body was found in her car three days after it mysteriously left the road, just outside Bosworth. You might recall the case,' he said.

'It rings a bell,' Peddyr replied. 'The family caused a stink if I remember rightly.'

'That's the one,' Kevin said with a curt nod. 'It wasn't as simple as they made out. For a start there were no skid marks, the vehicle ploughed through a hedge and buried itself in a thicket. The poor woman was reported missing within hours of failing to return home but, because it was so well hidden, we just didn't find the car – despite retracing her route home. We didn't look properly. Today we are going to look in every nook and cranny.'

Kevin Spratt was a sturdily built man in his early thirties with bright rounded eyes. His enthusiasm for his job was not dulled by the inclement January weather. 'The Housing Officer is a friend of mine, so I wangled a key for you,' he said with a wink. 'Take your time, have a good look round her flat and let me know anything you think may be of interest. Gloves on if you would. Our lot were in there on Thursday, but it was logged as a welfare visit. Which these days constitutes a quick pop in to see if she had keeled over and was lying in a puddle of her own making...' Passing Peddyr a key on a plastic fob, he shrugged. 'No sign of burglary, no forced entry anywhere, and no Mrs Hudson. When you're done, bell me. We should swap notes and because I need to record your visit, keep it legit, just in case she does show up.'

While Peddyr took possession of the key, Connie had taken the opportunity to dash to the railway station to make use of the facilities, and visit the cafe for hot drinks, determined also to seek out some food to keep them going. While there, she would ask questions of any station staff she could find, in the unlikely event that they could shed further light on Vera Hudson's disappearance.

The task for the day had become a longer exercise than

either of them had predicted because, however cold it might be, Peddyr was not going to turn down the chance to step inside Vera Hudson's home.

Like all the other ground floor maisonettes, number eighteen could only be accessed from Browns Court, and this meant potentially running into Jethro Dart again. Not that Peddyr was bothered by the prospect; he could still handle himself if necessary. Without his wife around to protect for a short while, Peddyr boldly marched to Vera Hudson's front door, which was in a far better state of repair than one next door at the Darts' unsavoury abode.

The key turned in the lock with ease, and removing his own gloves, Peddyr reached into his pocket for the blue nitrile ones he had at the ready, hiding them from prying eyes until he was out of sight and standing in the spartan hallway. Pulling the protective gloves onto his cold hands took longer than usual, so he used the time to check his surroundings before moving further into the property. A cardigan hung from a row of pegs, as did a lightweight waterproof jacket. 'No winter coat,' he noted and pulled out his trusty notebook. 'And no shopping trolley.' He glanced down at a shoe rack. 'One pair of well-worn trainers, one pair of sandals, a brand-new pair of knee-high boots.' He reached out to examine the material. 'Not leather. Price still on the sole. Size eight.' He sniffed. 'Big feet for a woman of her stature.' The description he had been given put her at a chunky five-foot-six.

He turned back to face the door and hunkered down to examine the post lying on the vinyl-tiled floor. No doormat. Among the flyers and advertising leaflets were several letters addressed to Mrs V A Hudson and one to another person by the name of E J Cooper. A name he recognised. 'Postie got the right address, but whoever sent it got the wrong person, or the other way round.' The letter had been sent to number eighteen, just as it said on the envelope, but he knew that an Esther Cooper lived at number thirteen. Her name was on the list of Browns Court residents given to him by the local authority and apart from Lois Finnegan she was one of the few residents who had answered her doorbell the evening before.

* * *

*E*sther lived above Jody Oakden and Timothy Taylor, two people Peddyr and Connie had yet to speak to. She, on the other hand, had given five minutes of her time, opening her door by a few inches to speak with him and Connie. A nervous woman, dressed in high-vis fluorescent orange from head to toe, she spoke from beneath a baseball cap.

'I work the railways. Cleaner. Trackside mostly.' At the time this had struck Peddyr as ironic, given that he could peek past her to see a midden, its smell emanating from the doorway was verging on the putrid. Her flat was rammed to the rafters with newspapers, magazines, clothing, books, boxes, and all manner of carrier bags – their contents unseen. She certainly didn't take her work home with her. Or perhaps she did, Peddyr had thought, a ripple of a smile making its way to his face.

'Do you know the lady at number eighteen?' he had asked.

'Don't know nobody. Keep to myself. Most of them are scum. Lazy benefit cheats. Drug dealers. Don't want to know none of them.'

Checking his list, Peddyr raised a query. 'But you've been here longer than most.' Esther Cooper hadn't been willing to say much more about her immediate neighbours and was even less forthcoming when asked about the people who had moved into the new flats opposite. 'Snobs with cars.'

* * *

he letter addressed to her remained in his hand as he weighed up options. He was unsure whether to post it through her door or to replace it on the floor of number eighteen with the other mail. 'It might be something important,' he muttered. Standing upright and tucking it into a jacket pocket, he cursed a sudden stiffness in his back as well as a protest from his right knee.

To his immediate left was the galley kitchen which contained a fridge almost bare of essentials. There was a dash of rancid-looking milk in a plastic carton, some butter substitute in a tub, two eggs, and a pack of sliced ham which was giving off an unpleasant smell. He checked all the drawers and cupboards, which contained a few utensils and lacked the usual household detritus confined to a specific drawer. The Random Shit Drawer. 'Everyone has an RSD, Vera. Where's yours? And where are your bills?'

Before moving into the bathroom and finally the bedroom, he checked once more for any receipts, mobile phone contracts, or guarantees for appliances, but found nothing. In the bathroom cabinet he at last came across packets of tablets with Vera's name on them. Apart from the post on the hall floor these were the only clue as to the name of the tenant. The tablets had been dispensed locally and well before Christmas. He made a note of the doses and the names of the medicines.

In the bedroom came possible evidence of Vera's prowess as a shoplifter: the wardrobe contained an unusually high number of items of clothing with labels attached. Jumpers, jeans, leggings. 'Our Vera isn't the kind to wear skirts,' Peddyr said as he slid hangers from one side of the hanging rail to the other. 'Favourite colour is blue. Black a close second.'

He stood back from the bed, the central whorl of cat hairs on the bedcovers defining where Vera's pet chose to sleep each night, and he folded his arms. Something wasn't fitting right.

Where were the trappings of a life lived? The lounge had one chair and a small TV on a coffee table. It barely looked lived in. That was the incongruity about the place. That was his overall impression. An empty flat. An empty life. There was no Wi-Fi router, no comforts of home, no personal items on display. Where were the photographs of her husband Ray? Where were the nick-knacks and the mementos picked up to remind a person of a day out at the seaside?

What finally convinced Peddyr that Vera Hudson was not due to return any day soon was the knitting, or rather the lack of it, and when he continued his search, there was nothing else to hint at a keen crafter or a creative. Not a painting hung on the walls, not even a crocheted loo-roll holder. He opened more drawers until eventually he found a half-completed scarf attached to a pair of knitting needles. 'That's your lot is it, Vera? Half a sodding scarf.'

THE GANG OF FOUR

*T*he offices of Bagshot & Laker solicitors were warm and welcoming as was the greeting from Fiona McFarland, secretary to Bernard Kershaw, senior partner. 'My two favourite private investigators,' Fiona announced in a sweet lilt as they stepped through the tall glass and stainless-steel doors and into a wood-panelled reception area; Fiona's domain and one which smelled of citrus. 'Any sign of Vera Hudson so far?' she asked, making her way towards them, her tartan skirt swinging in rhythm with her wide hips. 'I do hope you have some news for poor Mr Harkness.'

After an exchange of pleasantries and remarks about the icy air that had followed Peddyr and Connie in from the darkness of the street, she ushered them through to Bernard's office and dashed off to make hot drinks. 'I'll be back in a wee while. He's expecting you.'

Peddyr wasn't in a cheery state of mind. 'I truly thought we would be sitting in front of the fire by this time on a Saturday afternoon,' he called across the room to Bernard. Taking off his jacket, he hung it from a coat stand sited near the door and took Connie's coat from her to do the same.

There was a gentle tapping and into the room stepped Monica Morris. A tall smartly-besuited woman, she towered over Connie who was obliged to tip her head back to greet the newcomer with a wide smile.

'Ah, Grasshopper, to what do we owe this pleasure?' Peddyr interjected before anyone else could speak. The nickname had stuck for some years, ever since Monica had been mentored by Bernard Kershaw during her training to become a legal executive specialising in the Mental Health Act.

Bending to kiss Connie on both cheeks, Monica grinned. 'He still finds that so amusing,' she said to her before nodding to her boss and wagging a finger at her good friend Peddyr. 'And don't start. You know how Bernie gets all eggy when you mess about.'

'Me?'

At his expansive and expensive desk, Bernard deflated, letting out a long slow sigh and allowing his head to hang. His chin couldn't reach his chest, the rounded folds of his neck prevented any such landing. 'Here we go,' he said, despairingly. 'Can you two forego the comedy routine for once. We have all sacrificed our Saturday to respond to this, and time is precious.'

'Agreed,' replied Peddyr. 'And you're not the one who's been out in the bitter bloody cold freezing his fundamentals off.'

'I don't have any fundamentals,' Connie added, rubbing her hands together. 'But even I've had enough for today.' She turned to Monica with a look of despair. 'We daren't take the car to the ghetto, which is fine, the exercise will do us good. But having scrabbled about in bins and on occasion been verbally abused today, the final indignity came when I had to make use of the ladies' toilets at the station. I've perfected the art of the hover, and thank goodness I had wet wipes in my bag but really...' She left the rest to Monica's imagination and acknowledged Peddyr's look of gratitude for her willingness to spend so many hours with him on the trail of a missing woman.

Settled into leather button-backed chairs, sipping hot

drinks courtesy of Fiona, the four friends and work colleagues were at ease in each other's company. 'Decided to give the morning swim a miss then, old man?' Peddyr enquired, catching Bernard with an impish twinkle in his eye. 'The winter weather putting you off since you dropped some of that protective blubber?'

'I won't deny it, old bean. The duvet seemed much the preferable option this morning and my new abode is comfortable and welcoming, especially as there's no nearly ex-wife to harangue me. Maybe tomorrow.' He cleared his throat. 'To begin. Pedd, what have you and the lovely Mrs Q found out from friends and neighbours of Vera Hudson? I hear the police struggled to get much from them, which I understand was expected, given the nature of the neighbourhood.'

'We didn't do too badly, considering,' Connie said. 'And thanks for the photo you sent through yesterday, Bernie. It was of some help.' She smiled across at him. 'As you already know, police reacted promptly to Mr Isaac Harkness's missing person report. Apart from the visit to Vera Hudson's flat on Thursday, they have since carried out a very sensible search of the area. Tucked against the new development of Brookside is a large blue shipping container ostensibly still in use by the builders of the flats.'

Bernard raised his balding head. 'Please God, tell me the police searched inside.' He alternated his enquiry between Peddyr and Connie, a look of concern evident.

'Yes,' Connie replied, swiftly. 'They finally managed to contact the key holder at about midday today. We were still making headway into our doorstep interviews when the property developer Gary Wood turned up to meet with an officer from the VAIU.' She nodded at Bernard who had raised a query using his eyebrows. 'Bosworth police station houses a special safeguarding office,' she said, 'and Kevin Spratt, who doesn't have a brother called Jack, is one of a few officers making up the vulnerable adults investigation unit. A mental health and social care initiative by all accounts.'

'And Vera Hudson meets their criteria because of more than mere social circumstances, I assume. What did they find in this shipping container, may I ask?'

Peddyr stepped in to give a shortened version of events. 'Nothing out of the ordinary. Nothing in the container, nothing in the allotment sheds they could open without causing undue damage. Nothing in the abandoned car at the far end of the cul-de-sac. Nothing in the hedgerows and along the railway tracks. A big fat zero on CCTV from the station so far. No sign of Vera Hudson, plenty of evidence of drug use though,' he said, staring at a cluster of tea leaves in the base of the dainty cup in his hands. 'Sergeant Kevin Spratt is keen to pick up on anything we may find. Making house-to-house inquiries is a futile exercise for their officers. Several of the residents are more at home with blues and twos and a joy ride in a paddy-wagon.'

This embarrassing truth was common knowledge to the town as a whole and there had been a recent flurry of articles in the local paper, as well as several phone-in debates on BBC Valley radio. The area around the station had become synonymous with drug deals and antisocial behaviour, fuelled by visiting criminal gangs arriving by train. The new flats, laughingly called Brookside, were a cynical attempt on the part of town planners to raise the standard of the area. Vera Hudson's disappearance would do nothing to improve the already sullied reputation.

'What did Sergeant Spratt share with you about their missing persons search?' Bernard enquired.

'Everything really. In fact, I would hazard a guess that between us we probably know more about Vera Hudson than her own brother does,' Peddyr said, sliding a wayward tea leaf from the rim of his cup with a forefinger. It was time to inform Bernard of their findings. 'Connie, do your thing,' he instructed.

Refreshed by the tea, his diminutive wife rose from her seat and trotted over to the window to rest against the warmth of the radiator there. 'Right people, while I defrost my derrière a little more, here is what we know so far. Vera Hudson is sixty-two years old but from all accounts has had a hard life and as a result she looks somewhat older than her years, which is reflected in the photograph sent through by Mr Harkness the long-lost brother.' She stopped when Peddyr raised a hand.

'That photograph,' he began. 'Do we know where Mr Harkness laid his hands on it? Only to me it looks as if it was taken from some distance away and without her knowledge.'

With this Bernard tapped the notepad at his side. 'Yes, as a matter of fact I do know who took it. Isaac Harkness took a snap with his phone. This was fortunate because at least it gave him something to show to his father when he broke the news that Channel 7 were planning a TV programme about his life and work, during which *she* was to be the big reveal at the end.'

'And how did that go down?' Peddyr asked, both eyebrows dancing. 'I bet he was none too pleased.'

In response, Bernard nodded so aggressively his jowls rippled. 'When I spoke to him about it, Austin downplayed the whole issue somewhat, but I suspect you are right, Pedd. By the time he knew about it, Isaac and his Aunty Vera had already signed an agreement to participate. Thus, Austin was forced to involve his legal team to gain some control. It's all on hold now, of course.'

The hairs on the nape of Peddyr's neck stood to attention. He felt a motive presenting itself right then and there. 'Connie, tell our learned friend here what we know about Vera Hudson so far. I think he'll be pleased with our efforts.'

'With pleasure,' his wife replied, giving a small cough to clear her throat. 'Apparently, several decades ago, Vera unexpectedly found herself as a young widow and, as I have only had time to run brief checks, this would seem to be the case. Mr Ray

Hudson's untimely death made the papers because he had been in dispute with neighbours in an ongoing war about a boundary. It finally deteriorated to the level of physical violence and Ray Hudson was bound over to keep the peace.'

'And now he rests there...' Peddyr added, not able to resist the quip. Connie paused long enough to allow for the apology before she went on.

'At the time, his death was treated as suspicious.'

'And why was that, may I ask?' Bernard leaned forward.

'Because of the war with the neighbour it was thought to be too coincidental. Death threats had been made in front of witnesses. There was an altercation in the street, he collapsed. Nobody was ever charged with anything.'

Peddyr shifted in his seat, mulling this over. There was so much more to Vera Hudson than anyone had imagined, and he was beginning to see a winding investigation stretching out before him; a cold damp and dismal one. He tuned back in to what Connie was saying.

'She and Ray lived in Corby, Northamptonshire. We know not why, nor how, but somehow Vera Hudson secured a local authority property in this area... however it came about, she has only lived in Browns Court for the last six months, doesn't appear on the electoral register and is not a popular individual. Any thoughts of a stereotypical sad and lonely pensioner in need of sympathy should be wiped from your minds.'

Peddyr held his tongue and instead watched the audience for reactions. The impression given, when the case was referred urgently to P.Q. Investigations the previous day, was that Vera Hudson was a vulnerable soul who lived peacefully with her cat and enjoyed knitting. An occasional trip to church and to the shops was said to be her limited social world. If this was the life she had painted for the benefit of her long-lost brother, it was way wide of the mark.

Bernard Kershaw had merely repeated information from the

Harknesses to Peddyr and Connie over the phone when he called them into action. 'Find the sweet lady and return her to the bosom of her family. That is your remit. Mr Harkness will cover expenses, but this shouldn't take long. She can't be far. Perhaps she's visiting a friend.' Bernard's words echoed in Peddyr's head as he watched the solicitor's face fall with the new less palatable version of Vera Hudson.

To his left, Monica sat with a knowing smile lifting the corners of her mouth. She delved into her voluminous shoulder bag and produced a notepad. Finger licked with slow authority, she flipped a couple of pages before resting the pad on her lap, her legs crossed.

Bernard turned to her. 'It seems your hunch may have some validity after all, Monica,' he conceded, resting back in his chair, smoothing his silk tie. 'Do go on, Connie,' he said. 'I'm all ears.'

'You certainly are,' Peddyr chipped in, unable to help himself.

Bernard Kershaw, as well as being a respected lawyer, was gifted with ears of considerable size, and since losing a stone and a half in weight, in response to divorce proceedings and a determination to begin a healthier happier life, his most obvious facial features had somehow become more prominent. He rolled his good-natured eyes at Peddyr as a snort escaped from Monica. Peddyr daren't look at her for fear of encouraging more childish sniggering.

'Same old jokes. You keep wheeling them out and they don't get any funnier,' Bernard admonished. He raised an outstretched arm, palm uppermost. 'Connie, if you wouldn't mind.'

With his eyes focussed on the plush carpet beneath his feet, Peddyr composed himself by avoiding his wife's playful eyes, the ones he knew would be aimed at him. He heard the laugh in her voice as she spoke.

'Now where was I? … Oh, yes. Vera Hudson. Narrowing it down to find out exactly when she was last seen has been a struggle so far. You said Isaac Harkness last spoke to her on

New Year's Day. That was two and a half weeks ago. Mr Koslowski, the local shop keeper, reckons she hasn't been in for at least a week, but he couldn't be certain about that. His wife has been unwell and a cousin by the name of Marek was helping out, and he didn't know the regulars.' Connie pulled a face. 'Mr Koslowski wasn't a fan. He accused Vera of shoplifting on more than one occasion, stating she would squirrel things away in her shopping trolley; you know… the ones on wheels with zips at the top, the sort usually pulled along behind.'

Bernard straightened in his chair. 'And how old is she? Sixty-two, and she uses a trolley? Good God. What's wrong with the woman?'

'All sorts, depending on the day of the week, apparently. She told various people that she has COPD,' Connie replied. 'That's Chronic Obstructive Pulmonary Disease to you and me. Anyway, if true, it would restrict her ability to walk any distance. For that reason, the police initially confined themselves to the local neighbourhood. And today, we spoke to a number of those neighbours, two of whom accused her of kicking out at their dogs. Marie Delgado at number twelve stated that her Staffie – a lovely thing by the name of Petunia – was deliberately poisoned by Vera for having the temerity to bark at her cat. There's no proof of this but Marie was insistent. Any dog who so much as snarled at Vera's cat was at risk. Allegedly.'

'Conjecture and hearsay,' Monica said, tapping at her notebook with a biro. 'Unless you consider her past record.'

'Finally,' Peddyr said, leaning forward and rubbing his palms together. 'We get to find out why Monica is here.'

'I did wonder,' added his wife. 'It's lovely to see you, Monica, but it was odd for you to sit in on a meeting about a missing person. Not your usual remit.'

13

NEED A FAG?

*P*eddyr stared hard at Monica. 'Well? Why are you here?' he demanded. 'If I find out we've been freezing our assets off all day while you two have been snuggled up somewhere unravelling the mysterious disappearance of Vera Hudson without so much as getting slightly chilly, I'll...' The words faded as Bernard Kershaw shook his head and Monica reminded Peddyr that she had arrived minutes after the Quirks themselves.

'I've been digging out some paperwork, if you must know,' she added, pulling a slim spiral-bound folder from the shoulder bag by her feet. She balanced it delicately in front of her on Bernard's leather-topped desk.

'Pedd, old bean, do hold your tongue a minute and allow us to explain,' Bernard pleaded as he passed across a copy of Vera Hudson's photograph to Monica. 'Take a look. Is it her?'

She scanned it in silence, a puzzled look slowly appearing. 'Goodness me,' she said, sounding uncertain. 'I can't say it looks like her from what I can remember... The years have been extremely unkind.'

'You know Vera Hudson?' Connie gasped. 'Why didn't you say so?'

'If I'm right, I came across her some years ago, in a professional capacity,' Monica declared, glancing at the photograph once more. 'Bernie happened to mention her name while we were discussing another case over the phone last night.' She looked across the wide desk at her boss and pulled a face. 'Right name, right part of the country… but—'

'Try us,' Peddyr insisted. He'd had enough of being kept waiting and wanted a hot bath and a relaxing evening at home with his feet up. 'Spit it out, Grasshopper, for Christ's sake and that of my patience.'

Monica handed the folder to him. He flipped it open.

'But this is about someone called Julia,' Peddyr challenged. 'What has this got to do with Verity Hudson?'

'Years ago, decades in fact, when I was still a registered Mental Health Nurse, I stupidly decided to undertake a master's degree,' Monica explained. 'For one of the required modules, I made a case study of a woman by the name of Verity Hudson, Julia is the name I chose for her to ensure anonymity. She was at a psychiatric unit in Northamptonshire, admitted for her own safety following an episode of psychotic depression.'

Connie raised her hands to her face, touching her fingertips to her cheeks. 'And is there such a thing as psychotic depression?' she queried.

Monica nodded firmly. 'There is indeed, and in my experience, it usually occurs when an underlying depression remains untreated for a significant period of time or is of rapid onset, like some sort of complex grief reaction.' She pointed to the folder open in Peddyr's hands. 'It's all in there. The death of her husband from a heart attack, the unexpected pregnancy, the delusional beliefs. Great case study, tragic life.'

'Post-Partum Psychosis.' Peddyr read aloud, running his fingers down the summary in Monica's case study report.

'Referred from Fairfield Hospital when her baby was taken into local authority care. Risk of violence to others. So where did the kid end up?'

His question was met with a shrug from Monica who said, 'Shall we chat about this once you have read through my whole assignment?'

Bernard had been unusually quiet. He sat hunched over, making notes, and listening intently as the other three sifted through the salient points of the mystery as they arose. Without warning, he then picked up the phone and made an internal call to his secretary, asking if she would mind making a photocopy of Monica's case study.

As Fiona McFarland bustled in to take silent and efficient possession of the folder from Peddyr, Connie moved from the warmth of the radiator to stand at her husband's shoulder. 'What was she like when you interviewed her?' she asked of Monica.

After handing the folder over to Fiona with a grateful smile of thanks, Peddyr twisted to see Connie's face. 'Yes, Lao Po. That is the question to be asking.' He patted the tiny hand she had placed on his shoulder. 'And in those years since you last saw her, Monica, what has changed about Verity Hudson?'

'Everything has changed. Her health has gone down the pan for a start. She's put on weight, which I suppose you would especially if you were on steroids for COPD. We should check with her GP.'

Fiona busied herself. Tucking the folder under her arm, Bernard's secretary collected the crockery from the desk and with a full tray headed back out of the office again, never once interrupting the flow of conversation. Bernard mouthed his appreciation as he rose from his seat to open the door for her.

'The police already took the GP route. I asked Kevin Spratt for details of her medical history; it's standard practice for a missing person inquiry to ask for such things,' Connie confirmed. 'The mysterious Verity Anne Hudson has only very recently registered with the health centre and was on the books of a GP in Towcester where she hasn't been seen for over a year. Although she doesn't have a diagnosis of COPD, her mental health history and pregnancy are recorded in the GP summary. When she moved property, her previous GP practice furnished her with three months' worth of various tablets, mostly painkillers and night sedation. Peddyr can confirm that those medicines were in her bathroom cabinet. Apart from that, his visit to her flat told us nothing new because it was practically devoid of belongings. Very odd,' she said, writing down another reminder as it occurred to her, adding to her ever-growing list of things to follow up on. 'What *is* going on here?'

Peddyr cocked his head. 'Bernie? It's your client, do you have any idea what we might have got ourselves caught up in?'

Rubbing at the top of his head, Bernard Kershaw said, 'I'm flummoxed. This is a rum old do.'

When he used this expression, it was a sure sign that something untoward was in the pipeline. Peddyr knew this of old, even if Bernard failed to recognise it himself.

'How rum?' Peddyr asked with a note of insistence. From what he understood, Austin Harkness – the estranged brother of Verity Hudson – had been 'delighted and surprised' at the prospect of a reunion. His son had been instrumental in tracing Verity Hudson when diligent searches and cryptic social media appeals for anyone called Mrs V A Hudson aged sixty-two finally located the woman who preferred to be known as Vera.

Peddyr looked in puzzlement at his old friend. 'Why did Austin Harkness contact *you*? He has his own legal team and besides I thought you cherry-picked your cases these days and only deigned to work for known clients as part of your vain attempts to head towards retirement. Old boy network, is it?'

'We went to the same school, as a matter of fact,' Bernard replied. 'I was his fag for a term.'

Connie let out a gasp, Peddyr choked on his own laughter and Monica sat open mouthed as they listened to the man explain himself. 'He was a scholarship boy; his father was the headmaster. I was a junior in the same house as Austin. The sixth form boys all had a fag to run errands, make their beds and do their bidding.'

'Friggin' frogspawn!' Peddyr exclaimed, shaking his head in disapproval. 'A fag... don't let anyone else hear you say that. Sodding public schools; nothing but a breeding ground for perverts and politicians. Present company excepted.' He screwed up his nose.

'And here you are, doing his bidding again,' Connie said quietly. She threw a sad look towards Monica who stayed silent, fiddling with a pen.

'That's a little unfair of you, Mrs Q,' Bernard huffed. 'I must object to your unfounded assumption that just because I happen to practice law in a place convenient to oblige Austin Harkness with my services, that he is in some way using me. Need I remind you that I am held in high regard as far as my chosen profession is concerned and in legal circles my reputation is one to be applauded. I have accepted the case, and on this occasion, I have the opportunity to charge extortionate amounts of money for my time.'

'Revenge payment, is it?' Peddyr asked. 'What did he do to you? A flogging? Debagging in the toilets? Endless humiliation?'

'Don't be ridiculous, Peddyr. This isn't *Tom Brown's Schooldays*.'

14

SURROUNDED

*L*ois and Cara needed to update the scoreboard because the Brookside flats had filled up fast and the show of aggression from 16 Browns Court, witnessed by Lois and Dan, had galvanised them into action, as had the apparent disappearance of Vera Hudson. At Cara's insistence, they met for a natter on Sunday morning to build better profiles of their neighbours.

'What did you make of the private detectives?' Lois asked, stepping inside Cara's flat. 'And why didn't you send me an update yesterday?'

The Quirks had managed to catch several of the Brookside residents during their extended visit to Browns Court the day before. Although they had no need to speak to Lois again, they had been as good as their word and knocked on every door including that of number thirty where Cara lived.

'Sorry, I meant to, but I had work to catch up on,' she replied, apologetically. 'And there were some things I had to do to help the Quirks with their investigation. My Saturday disappeared in a flash, and it's been the same this morning.' She shot a look at her desk by the French windows. 'My brain has turned to fudge right enough.'

Saying an extended hello to the two budgies in their cage, Lois then settled into one of the inflatable chairs as best she could without toppling over. 'I guess she's still missing,' she said. 'Vera, from number eighteen.'

Cara had moved to the kettle and was staring distractedly out of the window. Her efforts to hide her excessive interest in Vera Hudson were taking their toll. 'The police were here again while you and Dan were out yesterday. Did you know?'

'And who would tell us? Apart from pristine Christine Fowler and her regular updates during Pilates and on Facebook, you're the only one who keeps me in the loop.'

Turning her attention to making coffee, Cara continued. 'Well, I'm telling you now. While you were out at Dunelm buying your funky coffee table, they searched the blue container and the allotments. Because they only had one photograph to go on, I gave the police and the Quirks a description of Vera, anything I knew about her habits and, I hope you don't mind, but I printed off a copy of our neighbourhood list so far.' She visibly winced. 'The police want the rest of our descriptions about the goings-on hereabouts, as we gather them, but not necessarily the scores. Although, when they were here, Mrs Quirk said they were "an unusual instinctive insight" and we should keep going. I liked her.'

'I like both of them,' Lois replied. 'If he wasn't so old and married, I could fall for a man like that.'

For Cara it was a relief that she had been able to provide some help in the search. Not only had she noticed more than most in the time she had been at Brookside while working from home, but because she watched Vera Hudson in particular. 'Let's get to it then.'

Cara put the mugs of coffee on a small table and gingerly lowered herself into the other inflatable chair.

Her ability to invent descriptive names for their neighbours was a habit developed to help aid her memory. On the ground floor was Hairy Toes, the tallest man in the world with the smallest car, who came and went to who-knows-where every day. He had a job, but Cara hoped for his sake that it wasn't a long commute.

In the other ground floor flat was Salesman Sam, a man in his mid-thirties with a regular girlfriend. The consensus was that the two ground floor residents were not the sort to take home to meet the parents. Lois declared she wouldn't have considered going on a date with either of them.

'Swipe left on Tinder.'

Cara shook her head with a despairing look. 'It's no wonder you've never had much luck finding a decent bloke until now. Steer clear of online dating. You'll not catch me poking my finger at a screen. I've had my share of scallywags. Men can swivel as far as I'm concerned.'

'Changing allegiances?'

'Cheeky mare! As it happens, I'm not that way inclined and not desperate enough to go looking for the next Mr Laidlaw on Tinder neither. That way lies disaster.'

Such wise words had Lois blushing with the embarrassment of what she had put herself through in the name of romance. 'My entanglements via dating sites have mostly involved bed sheets, been hot and sweaty, and lacking in meaningful conversation. Something I would rather forget.'

She turned her attention back to the scoreboard and to Salesman Sam. His SUV, which had clearly been in a spectacular prang just before he moved in, was still abandoned next to the metal shipping container at Cara's side of the building. She had a lovely view of it from her bedroom window.

The last people to arrive in the left-hand block, Posh and Becks, were neighbours to the elusive Mr Blue-Car-Football-Supporter. 'You'd hardly know he was there. I didn't hear a peep out of that floor until they moved in,' Lois remarked. 'But Posh and Becks have made up for it in spades.'

'Our scores for them?' Cara said, her head dropping with impatience because Lois was taking too long with her decision.

'Based on the fact that she's a rude cow, also because they are ignoring the allocated parking rules and wear nothing but designer clothing, and because he most definitely bleaches his hair; I award a generous two and a half out of ten,' she said, clearly satisfied with the justification for such a low score.

The approving nod from Cara was given to reassure her that she had not been too critical. 'I concur wholeheartedly,' Cara said, flicking a wavy ribbon of rose-blonde hair over her shoulder.

From above, the two girls had marvelled at the scene the day Posh and Becks moved in and had made comment as the removal men unloaded the lorry, valiantly ignoring Posh's shrill squawking from the windows of the middle floor flat where she was creating a designer nest to her taste. Although in Cara's view "taste" was somewhat of a misnomer, because there was nothing remotely classy about their choice of furnishings.

Predictably the TV was enormous, the sofa a zebra-print monstrosity, and the scatter cushions matched Beck's car. Hideous. All of it. And, in Cara's opinion, so were they.

Up until mid-December, Silver VW was the only resident of Brookside's right wing, which had made Lois and Cara envious of his peaceful existence. They hadn't been able to work him out, and most puzzling were his night-time forays. Every evening between about nine-thirty and ten o'clock, he would venture out for a maximum of twenty minutes in his car, music blasting loud and selfishly. 'Drug run,' Cara concluded.

Since then, there had been a flurry of arrivals in the right wing and these people had yet to be accounted for on the score-board. 'We must get our act together, I said we would email Connie Quirk with the updated version by lunchtime,' Cara announced. At this she placed her mug on the floor and tumbled awkwardly from the chair onto the carpet before making her way to her desk to sit at the laptop in her office chair. 'Who is on the top floor of the right wing?'

'Builder Bob,' Lois replied. He was a man who was rarely seen other than to give a grunted greeting in passing. There was a sour set to his expression, but Cara's theory was that his marriage had recently headed down the toilet and he was boiling with resentment.

His neighbours, White Van Woman and her husband, were unimpressive on the whole. She was tall, striking, with a head of dark wavy hair overwhelming her facial features, and from her generous mouth came a voice like a foghorn. 'She's a klazomaniac,' Lois announced.

'And what's that when it's at home?' Cara asked.

'Someone unable to speak without shouting. I heard it on *Countdown*.'

Matilda was the name given to the strange girl on the middle floor of the right wing. 'I still can't get over the fact that her elderly parents did all the hard work when she moved in,' Cara remarked, making notes on the laptop. 'I swear they fist pumped as they drove away.' Matilda scored very poorly.

'And on the ground floor we have Asian Prozzy with her string of male visitors,' Lois said. 'Leaving only two flats empty.'

'And not a single child between us,' Cara noted, rolling her computer mouse on its mat. 'And none in the rest of Browns Court, you'll notice.'

'Odd,' Lois said. 'You're right, and I hadn't even realised until you said that.'

There were no families living in Browns Court, in fact the demographic in the maisonettes was strikingly similar to the Brookside flats. One or two residents over the age of fifty, other than that the occupants were mostly single people with visiting romantic entanglements, and the occasional married couple.

Both sets of residents displayed the expected diversity in terms of race and sexuality. There were, however, some glaring differences which set them apart from each other.

Brooksiders were accepted by the landlord only if they could prove a regular income. None of them were on benefits to Cara's knowledge and, with the exception of her budgies and a goldfish owned by Posh and Becks, none of them had any pets. None of her neighbours in Brookside appeared to earn a living from selling drugs as far as they could tell, although there was a question mark about this when it came to Silver VW. Then there was the matter of illegal earnings and night-time visitors to Asian Prozzy.

'I think we should familiarise ourselves with our neighbours across the car park, from a safe distance,' Lois suggested. 'The way the Quirks were received, I wouldn't feel safe knocking doors to introduce myself. Make sure they don't catch you spying on them,' she said to Cara.

'Don't worry. No one has seen me so far,' she replied with a wink. 'Have a look at this. There's The Hoarder surrounded by her mountain of detritus.' Cara showed Lois a photo she'd taken with her phone. She placed her mobile on the kitchen work surface for Lois to see. 'And there's her funny looking uniform. Wonder what she does for living? If she does venture out…'

'And who is this lady?' Lois asked, aiming a finger at the next photograph.

'The Quiet Worker,' Cara replied, a small set of wrinkles appearing on her brow. 'She's West African, I think. She works, but I don't see much of her apart from the occasional glimpse before she closes her curtains. Which was the case for Vera at number eighteen. In the last week, all I catch is the cat going in and out.'

'And I've seen these two.'

Cara had captured a photo of a short man in a red baseball cap and red tracksuit, next to a taller woman in pointed ankle boots and jeans. 'I don't have names for them yet, but I'm pretty sure he's a dealer. The number of cars rolling in, stopping, and collecting a small bag of something after tapping on his window... He's not running a tuck shop.'

Lois acknowledged that she had spotted the man strutting in and out of number ten, the ground floor flat on the far side of the alleyway. 'The Red Dwarf.'

Picking up her pen with a brief chuckle, Cara added the label to the scoreboard notes on a pad by the side of her laptop. 'Brilliant. He can't be more than 160 centimetres. And have you noticed the way he walks? Giving it the big "I am" with those stumpy legs of his. Hilarious.'

'She's got hair like Sharon Osbourne, a dancing pole in her lounge, and at least two other blokes go round when Red Dwarf's not about,' Lois confirmed, grinning in delight at her own contributions. 'What about Taylor and Jody?' she asked, prodding at the box on the official scoreboard with their names written on it. 'Jody's Insta account is amazing. He says he's saving up for rhinoplasty, on account of a slight kink in the bridge of his nose. That's going to cost and those two must spend all their money on wigs, make-up, and clothes.'

Cara had discovered their names because they called to each other whenever they left their front door. Conversations outside drifted upwards and were easily heard if a window was open.

'And there are neighbours we know nothing about,' Lois remarked. 'Of course, they must know each other relatively well, but us Brooksiders are strangers to them, as we are to each other.'

Cara hadn't thought about it in that way before, but it was true. All the Brooksiders had been randomly selected by one man and thrown together with the assumption they would be socially responsible, respectful of the property and each other, and pay their rent. Strangers, sussing each other out from afar, watching and being watched.

15

TEA LEAVES

*C*onnie decided to make use of Peddyr's office while he was out on Sunday morning. Usually only attending for funerals and weddings, he announced that he was going to the morning service at the local church. 'The service is at ten-thirty, which fits in nicely,' he had said the evening before. 'I'll take a morning swim with Bernie, do my household chores and then go straight there. Even if I have to ask the vicar, I'm sure someone will point me in the direction of Pamela What's-er-name.'

'You'll have to stop referring to her that way. It's sure to slip out if you don't give the woman her proper name,' his wife chided.

'I do, and it is,' he replied, grinning. 'Pamela Watts *is* her name.'

Without him around to distract her, Connie could focus on her searches of genealogy sites. She looked up towards a picture of Columbo for inspiration. Peddyr's office walls were lined with photographs of famous fictional detectives, and the room was designed to resemble that of a Sam Spade set, proper film-noir stuff. She had purchased most of the items within the office after careful searching and presented the finished article to Peddyr as a gift to celebrate his final retirement from hands-on security consultation work. It was the manifestation of his promise to her, a solid reminder that P.Q. Investigations was in business and no longer a much-talked-about dream. With its birth, Peddyr Quirk left behind a career in the police, consultancy work for the film industry and other less obvious contracts that would never become common knowledge. He was now a part-time lecturer for the police and a fully-fledged private investigator. Connie was his right-hand woman.

'It's no good you winking at me like that,' she said to the wall. 'And what is your full name, anyway?' she continued to ask the picture. 'Even Madonna has a real full name. You can't just be Columbo.'

Annoyingly she couldn't recall if this had ever been mentioned in the TV series. 'Morse was finally exposed as being called Endeavour, which was a strange thing for his parents to do,' she mused as she looked across at some of the other prints. 'There's Sam Spade, Mike Hammer, Hercule Poirot, Sherlock Holmes, Jim Rockford... then there's you lot,' she said, flicking eyes around to the corners of the room. 'Petrocelli, Ironside, Cannon, Macmillan and Wife.' Connie smiled when her eyes settled on Rock Hudson and his co-star. This was her latest acquisition and had pleased Peddyr no end. He added it to his "Wall of Detective Cheese" almost as soon as he had unwrapped it on Christmas Day.

Tracing her gaze back to where she had started, she nodded. 'Something tells me your name was Frank,' she said. 'Frank Columbo.' Fingers intertwining, she rocked back in Peddyr's comfortable captain's chair, and it let out a squeak. 'But none of you will have the middle name of Thorn. Unusual, isn't it?'

It came to her like a punch to the arm. 'What is wrong with you?' she said to herself. 'Get on and search for Austin Thorn, not Harkness.'

Verity Hudson had been a cinch to find out about. Her marriage to Ray Hudson was on record, as was his death. Monica had said there was a child too, but the searches threw up nothing, which would confirm that the child had remained under some form of social services protection or been adopted. 'Damn,' Connie muttered. 'Where did you disappear to, you little so-and-so?'

Austin Harkness should have been an easy name to research, to trace his family tree, cross reference it with Verity Hudson's and to place them in the same world. This was basic background searching that Connie did with relish. Invariably it threw up something of interest, just as it had on this occasion.

As far as Austin Harkness was concerned, his business dealings were straightforward to account for. They were in the public domain. His fortune, his properties and assets were well documented and evidenced. He paid taxes, extortionate ones at that, and had never been accused of avoidance or any wrong-doing when it came to business practices. Indeed, the opposite applied: He was generous and philanthropic. The press loved him. Financiers loved him. He was a rags to riches success story. No great surprise then that Channel 7 had planned a programme about his life, and unexpectedly finding an estranged sister must have pleased the producers immensely.

Curiosity duly aroused, Connie wanted to know about the private man.

Little was ever published about his family. He mentioned in several articles and interviews that his parents were teachers, his father a headmaster at a public school, but there was no mention of a sister. His wife and son and extended family were kept out of the spotlight and although there had been rumours about Isaac Harkness failing to live up to his father's expectations, nothing was made public.

Lifting her head once more, Connie sighed. 'Come to think of it, Frank,' she said aloud to the picture of Columbo, 'I don't know anything about Alan Sugar's family, or if that scary woman on Dragon's Den has a husband.' Drumming a pen on the desk she tutted. 'But I do know that if his sister's maiden name was Thorn, and his middle name is Thorn, then we may have stumbled across something. Time to delve into the Thorn parentage.'

Sometime later she heard her name being called and turned her wrist to check the time on her watch against the time on the computer screen. 'That can't be right,' she gasped. It had gone midday. Peddyr was later than anticipated and still she hadn't begun to think about preparing lunch.

Sunday was sacrosanct in the Quirk household when cases allowed. A full roast dinner was expected today and, to make matters worse, she had invited Bernard Kershaw to join them. He was finding the life of the soon-to-be single man rather more taxing than he had imagined, and she felt sorry for him. He and his wife Deidre had finally separated, with divorce pending. Bernard had done the chivalrous thing by moving out of the spacious family home and was now ensconced in a comfortable modern apartment. So far, he had failed to expand his repertoire when it came to cooking for himself. If food didn't come ready prepared for the microwave, it would be beans on toast or the same but without the toast. Connie couldn't bear to think of him sat alone on a gloomy winter Sunday. 'Is that you, Lao Gong?' she queried.

The door opened and there stood Peddyr, rubbing his hands together to warm them, disappointment etched on his rosy cheeks. 'Don't tell me, menopausal brain fog has resulted in you not knowing what day it is.' He threw a look over his shoulder. 'Shouldn't the beef be in the oven by now?'

Connie shrank with embarrassment. 'Yes, to the last question but you are wrong about the brain fog. Actually, I have experienced the polar opposite this morning. My neurones have been firing at a rapid rate and I have news.' Judging by the look on

Peddyr's face she had not impressed. A better plan was required, and she knew just the thing to lighten his mood. 'Tell you what. How about you call for your playmate and trot off to the pub. Be back for a late lunch, say... two o'clock. A packet of peanuts should keep you going until then.'

The wrinkles on her husband's bold brow unfolded as the smile grew broad on his face. 'Mighty. I'll give the old codger a ring and let him know we have a free pass. No Dreary to nag at him and no pressure on time.' He tipped her a wink. 'You can tell us all about your findings over a pile of Yorkshire puddings and roast potatoes. Just the ticket for a Sunday afternoon snooze later.' He reached across his desk and picked up the handset of his retro Bakelite phone. He dialled without having to pause to recall the number.

'Bernie? Fancy a few bevvies down the Queen's Arse before lunch?'

Connie would have to get a move on if there was to be a lunch ready in two hours flat. Rare beef was on the cards as standard, but she had veg to prepare and hoped she could retrieve the two men from the pub before they reached a level of disinhibition which when added to wine could result in incoherency.

Then the mental image of two men slouched on the sofa snoring loudly for the afternoon, popped into her head. If this was to be the inevitable outcome then why fight it, she thought.

She could take advantage of the opportunity to fish for more information on Austin and Verity Thorn who were, it seemed, estranged siblings and the children of a pitiful scandal. One that Austin had secreted away behind a change of surname and a charmed existence. Verity had taken a different route in life.

Connie considered the file on her husband's desk. He had asked to read Monica's case study first but had so far only managed a flick through the first few pages or so, not fully absorbed in reading details. In his absence, the folder had called to Connie, and she had almost finished reading it.

'You take as long as you like at the pub,' she said to him when he had completed arrangements to meet his friend. 'It's about time you two let your hair down.'

Peddyr threw her a bemused look. 'Hair? Bernie hasn't got anything more than a few wisps on his rounded noggin and you mowed mine too bloody short again. Still... thanks. It's been a while since we had a man-to-man chat about life, divorce from Dreary, who said what to whom about custody of the cat, and whether he has plucked up courage to fiddle with Monica's bra strap yet.'

Connie remembered to laugh at the appropriate moment, but in truth her mind was elsewhere.

'Before you go out again, can I ask whether you managed to speak to Pamela Watts.'

He nodded in reply. 'I did. What she told me was exactly what I expected her to say. Vera Hudson was a lonely woman who kept herself to herself, didn't make friends easily and never volunteered much personal information, preferring to ask about other people. Pamela had never been invited to her home and only ever met her in church on the occasional Sunday or at the Knit and Natter group. By all accounts Vera wasn't a regular attender and did more knitting than nattering, although she seemed to enjoy listening in to what others had to say in terms of local gossip, the badmouthing of Christine Fowler, the latest crime wave to hit Browns Court, whether the vicar was a closet gay – that sort of thing.'

'Not a lot of cop then.'

'Not really. What Pamela did confirm was that our Vera is a professional tea leaf. The church wardens changed how the collection was made because of her. She wasn't accused or reported but was seen removing money from the offertory plate, so they replaced it with a bag. That was a disaster too –

hand in, scoop as many notes as possible, hand out again – so now there is a wooden box with a slit in the top which gets passed around. Those flipping do-gooders were too shit-scared to challenge her, apart from Christine Fowler of course who reportedly had a toe-to-toe moment with Vera behind the pulpit a couple of Sundays ago.'

'Oh, to have been a fly on the wall for that showdown.'

'Pamela did catch a few words.' He reached out to retrieve his notebook, which he had thrown casually onto the desk not moments earlier. 'Not that they made much sense. Christine apparently said something about being ignored. "Being ignored by Vera which didn't change what she had done",' he quoted from his jottings. 'Pamela recalled hearing Christine use the phrase "I was there, remember" and then the words "sparing the child".' He flipped the notebook shut and returned it to his desk. 'Nonsense as far as I can make out.' He shrugged. 'Apart from Christine, it seems that the majority of the congregation tolerated Vera Hudson, worked around her rather than accuse the old witch of anything untoward.'

'Now, now Pedd. None of this can be proven. We should keep an open mind.' What Connie said was right, and yet she knew that her husband's instincts were also correct. Everyone they had spoken to so far had been highly unflattering about Vera Hudson.

Peddyr hummed at her. 'You make a fair point but let me remind you, her shoplifting exploits are legendary and if Sergeant Kevin Spratt is correct, she doesn't have any need to carry oxygen in her unfashionable wheelie shopping bag. That is a simple ruse and a convenient place to hide the spoils. So, add liar to thief and potentially poisoner as well, and we have ourselves a downright nasty individual who has disappeared.' He looked deep into Connie's eyes. 'You have something to add to the story, I can tell.'

'I do.'

'Save it for the dinner table this afternoon, then on Monday I'll make beef sandwiches. Fancy a trip to Leighton-Be-Buggered?'

With a shiver of excitement, Connie reached out for his hand to squeeze it tight. 'Isaac Harkness? Yes please.'

'First off, we head to a little village on the River Ouse and a sodding great mansion to meet Austin himself and his wife Olivia. Following an offer from the Harkness family, Bernie has set up a meeting for midday Monday, so I thought we'd make a decent fist of things and book into an Air B&B for the night. This works out fine, as it happens, because our appointment is with Isaac on the Tuesday. His day off.' He grinned at Connie, happy to announce an escape from their hometown for a while. 'The Quirks are going on a road trip. It's a shame the weather is so shocking. It would have been a good place to explore on the bike...'

Connie sympathised, Peddyr was like a caged animal in the depths of winter. Chances to take one of his motorbikes out for a spin were few and far between if the weather was foul. He said it wasn't worth the risk of an accident or salt eating into his bikes, but the frustration resulted in a less relaxed husband. She looked out of the window and across to the park, only to sink inwardly at the sight of a grey drizzle coating the paths and the bare branches of the trees. January always seemed to drag its feet. She shook herself. 'Right, off you go, mister. I have lunch to rustle up out of thin air. See you at two.'

16

A LATE LUNCH

The beef was in the oven, the potatoes peeled and parboiling on the hob when Monica arrived at the back door. Connie shouted at her to let herself in. 'Don't stand on ceremony, hang your coat up, pour yourself a cuppa and talk me through that case study of yours,' she said.

'That's what I love about you, blatant bribery. You knew I'd drop everything for a chance to eat lunch at the Quirk's. Where's his lordship?' Monica asked. 'Tinkering with a motorbike or in his office?'

'At the pub with Bernie.'

'Is that wise?'

'Probably not, but I got so caught up in researching the Vera Hudson thing, I lost track of time. Hence the chaos.' Connie wiped her hands on a hand towel and reached for Monica's assignment that she had propped up against the bread bin. She passed it to Monica. 'Here. Do me a favour and run through this step by step with some explanations for lay people if you would. I can translate most things to and from several languages and dialects but some of the technical terms in the world of psychiatry are beyond my sphere of competence. I got lost on page one at "psychomotor retardation".'

Monica grinned with amusement. 'It's something you don't suffer from. Just the opposite in fact. Is there any prep I can help with? I know the case inside out, so no need to quote verbatim.'

Expressing her surprise at the news there was to be an additional guest who was due to arrive in the next hour or so, she set about laying the table. 'I thought this was Pedd's job,' she said, polishing and placing the required cutlery for five people.

'It's one of them. He has a list of blue macho jobs; clearing the guttering, plastering, mechanical stuff, anything involving a drill, taking out the rubbish... I have a set of girlie pink jobs such as most of the cooking and remembering birthdays. Then we have the purple jobs; decorating, cleaning the bathroom, vacuuming, shopping.'

'Poor old Bernie can't seem to master any of the pink jobs. He got himself trapped in a duvet cover last week.'

At the sink, Connie grinned to herself. 'And how do you know that may I ask?'

'It's not what you think. And for the record I haven't spent any time in my friend and esteemed colleague's bedroom. There may be the early signs of a possible romance on the cards but I'm going to make him work hard for it. I already willingly divorced a man who was unfaithful and who declined to play his part in household management. Here endeth the lesson.'

'Oh, give the man a break—'

With a mock reprimand to Connie in the form of a wagging finger, Monica said, 'In my own good time. Now, what was it you really wanted from me? Oh, yes... a missing person and her psychiatric history.' Having made a rapid change of subject, she proceeded to outline her contact with Verity Hudson; where they had met, her meetings with Verity and what she had found by trawling through her case notes at the time.

While Monica talked, Connie worked her magic on the

Yorkshire pudding batter and the rest of the vegetables, glancing at the clock every now and then.

'I met her at a unit in Northamptonshire. She was transferred there some three months after giving birth to her daughter, and her mental state was not thought to have improved in the time she'd been there.'

'Okay,' said Connie. 'Let me get this straight. Verity Hudson should not have been at Fairfield Hospital in the first place. Because of government policy, large mental hospitals like Fairfield were closing down but, because alternative provision hadn't been built quickly enough, there was a shortage of beds. Verity was admitted to Fairfield temporarily.'

'Yes. It was a cock-up.'

'Technical term for "there was nowhere else for her to go".'

'Precisely. She was on a section, deeply depressed, paranoid, delusional and not eating properly. Verity was therefore putting her unborn child at risk. Thus, there was a pressing need to detain her. She should have been placed in a mother and baby unit. There was not a bed to be found.'

The shocking details outlined in the hospital records, indicated that after the death of Ray Hudson from a massive heart attack, Verity sank into an all-consuming period of grief. The couple had lived in a council property in Corby where concerned neighbours raised the alarm after Verity was seen wandering in the street talking to her dead husband. 'She was heavily pregnant at the time,' Monica said. 'And she had missed several midwife appointments, so her GP had already referred her to local social services. They in turn had made an urgent referral to mental health services, but community provision at that time was very limited in the area.'

'Which is how she ended up in the nearest place that could offer a bed.'

'Yes. A hospital on the far side of the next county and she had no family. Not that anyone knew of.'

The colander was brought into play as Connie drained the potatoes and parsnips. Monica found some glasses and placed them carefully on the table. 'Tumblers *and* wine glasses or is that making an assumption?' she asked.

'Best go for both.' Wiping her brow with the back of one hand, Connie asked, 'Why was she still so unwell when you met her. Was it because of the baby?'

Beaming back at her, Monica nodded. 'You see. Common sense. That's exactly what I thought at the time. She was desperate, distraught, traumatised, and any other word you can think of to describe a woman whose only child has been whisked away straight after she was born.' Monica stared past Connie, looking out of the window to the trees in the park beyond. 'It was awful. The psychiatrists were convinced she was totally delusional.'

'Why? She had a real baby. The baby was really removed by real social services. What's delusional about that?'

Pulling out a chair, Monica sat at the table and thumbed through her assignment report. 'Here it is … this is what I wrote: "Julia" – remember I anonymised the whole thing – "Julia is adamant that a social worker contacted her brother. It should be noted that her current case notes which were at my disposal showed her as having no siblings and being brought up in care following the death of her parents. Details were limited".' She paused to take a breath and then continued to run a finger along the lines of typed words.

'"Julia states that before her transfer to this unit, the Fairfield hospital administrator was discussing her case with the solicitor representing her, and the fact that she had a brother was mentioned. She overheard them discussing matters as she waited to be called in to a Child Protection review meeting. She asserts that she heard everything. Julia repeated her brother's name several times to me during my assessment of her but was unable to recall the name of the female administrator concerned. She knew the solicitor by his surname.

'"It is Julia's firm belief that her brother failed to help her when approached by social services and the hospital. However, there are no records of these alleged attempted contacts or details of a brother recorded in hospital case notes. And whilst her presentation may be indicative of a fixed delusional belief, it should be recognised that Child Care Social Services' records are held in strictest confidence, and it is therefore not possible to corroborate Julia's assertions about the existence of a nearest relative, given that this information was not made available to me. I was reliably informed that the local authority had nominated a social worker regarding application of the Mental Health Act in lieu of a Nearest Relative.'"

Connie sighed, fiddling with a tea towel, 'And now we know she did have a brother all along.'

'Yes, a brother she vowed to make pay for the loss of her child to a system she despised. Julia... Verity, was blazing with anger. She'd whacked a few members of staff and trashed her room more than once. She made threats to find her brother and make him suffer.'

'But she never did.'

'Apparently not, but then she seemed not to know that he had changed his name. She told me he was called Thorn. William Thorn. I wrote it down in my notes and it's one of the reasons why I was unsure about the connection with this missing person request.'

'Do you know what happened to her when she finally left the unit?' Connie asked.

'I only know she was befriended by a couple of the other patients, one called Satwinda, I think, and the other... whose name I can't remember. It's all so long ago. The last I heard, she was moving into a group home with one of them. Somewhere in Northamptonshire. She would have had no trouble accessing a council tenancy agreement because she and Ray rubbed along for years, paid their rent, caused no major trouble other than a fall out with a neighbour over some leylandii.'

'Sad that they should have a child after so many years of trying but then he ups and dies,' Connie said, her mouth turned down in sympathy.

'A miracle baby, she called it. She always said her husband's death was the fault of the neighbour they were in dispute with. According to her, Ray became overprotective. They had a baby on the way and, not for the first time, he and the aggressive neighbour got to the point of fisticuffs when Ray simply dropped dead on the pavement.'

For a while the two ladies busied themselves, finding condiments, and making more tea. Connie thought through the next steps that she and Peddyr might take in their search for Vera Hudson. 'Do we know the address of the group home Verity went to when she was finally let out? Maybe we can find someone who she was friends with.'

'I can try to pull some strings and see what I can come up with.'

The front doorbell interrupted Connie's planned response and she picked up the intercom with a cheery welcome. 'Just come up the stairs, Cara. I'll meet you in our reception.'

ISAAC VISITS MOTHER

*I*saac knew where his mother would be on a Sunday morning: at the stables, preparing for a leisurely ride across the fields on her prized gelding, Tabasco Buchanan the Third, or Tabs for short. As a youngster, Isaac had spent many childhood hours finding ways to amuse himself at the stables. The horses held no interest for him, he had much preferred to study the work of the farrier when he made a visit, or to chat to the stable hands about saddlery. The way they cared for the leather fascinated him for some reason and they would play cowboys with him. Although he never did master the lasso, he became quite accurate when it came to throwing horseshoes at a target on the ground. However, his favourite treat was to drive the small tractor about the yard when his mother was out riding with her horsey friends. Nobody had objected to his use of any equipment, least of all Bevan who was assigned to watch over him while his mother was absent. Bevan worked for the family for years but was more like an uncle to Isaac.

Once his feet could reach the pedals, Bevan had taught him to handle all the vehicles at his disposal. Old Land Rovers, tractors, a quad bike, and best of all a Ford Escort rally car.

The smell of the stables always reminded Isaac of Bevan. He hoped the old man was pain free. He deserved some pampering in his old age but had succumbed to cancer in the last year and Isaac regularly phoned the nursing home to see how he was doing. His mother went to more trouble and took time to visit Bevan each month. Isaac always made excuses. He didn't like to see the old man so weakened by the infirmity of advancing years, preferring to think of him as the solid dependable guardian of the family he was when Isaac was a lad.

The physical strength of Bevan was awe-inspiring to a young child whose only goal in life was to beat Bevan at arm-wrestling – something he watched the man do at the stables, giving all the stable hands a drubbing. Nobody was as strong as Bevan and Isaac never developed much in the way of muscles and never beat Bevan at arm-wrestling.

Isaac spotted his mother leading Tabs from the stable to ready him for a ride, leaving the halter on while she tacked him up. The saddle cloth and saddle were at the ready and the bridle hung from a hook by the stable door.

He wouldn't have long.

'Morning, Mother. Lovely day for a chilly ride. Nothing stops you, does it?'

She swivelled her head. 'A bit early for you, isn't it?'

'Nothing else to do. Since Father laughingly suspended me from my job, I'm sick of staying at home waiting for a decision on my future. Besides, Natalie isn't back from Luxembourg until Tuesday evening, and I wanted to talk to you in private about Vera Hudson.'

'Found her, have they?'

'No. Not yet.'

'She'll be dead I expect.'

'What makes you think that?'

'Because your father has sent his band of merry henchmen out to track her down. And that's on top of the two private detectives he's hired through Bernard Kershaw. He doesn't like loose ends. Apparently, she made his life a misery when he was a child, and he doesn't want her in his life. Your so-called surprise has stirred it all up. She'll find that he serves revenge swiftly and efficiently. She might as well kill herself now and have done with it. If she hasn't already.'

Isaac folded his arms and leaned against the whitewashed wall of the stable block, watching his mother place the saddle on Tabs and tighten the girth straps with practised ease. 'If you knew she was so awful, why didn't you tell me when I set out to find the wretched woman?'

'Because I didn't know. I forced it out of your father on New Year's Day when you were stupid enough to get yourself over-heard talking to her on the phone. Couldn't you have waited until you got home? You know Watson lurks everywhere listening to everything. It's his blasted job for Christ's sake.'

Isaac had regretted his mistake ever since. He should have gone for a walk and taken his mobile phone with him, but he'd had a skinful of champagne and brandy to celebrate New Year and laziness had led him to make a simple error of judgement that could cost him dear. 'I'd made arrangements to call at a certain time,' he explained. 'Anyway, my home isn't exactly private either. Natalie nags me endlessly and the girls barely give me five minutes peace when they are home from school.'

'I wouldn't know. Your charming wife goes to great lengths to make sure your father and I are not welcome in her house. We see the girls once in a blue moon when they come here to ride, which isn't often. Their ponies see more of me than they do of the girls.' She threw a look at the far corner of the stable yard where Isaac knew the ponies were kept. They would be warm, fed and pampered by his mother. She loved her animals, but she was less keen on her daughter-in-law.

'Anyway, whatever you do, stay out of your father's way. He's gone onto a war footing. There's some do-gooder from

Bosworth Bishops who has been in touch with me. They sent a letter of all things. Nobody does that these days.'

'They? They who?'

'I don't know. Anonymous. They want to meet me. Something about this aunt of yours.'

'Have you told the police?'

'Don't be silly. I told your father. He's looking into it.' She busied herself, making adjustments to the bridle. 'Now if you don't mind. I'm off for a restorative ride. Oh, and don't forget, your father has arranged for the private detective people to see you on Tuesday at two o'clock sharp. They won't be long; you'll have time to collect Natalie from the airport.'

18

BRAVE

*E*arlier that Sunday morning, their conflab completed, Cara waved to Lois and closed the front door to her flat. On returning to her desk, to formulate an email to Connie Quirk, she felt heavy with the guilt that was creeping into her mind again. Lois was an ideal neighbour; a sweet girl who trusted too easily and asked for nothing more than friendship and honesty. Friendship, Cara could manage straightforwardly enough but honesty was not so freely available. Whenever asked, she dodged the facts about what research project she was working on, which wasn't unusual given the constraints of a non-disclosure contract.

'I can't tell you anything, Lois. If there's a breach, a release of information not agreed by the clients, then me and the TV production company will be dragged into court quicker than you can say public liability insurance.' She couldn't tell her why she was specifically interested in Vera Hudson at number eighteen. Nor could she divulge that she was not alone in that interest.

An unexpected payment still sat in Cara's bank account, untouched. It didn't have a name attached, only a reference code, and had come through the law firm of Chinieri, Maxwell & Stout. The payment was suspiciously large. Cara found evidence that the law company existed but had never had any dealings with them until she contacted their offices to query the deposit.

'I think there may have been a mistake,' she had said to the person dealing with her over the phone.

'No mistake. Our client wishes to remain anonymous.'

'So, it's not from Channel 7?'

'I'm not at liberty to say, I'm afraid.'

Unsuccessfully, she had then tried to arrange for the money to be returned, dubious about the origin of the payment. It was too much of a coincidence that the bonus had arrived shortly after she had been asked – no, *told,* – by the executive producer Rory West to rewrite the biographical information on Austin Harkness; a biography designed to explain and explore the facts behind a hitherto unknown sister. A past she had meticulously researched, reading through records already tainted with inconsistencies and glaring omissions.

'Forget the sister. She doesn't exist as far as this production is concerned. Stick to facts that are already in the public domain. Nothing else,' Rory had instructed.

'But—'

'Just do it, Cara. Don't push me on this or we could find ourselves at the shitty end of the stick. A whopping-great legal stick that will be rammed forcefully up my backside at the expense of my job and the reputation of Channel 7.'

The threats made by Rory West still rang in her ears and how she had reacted to them contradicted everything her parents had taught her about keeping a polite tongue in her head. Her father had asked her to be true to herself and yet, by capitulating to these forceful demands, she had let him down and let herself down. It was eating away at her.

Her own diligence had placed her in an awkward situation

because her research had led her somewhere incredibly unpleasant.

An emotional black hole appeared before her.

'There are times, wee Cara, when I wish I'd never started this.' In her head Cara pictured the gravestone in the churchyard where her namesake was buried. She had taken to calling her by name, adding a Scottish 'wee' to remind herself who she was talking to. To help separate the two Caras, she had conjured up a picture of what the real Cara Laidlaw may have looked like if she had survived beyond the first weeks. Despite efforts to the contrary, she was only able to see her as a child, one searching for a life to be lived. What she was about to do was for both of them, she told herself. As distressing as it was, it was the right thing to tell the whole truth as far as she knew it.

Accompanied by the cheerful tweeting of the two budgies in the cage close by, she began to type.

Dear Connie, As promised I attach an updated copy of the scoreboard spreadsheet developed by Lois Finnegan and myself to help with your profiling of people in the area who may know Vera Hudson.

She stopped and thrust her fingers into her hair. 'For God's sake, just do it! You must share this with someone at some point, Cara. If you carry on this way, you'll go round the twist and back again. This could all be your fault.'

A swift glance out of the window reminded her that Vera Hudson was the reason she had moved to the Brookside flats. Vera Hudson was, in all probability, her birth mother and Cara had found a way to approach her through Isaac Harkness without revealing herself as the child given up for adoption some three decades previously. Had this selfish drive to find answers and by-pass the customary routes to a mother and child reunion been the catalyst to Vera's disappearance?

Isaac as "Only Child 125" had proven to be an asset in some

ways but a liability in others. He had confided in his mother before anyone from Channel 7 had chance to approach the woman to ensure she could be counted on to keep quiet about the intended surprise. Had Olivia Harkness been the weak link? The one who had told Austin what was in store for him? All communication from Isaac Harkness as "Only Child 125" had now ceased, leaving Cara as "Timid Mouse" to suspect he had been frightened off, perhaps too scared to tell his cousin that her birth mother had gone missing.

Cara returned to the email she was writing to the Quirks and re-read the words. They were bland and perfunctory. Not good enough. As she started typing once more, a cold hollow of fear formed in her stomach, making her gag. She swallowed hard. 'Decide the path and walk it,' she said to herself as her fingers again moved rapidly across the keys.

I also have in my possession a file compiled during my research into Verity Hudson and Austin Harkness for the TV series I mentioned. The live show involving them was due to take place in April, however, the production has now been shelved as a result of Vera's disappearance and some legal technicalities. I am also aware of glaring anomalies in Mr Harkness's life story and most recent adaptations to the script for the live show would have avoided the true version of events entirely. I strongly believe that the request for these changes has a bearing on the disappearance of Vera Hudson. Would it be possible for me to meet with you and Mr Quirk at your convenience and in strictest confidence?

Cara Laidlaw

Before she could talk herself out of this course of action, she hit the send button and walked away from her desk. Jimmy and Rab, their usual twittering absent for a change, nodded at her as she opened their cage. Encouraging Jimmy to walk onto an extended forefinger, she found some comfort in stroking his soft blue feathered head.

* * *

*W*hen Peddyr stepped in through the back door, followed by Bernard Kershaw, he was chuckling at something his jovial friend had said about thermal long-johns. It was only after they had hung up their coats did he notice that the kitchen table had been laid for five people. 'Hello? More than one extra visitor, Lao Po?' he asked his wife, who was stirring the gravy with a long spoon and a self-satisfied grin. She had sent a text to forewarn Peddyr that Cara Laidlaw was to join them for lunch and had forwarded her email for him to see.

'They are admiring my amaryllis in the lounge,' she informed him. 'On your way to wash your hands, pop in and ask them both to come through, lunch is ready,' she said. 'You are carving, so please tell me you will not be drunk in charge of an offensive weapon if I let you loose with the knife.' The smile that passed between them was borne of mutual affection. 'Bernie. Good to see you. Can you take care of the drinks? Monica takes white wine, as you know, but you will have to ask our other guest what she prefers.'

'Monica is here? Are you up to your old shenanigans again?' Bernard said, an accusatory scowl aimed at Connie. Her attempts to matchmake between him and Monica were rather too obvious and yet there was little resistance from Bernard on this occasion, Peddyr noticed as he gave his wife a peck on the cheek.

'Just a glass of water for me,' came a voice from the doorway as Cara entered the kitchen. 'Can I give you a hand with anything, Mrs Quirk?'

Connie stopped her preparations and wiped her damp

fingers onto the apron she wore. 'Cara, please call me Connie. There's no need to be formal. We are all friends here.' She nodded towards Bernard. 'This is our good friend Bernard Kershaw.'

'Err, Connie... that was still rather too formal, we are not in the office now. I too am off duty, so call me Bernie.' There was a shake of hands and an exchange of smiles before Cara was tasked with transferring the platters of vegetables and Yorkshire puddings to the table, helped by Monica who chatted amicably to the visitor.

'I've been learning Yorkshire,' she told Bernard as she took her seat and stretched out for the glass of wine he poured for her.

'I think you'll find that Yorkshire is not a language, Monica,' he said, shaking his head at her apparent ignorance.

'Nah then, mardy bum,' Monica retorted, raising her glass. To which Cara reacted with an embarrassed grimace as she too took her place at the table. 'And that was one of the polite ones,' Monica added cheerily.

'Ah, Grasshopper,' Peddyr announced as he readied to carve the joint of beef that his wife placed in front of him. 'This is just what we need to add to our repertoire of insults that aren't swearwords. Keep up the good work.' He glanced over his shoulder and nodded for Connie to sit. 'Instead of saying grace, I would like to propose a toast to Connie. Not only has she produced a feast in record time, but she has invited some very important guests. Cara, welcome to Chez Quirk. Sorry to drag you here at short notice but my wife tells me you have "exceptionally important information to impart", as my good mate Bernie here might say.'

He sliced the meat with ease and Connie passed the plates around the table. On seeing Cara's worried expression, she reached out to touch her hand.

'Don't worry. Bernie is a solicitor and—' She stopped short. 'Oh, no. I should have realised…'

'What should you have realised, Lao Po?' Peddyr demanded, cross that she had interrupted the flow of the food to hungry mouths. He indicated for everyone to carry on loading their plates while Connie outlined her quandary.

'I asked Cara here today because we are due to see Isaac and Austin Harkness. I thought it would save time if she told all of us about her background research into the family.' She shook her head. 'But now I realise that this would constitute a conflict of interest. Austin Harkness is your client, Bernie. You are acting on his instructions.'

As Bernard nodded sagely, Cara cleared her throat. 'And what I have to say will require me to breach a non-disclosure agreement and it mustn't get back to Austin Harkness or to Isaac. I have to trust who I share this with. So, I'll not say a word while we are together at the table. I can't risk it.'

Noting her mounting anxiety, Peddyr sat down to his dinner, breathing in the delicious smells. 'Let's eat instead. Eat and think, people. How do we handle this so that Cara can be assured of absolute confidentiality? Without her inside knowledge we may take forever to find Vera Hudson.'

Sometime later, with knife and fork placed together on his plate, Bernard patted his rounded stomach. 'Wonderful, as always, Connie. Thank you. Now then,' he said, his mellifluous voice reverberating around the room. 'I've given this due thought. Cara, you will deal only with Peddyr and Connie. Monica, you will act in an advisory capacity only. P.Q. Investigations have been engaged to help in locating the whereabouts of Mrs Verity Hudson – known as Vera Hudson. How you both go about achieving this is not my business. Therefore, unless it is imperative that I know details pertaining to my client, I will not take any part in discussions. That way I can never be accused of a breach of trust or anything else untoward. Does that suit?'

'Agreed,' Monica stated, mentioning to Cara that she and Bernard were part of the same firm of solicitors and therefore compromised.

'We work in silos?' Connie queried. 'It's not how we usually function. Is it legal?'

'Bollocks to legal. What's the problem here?' Peddyr demanded to know. 'It won't be the first time we've used unconventional means to get a result.'

Connie held up her hand. 'Stop right there. Until we have heard details, I must agree with Bernie. You and I will be the only ones to hear what Cara has to say. We are jumping to conclusions without knowing the facts. I'm sorry. I thought this would save some time, but perhaps not. Monica, can we get back to you as soon as Peddyr has read your report thoroughly?'

'Of course, take your time. You know where to find me.'

Connie grinned her thanks and rose from her seat. 'And, Cara, would you like to come with me? You and I are sober as judges, so we will use Peddyr's office while the rest of these lovely people do the washing up as payment for my hard work in doing the cooking. Pudding is in the fridge. Lemon cheesecake. I'm sure Peddyr can bring us a slice with a cup of tea when the clearing up is all done.'

Peddyr was too shocked to speak up in his defence. Instead, he resigned himself to his fate. 'Chief scullery maid… that's me. If my dishpan hands require medical treatment, I'll blame you, Lao Po.'

Bernard was more sanguine. 'I'll wash, you dry,' he said to Monica as he braced hands on the table and rolled to his feet.

When Connie and Cara were out of earshot, Peddyr spoke to his two friends at the sink while he set about returning crockery to rightful places in the kitchen cupboards. 'She's really off on one at the moment. Connie reckons Cara holds the key to this whole case. She also trusts the girl. A woman we have met once. I ask you… Last night when we got home, we had the bloody

Chinese horoscope going on as well as that spooky mindreading thing she does when she looks into my eyes. There is something about Cara Laidlaw that has my wife in a tizzy. Not the usual hundred mile an hour whirlwind. No, this time it involves dithering. Luckily, Cara made the first move and has come to us for help.'

Monica flicked at him with a tea towel. 'Well, I suggest you follow Mrs Q's instincts, Pedd, because she's usually right. Uncanny, unorthodox but right.'

Grateful for her encouragement, Peddyr gave her a smile and peered into the sink at Bernie's pudgy hands as they worked to scour the roasting tin. 'I tell you what, old mate, you'll make someone a lovely wife. That scrubbing action is something else.'

19

CONNIE LISTENS

*W*ith her appetite abandoning her stomach in favour of butterflies, Cara hadn't eaten as much as she should have. The food lovingly prepared by Connie Quirk looked and tasted as good as any restaurant meal, however, when Bernard had been revealed as Austin Harkness's solicitor, Cara had almost choked before a single morsel had passed her lips. Her instinct was to make her excuses and leave the table, but her strict upbringing prevented her from acting in such a way. Besides, the Quirks didn't deserve to be insulted.

It took a few anxiety-ridden moments but once she had established that Bernard Kershaw had only been asked to deal with locating Vera Hudson and was not a partner in Chinieri, Maxwell & Stout, Cara's trepidation eased considerably. She wasn't sure if it was Konrad Neale or Austin Harkness playing games by bribing her with money, but for some reason Austin Harkness had chosen to use a local lawyer to help in the search for his sister and that fact did not sit well.

Cara was led through the flat and into an adjoining reception area, sparkling clean, stark, and functional. Behind the desk were certification of the Quirks' insurance and security industry membership. On the shelves were a variety of sorry-looking cacti and succulents. Among them nestled the obligatory family snaps. 'Proud grandparents, I see,' she commented. It reassured her to know that she was dealing with a couple dedicated to each other and their family, and she began to feel more confident in her choice of ally.

The most obvious indicators of the Quirks' background and career history came as a pleasant surprise to Cara. 'Mr Quirk is into his motorbikes then,' she stated, pointing at the poster-sized framed pictures on the walls. 'Oh, and he worked on these films, did he? I didn't have him down as a stuntman.' She was disarmed by the evidence of an unusual past life. A much younger Peddyr Quirk, tousled hair, and dimpled grin, appeared in nearly every photograph, standing with a well-known actor, a variety of motorbikes featuring in every single one.

'He's not that stupid,' Connie replied with a titter. 'He left the stunts well alone. No, he used to be a consultant for the film and television industry and sometimes taught famous faces how to handle a bike. Not so much these days. Once he retired from the police service, he needed something to keep him busy between less publicised private security jobs, shall we say.' The look from Connie warned Cara not to ask her to elaborate.

'Motorbikes are still very much in our lives,' Connie continued. 'Peddyr can't imagine ever not being able to ride.'

Cara spent a few more moments examining the pictures and the hints at Connie's upbringing in Hong Kong. 'So, what does Lao Po mean? I heard you calling each other by Chinese names, but I don't know what they mean.'

Connie laughed in response. 'Oh, yes. We do it without thinking when we are at home. Sorry.'

'Don't apologise. It sounded so affectionate. I just wondered, that's all.'

'Lao Po just means wife or wifey, and Lao Gong is the equivalent of hubby, I suppose. Nothing too soppy.'

'How did you two meet?' Cara asked. Although she was posing questions designed to reassure her that Connie and her husband were to be trusted, she was also genuinely interested.

'You can talk to me through here,' Connie said, opening a part-glazed wooden door. 'It's cosier and more conducive to a private discussion.'

The glass in the top half of the door was acid etched and when Cara entered the room it immediately evoked scenes from old fashioned gumshoe movies and 1930s private detective films that she had only ever seen because her parents used to watch them on a rainy Sunday now and again. The smell of beeswax and leather made her smile, as did pictures of fictional detectives on the walls. The humour of the household was condensed in this one room.

'We met when Pedd was a senior British officer in the Royal Hong Kong Police. I worked for the Foreign and Commonwealth Office as a translator. He pestered me until I gave in and agreed to marry him. My parents were furious and never forgave me.' At this statement, a shadow of sadness crossed Connie's face and Cara recognised the emotion. She had felt it often enough of late.

A change of subject came rapidly on the back of that unguarded moment. 'So, whereabouts in Yorkshire were you born?' Connie enquired, taking a seat at her husband's desk.

It was hard to know how to begin her story, but with that question Connie Quirk had opened the door, inviting Cara to take a bold step; to put her faith in someone other than herself. Her hesitation resulted in a stammering, stumbling attempt to explain as she sat in one of the upright chairs placed beside the desk.

'I… Well… My parents were Scottish, and I thought I was born in Yorkshire, but it turns out not to be so. I think of myself as a Yorkshire lass, but I'm not who I thought I was. My name isn't even my own.'

'Neither is mine,' Connie said, sharing a gentle smile. 'My name is Fen Fang Wong. At least that was the name I was given at birth.'

Shocked at the honesty and openness, Cara felt unexpectedly buoyed up by the words from the woman who had been so generous with her time and her hospitality. Cara stared into her eyes and saw nothing but a true soul. 'I only found out recently that my name should be Caroline,' she said. 'And I don't even have a middle name.'

There was only a second's delay before Connie clutched at her heart. 'Oh, my,' she said.

With a shrug Cara expanded further. 'I was adopted as a baby by the Laidlaws, who were much older parents than most but who were just the kindest of folk. I would never have known any different had my dad not decided to unburden himself in a deathbed confession letter.' The rest of the story came spilling out in a torrent, Cara unable to stop herself. The need to confide in another person was outweighing her caution. Even her oldest friend Bev had not been party to the details she now shared with Connie Quirk.

'I believe that my real mother is the woman you are looking for: Verity Anne Thorn. My father is unknown – at least that's what it says on the birth certificate.' Releasing a sigh, she went on. 'I was born in a hospital, a mental hospital would you believe, and then placed in the hands of social services.'

'Which is why I couldn't find any trace of you,' Connie said, a sorrowful edge to her voice.

A breath caught in Cara's throat. She hadn't expected the Quirks to be so thorough in their search for Vera but looking at the intelligent eyes of the woman opposite she shouldn't have been surprised. 'It's been bothering me,' Connie went on, 'that I couldn't find what happened to Verity's child. Those records are not accessible to the likes of a private investigation company.'

Placing her hands to her cheeks, she smiled gently. 'Well,

hello there Caroline Hudson. Nice to meet you and to know you are safe and sound and had a good life. What a relief.'

Cara felt light-headed and clutched the arms of the chair. 'How the hell did you know I even existed then?' Panic threatening to overwhelm her. 'Who else knows about me?'

Immediately, Connie reached out for a file. 'An anonymised case study was carried out many years ago, some months after you were born. As part of that study, your mother was interviewed at length by the researcher. The medical history section stated that the participant was three months post partem, and the child had been removed into care. The subject of that case study was your mother. I know this because the author is Monica Morris who you met today.'

When Cara reached out, mouth agape, Connie shook her head. 'I'm sorry, I can't let you see this without Monica's express permission.' There was an apology in her eyes as she slid the folder back into place within the pile of documents she had at hand. 'I'm reading through it again later today to dissect it properly. Then I will speak to Monica about what to do for the best.'

Reluctantly, Cara had to concede. 'I understand, but it's so tantalising to know that file exists, that Monica met my mother. Will she speak with me in private?'

'I'll ask her.' Pausing as if to reset, Connie inhaled deeply. 'And you really are a researcher for Channel 7?'

'Oh, aye. After university in Leeds, I wangled a post on a local newspaper. I studied journalism but had more flare for the background searches than I did as a writer. From there I worked freelance mostly for the *Daily Albion* covering business and finance issues. Not very exciting but I was good at it and unearthed a couple of stories regarding tax fraud and business misdemeanours. Then I was headhunted by Channel 7 about four years ago to work on programmes with the likes of Konrad Neale.'

'Oh, him,' Connie said with a knowing sigh. 'He's full of

himself, that one. "Welcome to *The Truth Behind the Lies* with me Konrad Neale," … God's gift to TV investigative journalism.' Connie imitated the familiar TV programme introduction. 'He can't be much fun to work for.'

Cara allowed herself a smile. 'I couldn't possibly say… his wife – wife number two – is lovely though. Fortunately, most of the time I deal with her and keep well away from the giant ego of her husband.'

'So, as a researcher, you were ideally placed to go in search of yourself when the truth about your adoption came to light.'

'I was. I am, but now I wish I'd never started. I opened the lid on something much bigger than a can of worms.'

'Did this giant can of worms come to light when you used Isaac Harkness to delve into the private life of his father? The press is always after a story about Austin Harkness, I get that. But how on earth did you find out he had a long-lost sister, and how did you know it was your birth mother and how did you connect the two?' The questions came thick and fast, Connie on the edge of her seat.

MRS OVERALL

a shadow appeared against the opaque glass of the door, accompanied by a mumbled request for help. Connie bounced to her feet to allow her husband in, carrying a tray, wearing a floral apron tied at his waist.

'Mrs Overall, I presume,' Connie said with a laugh. 'Honestly, Pedd. This is work. Where is your sense of professionalism?'

'Sorry, Lao Po. Left it at the pub.' He smiled at Cara as he rested the tray on his desk. 'Now then, how are you two getting on? What have I missed?'

With a sigh and a wink to Cara, Connie shooed Peddyr back out through the door, giving him a humorous ticking off and ordering him to watch television for an hour or two. 'I'll tell you later when the beer has worn off,' she said.

Returning to the desk, she apologised for her husband's flippancy, explaining her reasoning. 'He'll have a sleep this afternoon and I can get on with some more research. We are due to meet the Harkness family in person tomorrow and I want to be forearmed. Cup of tea?'

Once again, Cara was rattled at the thought of how easy it would be for her real identity to be exposed. 'You may want to read this then,' she said to Connie, delving into her bag to produce a USB flash drive. 'I'll download the file onto your computer now. Save me emailing it to you after I get home.' With time pressing, she gave Connie Quirk a potted version of Harkness family history, one that would never make it to any documentary series.

'I was supposed to have destroyed the file, but I couldn't bring myself to do it. This information is highly confidential and I'm trusting you because there is nobody else I *can* trust.' She leaned over Connie's shoulder and pressed the keys to download the file. 'When Vera Hudson met with Isaac for the first time, she told him that she and Austin had been taken into care as children because their parents had committed suicide. A suicide pact. The file I've just given you outlines why that might have been. According to newspaper archives, the Thorn parents had been accused of and charged with child abuse, something they emphatically denied. On bail, they killed themselves while awaiting trial.'

Connie shot her an admiring smile. 'I read the same information only this morning. The coroner's report makes for difficult reading. Fancy finding the pair of them hanging side by side; that poor neighbour. Peddyr wondered if it was murder suicide. You know, he kills her then tops himself...' she left the comment dangling before begging forgiveness for being thoughtless. 'They were your grandparents. I should have been more tactful.'

There was so much more to the story, but Cara knew that Connie had already immersed herself in it and she began to believe that if they worked together, they could perhaps fill in the missing years and find Vera Hudson. 'Most of the records are impossible to access but it looks like Austin was successfully fostered. Verity didn't do so well.'

Connie sat patiently taking in every word, allowing Cara time. Much needed time. The only living creatures to hear all these facts until now had been Jimmy and Rab. For tiny birds they were good listeners, but Connie Quirk was more than a sounding board, she was there to help. Each time she spoke, she reassured Cara of her honesty and diligence. When she listened, she did it with an attentive ear.

'Although only two and a half years older than his sister, Austin seemed to thrive and eventually adopted the Harkness name officially. Verity floundered, got in with a bad crowd, drink, some drugs, a police record for public order offences and making a general nuisance of herself at animal rights protests. She met Ray Hudson, several years her senior, married him and settled into a life of work in a tea packing company until Ray died. In all that time, not once did her brother attempt to find her, or the other way round, according to what she told Isaac. So, there we have it, he was adopted into a caring family, I was adopted into a caring family. Verity...' Cara allowed the thought to dissipate, she didn't want to dwell further on how poorly her birth mother had faired in life.

Connie jumped in at this point. 'I know about Vera's marriage, and I have pretty much the same details about what happened to her as you have found.' She cocked her head. 'But exactly how *did* you find out that Verity Anne Hudson was your mother and the sister of Austin Harkness?'

Cara knew then that she had been sussed out. Connie Quirk hadn't fallen for the barrage of information being used as a devise to avoid that one simple question. Cara sat back in her chair and inhaled deeply.

'Thinking I knew best, I ignored all the advice. My parents were both dead and then I discover I'm not only adopted but a replacement for their own child. They also gave me her name which left me wondering who I am. So, I blindly went on a mission to find my real mother.' Saying the words, she felt the emptiness engulf her again and the tears came. 'And I didn't like what I found...'

Taking time to compose herself, she dabbed at her eyes

before telling Connie the truth about the DNA test and how she had discovered a cousin, a blood relative. 'All I wanted to do was to understand what happened to my birth mother but it's a right mess,' she said. 'My Subject Records Request to Child Care Social Services was all but useless and, in the end, I was only given access to what was, in effect, a hugely redacted summary.'

'Why?' Connie asked. 'Can they do that?'

'Oh, aye. Like you did just now with Monica's case study. They cited discretionary access, third party confidentiality and a duty to protect me because the content of the records was not in my best interests. Instead of dragging out an appeal process, I stupidly thought I could circumvent the whole system by suggesting to Rory West at Channel 7 that Austin Harkness would make an excellent subject for their new series. And I lied, telling him that I had stumbled across a sister in the Harkness family tree while researching for a radio programme about self-made millionaires. I told Isaac Harkness the same thing. Luckily for me, Rory West at Channel 7 is the type of narcissist who absorbs other people's ideas, because if Austin Harkness finds out the suggestion came from me, I'm done for. Thank God I remembered all the lies I've told when I spoke to Isaac, because if he discovers that I'm "Timid Mouse" *and* Cara Laidlaw free-lance researcher, then his father will take me to court or have me disappeared like he's done to Vera. As they say in bonnie Scotland, "shadows dunnae make a noise". I'm on my guard.'

Connie spluttered into a clenched fist. 'That's a bold accusation. What makes you so sure he's behind this?'

'Who else could it be?'

21

THE MOP

*P*eddyr stirred at the sound of his wife opening the lounge door and took a moment to come to life. The clock on the mantlepiece informed him of the time and he stretched and yawned, orientating himself. 'Where have you been?' he asked.

'I gave Cara a lift back home. It was too dark to let her walk there alone. Then I went back to your office and began reading lots of very convoluted information. My eyes and my head are now protesting.'

Drinking at lunchtime had done Peddyr no favours, either. His mouth felt claggy and his head too fuzzy to think with clarity. 'I've wasted a whole afternoon,' he said, apologising and annoyed with himself. 'What I should be doing is reading that folder Monica gave us.' He roused himself and got slowly to his feet. 'I'll hit the shower and see if I can't wake myself up. Any chance of a strong coffee?' he asked with a puckered air kiss. 'After all, I did do the washing up, and I brought you tea and cake earlier.'

'I thought you might mention that,' Connie replied with a

tolerant grin. 'Actually, I'm in need of a drink too. Coffee coming right up.' Turning in the doorway, she added, 'Then it's my turn to examine the inside of my eyelids for a while. I feel quite weary.' Heading towards the kitchen, Peddyr followed on behind when, without warning, his wife stopped suddenly, causing him to take evasive action by catching hold of her shoulders. Something significant had crossed her mind. He could tell by her earnest expression as she faced him. 'You should know... I was right about Cara being the key to Verity Hudson's disappearance.'

'Go on.'

'She is the missing child. Verity Hudson's missing baby.'

The pause from Peddyr lasted several seconds as he blinked himself wider awake. 'Is she now. Do tell.'

Delaying a visit to the bathroom for a shower, he parked himself against a kitchen worktop and listened to his wife as she regaled him with the story told to her by Cara Laidlaw. When she handed him a mug of strong ground coffee, all he could think about was how disappointed Cara must have been when her search ended in this way. 'That poor girl. Fancy finding out you were born in an asylum, then discovering that your mother is a nasty piece of work and the disowned sister of a very rich man.'

'A man who has gone to some lengths and expense to keep his sister out of the press. If I was Cara, I too would have my suspicions about Mr Harkness,' Connie suggested. 'He gets wind of the discovery and closes the proverbial doors on a reunion. Then Vera vanishes.'

Peddyr thought about the implications. 'You're right. Cara's decision to involve Channel 7 may be at the heart of this and what I'm struggling to understand is why she moved to Bosworth simply to spy on the woman. Why so close?'

Connie narrowed her eyes. There was more to come. He risked a sip of the hot coffee, only to be met with searing pain as the liquid burned his throat. With some difficulty he covered this up, blowing into his hand.

'To watch her movements, to see how things unfolded, I suppose. Being in the immediate vicinity she could learn about how Vera Hudson lived her life,' Connie said, pouring a mug of coffee for herself. 'Cara's background research is of a very high standard indeed. You have lots of reading to do and it's gripping stuff, so get that caffeine down you.'

Connie had been right about Cara. The girl had been single-minded in her attempts to seek out her birth mother and in her haste she had chosen a high-risk strategy. Remaining so physically close whilst at the same time driving her search forward, had placed Cara in an awkward personal and professional position. Isaac Harkness was all too aware of a cousin being out there somewhere. The question was, just how much did Isaac Harkness know about this cousin, and how much had he, in turn, disclosed to his parents and to Vera Hudson?

'For argument's sake,' he said to Connie as he opened the door that led to their upstairs bedrooms, 'If Austin Harkness *is* behind Vera's disappearance, then Cara herself could be at considerable risk. Someone is mopping up.'

'Mopping up?'

'Yes. It makes sense. Austin Harkness has an unsullied reputation as an honest, hardworking industrialist. A man generous with his time supporting entrepreneurship. Scandal would ruin him. Therefore, he has a lot to protect, so is he taking steps to remove blots on his landscape?'

'Now there's a turn of phrase,' his wife commented. 'And you have no proof whatsoever.'

He considered this while the steaming shower and minty shower gel combined to bring him to life again. Once enlivened with another aromatic dose of caffeine, he sat down to read Cara's research file on the computer. Monica's information would have to wait in line.

By the time he returned to the lounge he had missed *The Antiques Road Show* and Connie was up and about packing a bag for their road trip. 'I've booked somewhere for us to stay tomorrow night on a farm near a place called Marston Moreteyne. There's a pub in the village where we can have dinner,' she said. 'One small problem...'

'Oh, yes?'

'Alleyn and Joe are on their way here with Roger the Dog. Joe's mother was supposed to have him for the week, but she's broken her ankle.' She looked at Peddyr sheepishly. 'Well, I couldn't say no. And the B&B takes dogs... he's no trouble.'

'Oh, brilliant. And what do we do with him while we are guests at the Harkness mansion?'

As was her way, Connie was persuasive. She had an answer to each of Peddyr's questions. It was fait accompli and he knew it. He gave in with a simple shrug. 'You never know, Roger could be helpful.'

In truth, Peddyr had a soft spot for his son's dog. A scruffy mongrel of indeterminate parentage, with a wiry coat, a waggy tail and a cute face, Roger was also small enough not to be a nuisance and large enough not to be an embarrassment. Neither was he prone to yapping and added to this, his love of playing fetch meant he ranked high in Peddyr's estimation as far as pets went.

'Best pack a couple of old towels and make sure to spread a picnic rug on the back seat of the car,' he said. 'I'll hook out the welly boots, shall I?'

As he fumbled about in the cupboard under the stairs where all manner of coats and boots were stored, he ruminated over the damning contents of Cara's documented evidence. Isaac Harkness had reportedly paid cash to Verity Hudson. Why? A bribe to persuade her to meet her long-lost brother? Perhaps. Or was there more to it?

Channel 7 had forced Cara to alter the biographical detail

she had unearthed about Austin Harkness, which made little sense unless Austin Harkness was behind the move to fiction-alise the truth. Even then, as skeletons in cupboards went, and despite her association with animal rights activists and some past drug use, Vera Hudson wasn't a source of significant shame. Therefore, Peddyr deduced, there had to be a bigger and darker secret being covered up.

Austin could easily afford to pay for a fake version of his life to be presented to the world, but only if his sister kept her mouth shut and only if Konrad Neale and the production team stuck to their contracted non-disclosure agreements, which Cara hadn't, making her either plucky or foolish.

There were too many questions yet to be answered and getting to the truth was going to be extremely difficult to achieve without compromising sources, Peddyr realised. His old friend Bernie had foreseen the difficulties and said as much when he uttered the words that this was "a rum old do". It certainly was.

22

ROAD TRIP

*C*onnie argued the case for driving to Bedfordshire. 'Oh, come on,' she protested. 'I've already set up Sat-Nav-Suzie with the post codes. Don't be a spoilsport, Pedd. You can look up all the current stuff online about Austin Harkness, while I drive.'

'No chance,' he stated flatly. 'In this weather, you and your heavy accelerator foot will have us in a ditch. I'll drive, you do the homework and read it out to me as we go along.'

A keen driver, Connie also had a love of speed. Peddyr found it hard to admit that at times he sought the same thrill when it came to riding motorbikes and his wife knew as much. Even so, he much preferred to be the one in charge of the steering wheel. Sedate and sensible wasn't his style nor Connie's but of the two he deemed himself the better driver.

Knowing she was beaten, Connie settled into the passenger seat and turned on the in-car stereo. BBC Valley Radio was her favoured station for local news and their phone-ins were highly entertaining. That Monday morning was no exception. Vic Yarbury from the breakfast show was in the process of handing over to the gregarious Talbot Howkins who outlined the subject matter for his daily show.

'We have local councillor Christine Fowler coming in to discuss the announcement that Bosworth will be holding its inaugural Gay Pride festival in June next year despite her objections. The debate should be a lively one. So lovely listeners, if you have an opinion then give us a call on the usual number or find us on Twitter and Facebook and have your say.'

'And do we have any update on the missing lady from Browns Court?' Vic asked.

'I'm afraid to say that there wasn't much of a response to our appeal for information on my Saturday show, Vic. But the public are being asked to come forward with any information no matter how insignificant it may seem. I dare say Christine Fowler as Neighbourhood Watch Coordinator will be able to enlighten us with further news should there be any.' The chatter continued as background noise, followed by a cheery jingle as precursor to the local news and weather.

'That's a shame,' Peddyr said. 'We'll miss what Christine Fowl-Mouth has to say. We'll be out of range by the time she comes on to spout her bigoted opinions and tell us how important she is. I can't think why she keeps being voted back on the local council.'

The roads had been gritted, the sky heavily laden with ominous clouds. 'I don't mind winter if it's properly cold, but this sleety rain gets in your bones,' Connie said, looking forlornly out of the passenger window of the car as they headed onto the slip road of the M40. 'I hope it cheers up.' She swivelled in her seat to check on Roger who was curled up fast asleep, gently snoring on the back seat. 'He seems oblivious.'

'I expect that's what Austin Harkness will say when we ask him about the plans for him to appear on *This is Your Life*. What if he wasn't aware of the intended surprise until *after* Vera Hudson disappeared which then forced Isaac's hand? He had to tell his father what he'd been up to because the police would be bound to make inquiries of the family and he was the one who reported Vera as missing. But is that right?' he mused. 'Tell me, what was the date when Cara last saw Vera Hudson? She was watching Browns Court like a sodding hawk. She'll have the nearest best guess.'

Connie flipped the pages of a notebook. Like her husband, she too favoured writing a timeline down on a handy handbag-sized notepad rather than make use of a laptop when out and about. 'She and Lois Finnegan went to Pilates on the first Tuesday and Thursday of the New Year and saw Vera pull her bedroom curtains closed as they walked past on Station Road. That's Thursday the second and Tuesday the seventh. On both occasions she was clearly visible. They both say they saw her bedroom lights on during the evening of the ninth and Cara reckons she most definitely saw Vera on Saturday the eleventh going out with her shopping trolley. There was no Pilates last week, Wigmore Memorial Hall is closed for boiler repairs and other maintenance so they—'

Connie was interrupted when Peddyr's phone rang. Connected to the car Bluetooth system, the number showed the caller to be Kevin Spratt. 'P.Q. Investigations, Peddyr Quirk speaking. Any news from your end, Sergeant Spratt? Found our lady yet?'

'Not yet, Mr Quirk, but thanks to National Missing Persons, we have uncovered a previous missing persons file for Verity Anne Hudson. She's done a disappearing act before. Reported missing by a housemate years ago. Her brother was informed but as they were completely estranged by then, it was of no real consequence; he hadn't seen her since childhood. She then bobs up in Kettering, then Oxford, then Bicester where she does another flit. We also knew about Towcester from the GP searches. After that there's no sign of her until she rocks up here in Bosworth Bishops. Our local authority said she was a relocation transfer on medical grounds but failed to elaborate other than to cite mental health issues. However,' he drew breath, 'when we asked Vale Housing Association for information, we uncovered a number of complaints from neighbours which resulted in a housing transfer request out of area. Vera Hudson may well be the archetypal neighbour from hell.'

Peddyr wasn't surprised at this news; it fitted the picture that was forming of the elusive Vera Hudson. 'Have you checked with mental health services?' he asked. 'Maybe she's languishing on a ward somewhere.'

'Already thought of that,' Kevin replied, his voice full of confidence. 'No sign of her. Back to the drawing board. Hope you have more luck with the Harkness family than we did. None of them seem to know anything much about her.'

Kevin Spratt had been in touch with P.Q. Investigations on a regular basis since Saturday and his dedication to the job had impressed Connie. 'It amazes me that an officer as thorough as that remains a sergeant, and yet an idiot like Whiffy-Breath Webster is made a detective inspector.' DI Duncan Webster had led the investigation into the murder of Scott Fletcher the previous summer and had bumbled his way through the whole process, needing P.Q. Investigations to unravel the mystery for him. So far, Kevin Spratt was proving much more professional and a pleasure to deal with.

Peddyr had been struck by the quality of information given in the relatively short update from Kevin Spratt. 'I should have asked Kevin to send me a copy of the first missing persons report. There was a housemate, he said, someone who cared enough about Vera Hudson to report her missing the first-time round. The only people to do the same this time were the saintly Pamela Watts and the self-serving Isaac Harkness.'

Connie perked up at this. 'Self-serving? What makes you say that?'

A VERY BIG HOUSE

*T*hey entered through an automated gate in a stone wall and access was only permitted once Peddyr had given his verbal credentials to a turgid voice on the intercom and waved at the security camera. 'Right on time. You ready?' he asked Connie as the sight of a substantial country house came into view at the end of a tree-lined drive.

Dipping her head to the car audio system she said, 'This song is very apt. Blur, if I'm not mistaken.'

The chortle that came from Peddyr's throat was child-like and when she sang the first line, he joined in. '"Lives in a house, a very big house, in the country..."' Connie gave herself a round of applause.

Before reaching Sharnbrook, they had stopped in the market town of Olney to make use of the sub-zero public toilets on the market square and to give Roger a short walk, a comfort break of his own, and some water to drink. During the brief stop they agreed a plan. 'I'll take Austin, you ask Olivia to give you the grand tour of the house and grounds and if she's alright with dogs then perhaps bring out the secret weapon,' Peddyr said, pointing at Roger who duly wagged his tail with enthusiasm. 'She won't be able to resist.'

'And you are going to ask to see her husband's classic car collection. Find common ground. Disarm him with your knowledge of engines and then confound him with questions about his sister?'

Peddyr tilted his head at her. 'No, actually. I'm going to play it straight. He will say what he wants me to hear but his wife will trip up because she'll fall for your devious little tricks.' He smiled down at Connie who was opening the rear car door for Roger to bound onto the back seat again.

'Objection, your honour,' she protested with a laugh in her voice. 'I'm not devious. Intuitive is the word you're looking for. Let's see how we get on. My head tells me she'll be one of the twinset and pearl gang. Horribly snobbish and stiff as a board. A Phwaa-Phwaa, like Deidre Kershaw.'

Connie and Peddyr didn't have much love for their friend Bernard's wife and had been delighted when he announced they were to divorce. Deidre Kershaw was a lady who lunched, usually at the golf club with a group of sycophantic social climbers who loved nothing more than to boast about how well-off they were. Christine Fowler was also one of the over-privileged pack of individuals that Connie referred to as the Phwaa-Phwaas because that was the noise they made when talking loudly together in haughty tones.

Sadly for her, Connie's prediction about Olivia Harkness looked potentially to be an accurate one. She groaned as the car pulled to a halt on the gravel driveway. 'Everything is so horribly perfect,' she announced. 'The house, the garden, the outbuildings, the butler.' She took a deep breath. 'Let's hope we make the right impression on Mr Harkness because if Bernie doesn't get paid, then neither do we.' Picking up her handbag from the footwell and opening the car door, she pasted a smile on her face and smoothed her skirt.

A wiry man dressed in a dark suit was standing by the open entrance, his face stony, his voice gruff. 'I'm Watson.'

'And I'm Quirk,' Peddyr replied. 'Peddyr Quirk. This is my wife Connie.' No handshakes were exchanged but nevertheless Watson threw forth a palm.

'Mobile phones and any other recording devices. If you would.'

The man was no taller than Peddyr, but a good ten years younger and infinitely more toned. His bearing gave him away as ex-military and he was no butler, Peddyr decided. While he studied the man carefully, Watson took Connie's handbag and emptied the contents onto a table tucked away to one side of the main doors. The way he deftly fingered the lining and straps left Peddyr in no doubt as to the intentions of the search. He was correct. They were scanned and patted down, shoes were removed and examined, and their ID was scrutinised thoroughly before Watson was satisfied. 'Keys to your car will remain with me. You can have them back when you leave,' he said. His face remained expressionless until he turned to Connie. 'And don't worry about the dog. Humans are fair game, but dogs should be treated with the love and care they deserve,' he said, pocketing the car keys and scooting around on the balls of his feet to lead them into the hallway beyond a second set of doors.

Connie shot a look at Peddyr. 'They probably read our lips in the car too,' she whispered, echoing Peddyr's thoughts about the level of surveillance they were under. He had also been struck by Watson's turn of phrase. *Humans are fair game.*

'I bloody well hope they didn't read our lips,' he replied lightly, striding out to catch up with Watson who had knocked and opened another door to allow the Quirks into a starkly modern office at the rear of the house, splashes of colour coming only from art works on white walls and pricey-looking ceramics perched precariously on glass shelving.

'Mr and Mrs Quirk. Welcome.' Austin Harkness, who had

been featured on every form of media in the last thirty years, was instantly recognisable from the gap in his front teeth, the neatly trimmed beard, slick suit, and impeccable manners. An athletic man, almost a decade older than Peddyr, he moved with an easy confident gait. Dressed for business, he made his way from behind a large desk and approached them both. 'I have a conference call in an hour, but until then you have my undivided attention, Mr Quirk. No offence, but my wife Olivia has asked if Mrs Quirk would like to join her in the orangery?'

The Harknesses were playing divide and conquer too, or so it seemed to Peddyr. Helpfully, Austin Harkness had orchestrated the exact plan he and Connie had agreed upon earlier.

'I'm not offended in the least, I'd love to see your orangery,' Connie said smiling broadly at Austin Harkness before following Watson across the polished floors of the hallway.

* * *

After the customary compliments about the location of the house and stating his pleasure at meeting an old school friend of Bernard Kershaw, Peddyr came straight out with his concerns.

'Before we waste too much time going over unnecessary ground, there are a couple of things bothering me, Mr Harkness.' With a nod from his host, he continued. 'If Watson is anything to go by, you already have excellent security staff at your disposal; people who could help locate your sister without the need to approach outside agencies. So, I must ask why you have chosen to make use of a firm of solicitors in a parochial town like Bosworth Bishops.'

There was a brief pause while this was considered, during which time Peddyr watched Austin Harkness closely, picking up on micro-expressions. Tiny and fleeting signs of unease were on show as the man sank into his chair and leaned back to listen.

'And the other? You said a couple of things were bothering you, Mr Quirk. What is your second concern?' He indicated for Peddyr to make use of a black leather and chrome chair which basked in the weak winter sunlight coming through trifold glass doors. The view beyond was of a sweeping patio, mature trees and immaculate frost-covered grounds which led to the river beyond.

Peddyr took out his trusty notebook before he spoke again. 'The second is a more personal question, Mr Harkness. Apart from the fact that she is your sister, and she left her cat behind, I'm wondering what all the fuss is about. People go wandering off all the time. From what I know, you and Verity Hudson have been estranged for some years, decades in fact, so why worry that she upped and left? I appreciate that there was a potential reunion on the cards, organised by your son as a surprise which backfired for assorted reasons, but… all things considered, if I were in your shoes… I'd let things lie.'

Austin Harkness inhaled loudly through his nose. 'Well now, Mr Quirk. You have me at a distinct disadvantage. Much has been written about me, whereas I know very little about you or your wife, other than what I have been told by Bernie Kershaw. However, I see before me a man who has bothered to see past the window dressing, a man who revels in solving problems by first defining what that problem actually is. I commend you for that, Mr Quirk.'

'Peddyr. Please call me Peddyr. I'm not great with formality, it makes me nervous.'

'Somehow, I doubt that,' Austin replied with a twitch of his lips. 'Your analysis of the situation is remarkable.'

Despite Austin asserting otherwise, Peddyr could sense that his background and professional career had been very thoroughly scrutinised. Austin Harkness was wary of him. 'I'm not here to take your money for doing a half-hearted job, Mr Harkness. I take my work very seriously. So, if I'm expected to be part of your window dressing – as you put it – then I suggest we end our business arrangements with immediate effect. Being made a fool of doesn't sit well with me or my wife.'

His pitch had hit its mark. Austin Harkness held up his hands in surrender. 'I owe you and Bernie an apology,' he said. 'I preyed on Bernie's good nature, and I underestimated to what lengths he would go in order to meet my simple request for help. You are quite right, Mr Quirk. For anyone interested in the story – namely one very irritating and persistent Konrad Neale and his journalist cronies – I wanted to be seen to care about Verity. I played along with the idea of a miraculous reconciliation, while in the background I sharpened my pencil and thrashed out the options for legal action against Channel 7 for invasion of privacy. I'm furious about the whole shambles.'

Peddyr tucked his notebook away into the inside pocket of his suit jacket and readied himself to leave. His valuable time and expenses would be paid for, but his annoyance still bubbled beneath the surface. 'I'll leave you to it then,' he said. 'Which way to the orangery? I'll collect my wife and direct her out of the building before I break the news to her. She's formidable when roused.'

He made it halfway to the door before Austin spoke. 'Mr Quirk. I would like you to continue working for me.'

With a sarcastic laugh, Peddyr swivelled on the balls of his feet and announced his verdict. 'I'm free to choose the clients I take on, Mr Harkness, whether they come through Bernie or not. I don't work for anyone but myself and my wife.' He raised a forefinger and aimed it at Austin. 'You have just failed the interview because, for all I know, you could have arranged for your sister to disappear. Your capable security team could have snatched her and dispatched her. I'm not here as your smoke-screen, your window dressing, or any other chicanery you may wish to serve up to the likes of Konrad Neale. Cheerio.' He threw Austin a flat smile and reached out for the door handle.

'Those are strong words, Mr Quirk,' came the response from the far side of the room. Peddyr heard the chair scraping on the polished floor. Austin had taken to his feet. 'So, I can only assume I have caused offence with my attempts to shake off media interest. What can I do to make amends? Apologise for abusing your trust and ask you to continue on the case? Locate Vera Hudson.'

'Why?' Peddyr demanded. 'Why me and why do you want her located?' He allowed the door handle to reset to its default position and turned around once more. 'I'll give you a second chance here, but only if I hear the truth.'

With a shake of his head Austin Harkness gave a short laugh. 'You are a clever man. The sort of man I would have on my team... and, believe me when I say, that is a huge compliment. I only employ the best. The truth is that my son should have left well alone. He has no idea how evil Verity can be, which is hardly surprising. There are things I keep secret for good reason and what my sister gets up to is one of them.' He thrust out his hand. 'Shall we start again? How much do you already know, Mr Quirk?'

Having at least been acknowledged to have some level of intelligence, Peddyr selected carefully what to tell Austin Harkness. 'My wife and I gathered much information from neighbours and acquaintances. We like to know the type of person we are looking for. It often pays to profile thoroughly.' The time was right to open old wounds and Peddyr wasn't in the mood for being considerate. It wasn't his style.

'Connie has a knack with family searches. She was surprised that you kept the name Thorn as a middle name. It made her life too easy when it came to researching your family history. However, we have no access to local authority records, and you have done a remarkable job in keeping your private life tucked away.'

'This has nothing to do with my sister's disappearance, Mr Quirk.'

'Oh, but it does, Mr Harkness. As I said, if we can understand the person, we can often predict habits and patterns of behaviour. Verity, or Vera as she prefers to be called these days, has moved around the country frequently, she bounces from one place to the next, rarely putting down roots of any sort and not making friends along the way. Since the death of her husband some years ago, you are her only family. This pattern has repeated without her ever coming near you or attempting to get in touch. Or am I wrong about that?'

Austin raised his chin and frowned. 'You are correct. If Isaac hadn't made such overt attempts to track my sister down this could have been avoided. The great idiot thought he could bring off a birthday surprise without even knowing the facts. He should have left well alone, because now it will all come out.'

He placed both hands onto the sleek surface of his desk. 'This goes no further. If any of this leaks into the press I will slap you with the worst law suit you have ever seen. I will ruin you.'

'Fair enough,' Peddyr replied. He had expected no less from a man capable of unleashing a whole courtroom full of barristers if necessary.

Austin Harkness straightened, catching Peddyr's eye as he strolled to the window to stare into the middle distance. 'I have wanted nothing to do with my sister because she's an out-and-out psychopath. Always has been. Our parents died when she was ten years old, I was thirteen and she despised me for breathing, for existing, for being the first child, for anything I said or did. She hated me. Verity was the bane of our parents' lives. She destroyed anything worth having, she lied, she ranted, she screamed, she hit out. What did my parents do?' He threw his hands into the air and faced Peddyr. 'Asked a child psychotherapist for help, who then recommended non-confrontational approaches to understanding something he called an "unusual attachment disorder". I call it evil. Pure unadulterated evil. What she needed was an exorcism not psychology.'

Peddyr laid his pen to one side. He was transfixed. This was the last thing he expected of Austin Harkness. The truth, or something that resembled it, was being told. The man sounded genuine, there were no tell-tale signs of lying. However, the story was recounted without emotion and there was no pain etched on his face.

'Going into the care system was the best thing that ever happened to me. A reprieve, a break from her endless anger. What do I get now? This mess.' He opened a desk drawer, flipped open a file and withdrew a piece of paper on which he scribbled down a few words. 'I want you to deal directly with me or Watson. Don't bother Olivia. The last time my sister was reported missing, my wife didn't handle the news well. Isaac was very young and given what I knew about Verity, Olivia convinced herself that we were going to be murdered in our beds by a madwoman. She turned this place into Fort Knox.' He shrugged. 'As it turned out we never saw hide nor hair of Verity... but consequently Olivia doesn't respond well to conversations about my sister and this latest chapter has set her off again. She's a bag of nerves lately.'

Peddyr nodded as he took hold of the folded paper. 'I'll do my best to spare her any more stress.'

'I believe it should cover your costs,' Austin said.

Peddyr took hold of the paper and bit his bottom lip to stifle the wholly unacceptable expletives he was about to let loose when he read the contents. 'There's been a mistake on this offer, I'm afraid. Too many noughts. If it's all the same to you, I'll send my bill through Bernard Kershaw. He'll ensure P.Q. Investigations are paid the amount owed and, to avoid any misunderstandings, we will provide a breakdown of costs to satisfy your accountant. Cheerio.'

24

SOUND, BUT NO PICTURE

*C*ara stared out of the window and down into a gloomy Browns Court. After only three hours sleep, she had awoken early that Monday morning and was passing the time until she could reasonably call her friend Bev. With lights on and curtains being drawn back in a few of the other windows, there were signs of life in the Brookside flats despite many residents likely to be as sleep deprived as she was.

The previous night, a raucous party had been going on at number fourteen and at about midnight Cara had received a call from Lois. 'Don't they realise people have work in the morning? Should we call the police?'

'I'm not sure we have enough grounds to call them just yet. If in doubt, do nowt,' Cara said. They were still debating what course of action to take, staring at the buildings opposite, when the door to number sixteen Browns Court burst open and the occupiers stumbled onto the path; Jethro Dart had his wife Tracey by her hair. Their dog raced past, tail tucked between hind legs, and headed for the alleyway as Tracey screamed. She had fallen to her knees, trying to prevent her raging husband from taking her beyond the boundary of the garden, its grass strewn with dog mess and litter. One hand balled into a fist against a pair of filthy combat trousers, Jethro Dart began swearing loudly as he released his wife, allowing her to get to her feet. Righting herself, she pointed up towards Brookside and began screeching at him.

'Turn your lights off,' Cara said to Lois over the phone. 'Don't let them see you.' Sharing the drama that was being played out below, she made commentary for her friend to hear. 'And here we have the wazzock who goes by the name of Jed. Why the gormless twonk feels it necessary to kick the fence and throw a bottle at his dog, is anyone's guess. Of course, assaulting his undernourished wife shows just what a charmer he is.'

'Now we should call the police,' Lois said, quavering.

She didn't receive a response because the violence escalated a notch or two with the arrival of the Red Dwarf and his girl-friend who looked more like a young Sharon Osbourne each time Cara caught sight of her. They emerged together from the party at number fourteen to intervene.

'The wife-beater isn't taking kindly to this is he?' Cara stated, fascinated by the scene as it unfolded in the gardens below. 'I think now might be the time to call the police,' she conceded, ending the call to Lois to dial triple nine and report a domestic violence incident and affray.

While on the phone, standing in the darkness of her lounge, she watched as the beleaguered fence was battered once more by a flying kick, and plastic patio furniture was hurled across the patch of dog-turd-dappled lawn by a thunderous Jethro Dart. During the chaos, his wife Tracey was led into the darkness and to the safety of Sharon's flat while Jed was distracted by the Red Dwarf who, to diffuse the situation, produced a small packet from his baggy tracksuit bottoms and waved it in front of Jed's face.

'Oh, and can you add illicit substance use and intent to supply to the list?' Cara asked the police call handler.

The pounding and riotous goings on, emanating from the impromptu party at number fourteen, lasted well past midnight accompanied by doors slamming and shouting of obscenities from both sides of Browns Court. Eventually a visit from two police cars at around one in the morning settled things down, but by that time the revelry had morphed into a drug-fuelled free-for-all. A few hours later, as the clock hit six forty-five, the only evidence to show for the night was the broken plastic chair, which lay abandoned on the lawn of number sixteen, beside it a tatty baseball cap. Outside number fourteen were several black bin bags overflowing with cans and pizza boxes and a large cardboard box which looked to contain a pile of empty bottles. The partial fence between the two properties showed clear signs of damage: it lay flat, its panels shattered and splintered.

From the glow of the streetlamps, Cara watched in admiration as Hairy Toes, once again, forced himself into his car before driving off to work and this was when she noticed that lights were on in Lois's flat next door. Her new friend had set about preparing for another week at the lower school on very little sleep. The thought of a classroom full of shrill voices and unreasonable demands made Cara shudder. 'Thank, God I'm my own boss,' she said to herself.

Prompted by this thought, she uncovered the budgies and whistled to them as she composed an email to executive producer Rory at Channel 7 who was battling to salvage something from the final episode of *This is Your Life.* Austin Harkness, having been told of the plans, was exercising his right to withdraw all permissions and in the circumstances the TV company could do nothing about it. The series would be one episode short. She read aloud her email to Rory with a possible alternative solution.

'Mr Neale will no doubt expect a replacement for the sixth episode. I have some interesting background already in place on Professor Ernesto Sycamore. Radio Four ran a feature some time ago and his pioneering work in the field of genetic modification and gender transition is fascinating. If Mr Neale is interested, I can forward the details. Kind regards Cara Laidlaw, Laidlaw Freelance Research Services.' She sat back in her chair and nodded approval. 'Aye, that should do it.'

With the ball rolling in the right direction to keep money coming in from Channel 7, she chanced an early call to Bev who she knew would be about to set off on the long bus ride to the office where she worked. An ideal time for Cara to come clean and admit she needed help.

'Bev, I've got some news.'

'Oh, aye? She's turned up again, has she?' Bev sounded excited. 'Have you got all courageous and spoken to her? What's she like in the flesh?' In the background Cara could hear the bus changing gear, grinding uphill on its journey to Grassington.

She had tempered Bev's enthusiasm for the last ten days by explaining away Vera Hudson's absence as entirely normal behaviour. She now had to be truthful, to a degree. 'Actually, it seems that Vera Hudson has disappeared. The police have launched a missing persons investigation and the locals hereabouts are worried. Her cat is still around but the woman seems to have vanished. Some folk think she's dead.'

There was a gasp from Bev who launched into a torrent of placatory statements after which she arrived at her own optimistic conclusion. 'She'll turn up right enough. And anyway, why listen to tittle-tattle?'

'Because tactless folk are just saying what everyone else is thinking. I had my chance, but I didn't speak to her, I didn't even drop a note through her door. Nowt. I just watched her like some perverted stalker, trying to work out if I liked her enough to bother with. What's wrong with me, Bev?'

The chat continued for the full length of Bev's journey to work and during that time Cara managed to avoid any mention of DNA tests, Austin Harkness, suicidal grandparents, and mental institutions. For some reason she wanted to avoid staining her old world as Cara Laidlaw with the decidedly unpleasant family background of Caroline Hudson. The fewer people who knew, the better, she told herself.

'There's no rule book to say you have to like her. You don't have to meet with her. But then… why are you staying there? What do you want?' Bev asked.

'I want to understand why. I need to know the full story.'

Having spoken to her oldest friend, she turned to the mundane to occupy her, but emails and policy amendments failed to be a worthwhile distraction as she waited for a reply from Rory West. Soon enough she was back on Facebook where she checked in on the Bosworth Bishops Neighbourhood Watch page. She had done this several times since Friday to monitor how well the town was responding to requests for help to find Vera Hudson. Today the page was monopolised by an indignant Christine Fowler. She was announcing to all and sundry that she would be on BBC Valley Radio later that morning.

'Looks like dear Christine is a little homophobic, Jimmy,' she said to the vibrant blue budgie sitting on his perch watching her work. Smiling, she allowed herself a short laugh. 'Apparently, our neighbours Jody and Taylor – the ones who were up all night, partying – had something worthwhile to celebrate. Gay Pride is coming to Bosworth in the summer, for the first time ever, and this is causing a stir with the not-in-my-backyarders and the unenlightened prudish types.'

A glance across to the silent maisonettes confirmed that the instigators were still in their beds. 'The Bosworth Influencers,' she declared, arriving at a suitable collective name for Jody and Taylor, whose personal Facebook pages made it clear where their interests lay: fashion, cosmetics, hip-hop music and living their lives as females. They were curvaceous and well-manicured females, Cara noted with an embarrassed glance at her own much neglected fingernails.

Making use of her computer, she tuned into the local radio station, knowing they would be debating diversity and the reactions to a pride march.

Later, distracting herself from work in whatever way she could, she was in the middle of generating a message to send to Lois about the latest developments, when an email notification arrived from Rory. It had taken until the afternoon, but he had taken the bait.

'Stand by,' she said to Jimmy and Rab who had perked up at the sound of her voice and were twittering to each other.

The message from Rory was rather cryptic. 'What does he mean?' Cara asked aloud. 'Why is he asking me whether or not I destroyed anything on record about Vera Hudson?' The frown on her forehead deepened. 'Why does he want me to keep what I have? What's he up to?'

In his reply, Rory had sent through a digital file of Verity Hudson being interviewed by Konrad Neale, with instructions that it was to be deleted once Cara had extracted what she needed. 'Mixed messages,' Cara declared to the budgies. 'He is most definitely hedging his bets.' She smiled nervously at the two birds again and opened the file.

With pulse quickening she sat back in her office chair preparing to take in every movement, hoping to find an emotional connection with the woman who had given birth to her.

When no image of Vera Hudson filled the screen, as Cara had expected, she tried again. The file was open, but only the audio recording could be heard, unsettling her already shredded nerves.

Konrad Neale led the interview and had filled time with some commentary. 'As you can tell, Vera withdrew her permission for us to film the interview and ultimately refused to detail her time in care. However, away from the studio she claimed that she had been traumatised by the experience. So much so that she was admitted to a special children's mental health unit, thus separating her from her brother.'

Cara listened on to hear the words from Vera. The voice was scratchy, the diction that of an undereducated woman, the story told in vague terms. After a few minutes Cara let loose a sarcastic laugh. 'Really? She tells Isaac one thing and then a different version to Konrad. No wonder Austin bloody Harkness wanted to pull the plug on this nonsense. Anyone with half a brain can tell that's a load of crap. She's lying.' She stared at her laptop as the voice-over continued without any video footage, Konrad making full use of empathetic tones.

'A catalogue of errors later and she became the victim of an uncaring system. Rebelling and experimenting with drugs in her teenage years, Vera became homeless on leaving care, only to be trapped in a loveless marriage as she describes here.' With no visuals to scrutinise, Cara was left to imagine what Vera Hudson was wearing, what body language she used, and what her facial expressions might be. There was only the gravelly voice loaded with irritation to go on.

'Everyone deserves a second chance,' Vera said in a monotone devoid of any emotion, save that of resentment.

The most telling reaction came with the next set of questions from Konrad.

'You said you knew for years that Austin Harkness was your brother, so why didn't you get in touch with him? Why has it taken your nephew to bring the two of you back together and why did the Harkness family never acknowledge your existence?'

After a brief pause Vera said simply, 'I was an embarrassment, I know that. You ask Austin, not me.'

Known for his incisive and at times ruthless interviewing techniques, Konrad wasn't to be silenced. 'That's as maybe, Vera, but you said to me that you wanted people to know the truth about what happened. This is your chance.'

'Look, sunshine. I had a shit time in care, he didn't. Simple as that. He made something of his life. There's nothing to tell. It's time to meet up again, say hello and move on with our lives. Nice to know I'm not alone in the world.'

'Never had children of your own?' Konrad asked.

A stunned Cara held her breath, dreading the answer.

'Interview finished,' Vera barked.

25

THE ORANGERY

*W*atson wasn't one for small talk, Connie realised. He grunted on occasion to acknowledge her comments about the decor and how thrilled she was to have met Austin Harkness in person. 'I'm not sure what I was expecting,' she said, aiming comments to the back of Watson's head. 'Within seconds I could tell he's one of those magnetic people, the sort that command respect without being pompous about it. Taller than he looks on the telly too.'

She stopped as something caught her attention. 'What's that man doing?' she asked.

'Burying what's left of the chickens.' The response was blunt, for which Watson immediately apologised. 'You should probably avoid talking about pets to Mrs Harkness. They weren't just egg layers, they all had names.' He stood next to her, staring into the extensive grounds. 'That's their very own pet cemetery. Dogs, cats, a couple of guinea pigs, a pet sheep and several fish are laid to rest by the trees. Their son Isaac started it when he was about four. Before my time.'

'What happened to the chickens?'

'Let's put it this way. They didn't die of old age and one of the estate workers, a half-wit by the name of Neville, didn't notice the clues to a den on the far side of the woods. A fox got in. Two birds were missing from the coop, so they must have been taken for food. Two others died of their injuries and three more had to be put out of their misery.' He sighed. 'Mrs Harkness loved those chickens.'

'How dreadful.'

'Neville was stupid enough to argue with Mrs Harkness about whose fault it was, but as vermin control is his job...' He shrugged, leaving the end of the tale unspoken. 'Foxes are not as indiscriminate as some people think.' He moved away from the window, beckoning for Connie to follow on as a strident voice echoed from the orangery.

'I can hear you, Watson. I'm almost certain our guest doesn't want to hear of such horrific events. Just because you have a cast-iron stomach doesn't give you the right to share such gruesome tales.'

'No, ma'am. Sorry, ma'am.' Duly rebuked, Watson ushered Connie forward to greet Mrs Harkness who looked like she sounded.

The obligatory twinset and pearls were not on display. A Guernsey jumper with Barbour gilet, jodhpurs, and leather Dubarry boots were on show instead. Wearing floral gardening gloves and wielding a pair of secateurs, Olivia Harkness set about completing the task she had set herself, trimming a glossy-leaved shrub. She was sturdier than Connie had expected, more reminiscent of a farmer's wife than the glamorous type she had imagined would be married to Austin Harkness.

'Shall we skip the remarks about the weather and get to the point? You are here because you have been asked to investigate the disappearance of my husband's unfortunate sister. You will talk to me to find out what I know. Then you and your husband will compare notes.'

'Correct,' Connie replied, pausing to admire the calming impact made by the variety of trees, climbers and ferns that surrounded her. 'Although I'd rather hear about how to grow such healthy plants. These are amazing,' she said. 'I managed to grow an amaryllis this winter.'

Olivia raised a plucked and pencilled eyebrow. 'Really, how fascinating.' The response was not enthusiastic, and Connie realised she was being tolerated not welcomed. The lady of the house spoke in clipped tones and short bursts. 'Shall we get on with it. I'd usually be out at the stables. Horses require regular exercise, Mrs Quirk.'

'Of course, I won't keep you long.'

Olivia's forearms were the giveaway. They were too muscular for a woman who lunched. She came from aristocratic stock and horses came with the territory, they were her priority; it had said as much in a copy of *Horse and Hounds* magazine that Connie had read as part of her Harkness family research in the car.

'When your son told you that he was planning to find out what happened to Verity Hudson, did you discourage him?'

'Yes, I did. He had no idea what he was getting into. I never imagined he'd be successful or that he would be so persistent. It took him several long months and a couple of lucky breaks. To be frank, I thought he'd given up the search. Then it was too late. He'd met the wretched woman and was deeply embroiled in negotiating with her about a grand surprise. He even bribed her with money.'

Being careful what she said and how to phrase the question, Connie pretended to be admiring a man-sized cactus while she marshalled her thoughts. 'In which case I guess you had to tell your husband that your son had signed a deal with Channel 7 for the rights to film the reunion. A shame about ruining the surprise but I think I would have done the same.'

Olivia's arms dropped to her sides, and she removed her

gloves, laying them and the secateurs on the rim of a large earthenware pot. Her fingers trembled slightly. 'Isaac confessed when confronted but only because he had to. His father was furious about the whole thing, and as for agreeing to a television programme... Isaac really did himself no favours there. I can't think what possessed him.'

Connie had so many questions she wanted to ask, but she held back, allowing Olivia Harkness to do the talking, just as Peddyr had taught her to do.

'After that, the blasted woman did a bunk anyway. Verity Hudson turned out to be—' she stopped herself, lowering her gaze to the floor and turning her head as she spoke. 'The same horrendous shit-stirrer she was all those years ago.' Pronounced so perfectly, these words struck Connie as an accurate reflection of what she and Peddyr already knew of Vera Hudson.

Olivia's eyes were beseeching. '*If* you find her, please tell her to...' She shrugged, unable to verbalise the unpalatable sentiment written large on her face.

'Curl up and die?' Connie suggested.

With a knowing smile, Olivia let out a snort. 'I never said that.'

'But you thought it.'

'Look, Mrs Quirk...We always assumed she was dead, you know. We never heard from her after—'

'After?'

Resting on a slatted wooden bench, Olivia asked Connie to join her. 'Better you know the truth now, rather than hear a pack of lies from anyone else. Isaac isn't aware of this because he was only ten at the time. But out of the blue, we were contacted by a social services legal department asking if we wanted to be involved in the care provision for Verity's child.'

'So, you *do* know,' Connie said. 'Did Isaac tell you?'

Olivia looked at her askance and rocked back. 'Don't be ridiculous. Isaac doesn't know anything about Verity's baby.

Nobody does. The legal wheels turned. Links were severed. The child was adopted, apparently. We let sleeping dogs lie.'

Connie held herself in check. In an unguarded moment she had almost exposed Cara Laidlaw's deception and, unfortunately for her, Olivia was astute and hadn't missed the anomaly.

'Mrs Quirk, how did *you* know there was a child?'

The lies came quickly enough for Connie to bluff her way through. 'Vera Hudson mentioned the adoption to someone at a church group. We were obliged to interview people who knew her. Locals and neighbours. It looks as if the sleeping dogs woke up... probably disturbed by Isaac.'

'Because?'

'Because someone went looking?' Connie couldn't give an answer. Not one she could share with Olivia Harkness. 'Did Verity know about you and Austin being involved with safeguarding procedures involving her baby? Could she hold you responsible for allowing the courts to take her child from her?'

A stunned Olivia gulped and plunged her fists into the pockets of her gilet. 'I don't know. I used to worry about that sometimes. From what we knew, she was unhinged as a child and locked up in mental institutions as an adult, what was I meant to think? The childcare arrangements were supposed to have been kept confidential... We declined to have anything to do with them, or with Verity.'

TWO FOR THE PRICE OF ONE

*O*nce back in the car, Roger patted and praised for being so well behaved, Peddyr drove out through the manor house gates and onto the road. Without consulting Sat-Nav-Suzie, he headed towards the village of Felmersham, finding a place to park by a bridge which crossed the river Ouse. 'Time to walk and talk,' he said. 'Beef sandwiches after that. I'll get the wellies and coats out of the boot.'

Connie had remained silent during the short journey, understanding her husband's mood. Her meeting with Olivia Harkness had been unsatisfactory in many ways and she could see that Peddyr had experienced something similar when it came to Austin. Now was the time to join up some dots.

Standing behind the car, Peddyr stretched, put on his jacket, and repositioned his hat, waiting for Connie to put Roger on a lead and head through the gate onto a footpath which followed the river back towards Sharnbrook. The stone houses of the village made for a picturesque backdrop, but the day remained grey and uninspiring, the grass still frosty beneath their boots.

In the stillness Connie was the first to speak. 'She sounded like a first class Phwaa-Phwaa to begin with, but then I confessed to being a plant-killer and eventually we made a joke out of it. An icebreaker if you like.'

She recounted how Watson had retreated silently once the two ladies began chatting, leaving her to it, but that she could sense his presence nearby, listening in. 'Watson knows everything that goes on in that house. He's the one we should interview,' she said. 'Anyway, Mrs Harkness said Isaac confessed on New Year's Day and ruined his father's hangover as well as his own.'

Woolly hat rammed low over his ears, Peddyr stopped walking. 'So, when Isaac rang Vera that day, his father knew the secret?'

'His father overheard the call. By all accounts Austin went ballistic, and with Isaac and his wife Natalie staying over for the annual party and fireworks there was a massive family row. More fireworks.'

She linked arms with Peddyr dragging him along. Walking and talking, doing, and thinking all at the same time came naturally to her, but her husband preferred to park himself somewhere while his brain whirred at full pelt – using up all available energy in the process. Connie squeezed his arm with hers. 'Mild embarrassment at a socially unacceptable sister is not good enough reason for his extreme reaction to being told the news of a possible reunion. What did *he* say?'

'He confessed to a top-notch motive for making his sister disappear.'

Once Connie had listened to his verbatim report on Austin's story, she too was perturbed by what this could imply. 'He certainly went to extreme lengths to stay hidden from his sister for all this time. I don't think I've ever come across a child who had their name changed by Deed Poll to protect them from an evil younger sibling. No wonder he blew his top at Isaac for raking it all up.'

'The Harkness family wrapped their protective arms around

William Thorn very tightly. So tightly he was practically reinvented. In effect it was like a witness protection programme.' Peddyr walked on in quiet contemplation for a minute before he spoke again. 'Whatever went on in the Thorn household with those kids must have been horrific, but the papers said it was the parents who were at fault. Verity's supposed wild behaviour wasn't mentioned in dispatches.' He aimed his eyes at the horizon and sighed. 'Child protection cases are shrouded in secrecy. We may never find out the truth about what went on between them. All we really know is that when Verity's baby was born, social services found her brother, tried to include him in care proceedings as nearest relative and he refused. Then low and behold, nearly thirty years later, Channel 7 and Isaac come looking for her story. In doing so they put a tempting morsel on the table.'

Connie nodded her agreement. 'Even if Isaac told her the deal was off because Austin had found out about the *This is Your Life* caper, she still had a golden opportunity to confront her brother through Isaac.' She grabbed at her husband's upper arm again, her grip much firmer this time. 'Hang on though... She could have done that years ago, she could have written a letter, dropped by, and knocked on the door anytime between then and now. On any given day since her child was taken away, she could have gone to the press, blackmailed him, taken revenge.'

Peddyr agreed. 'My thoughts exactly. But, how about this as a possibility, what if Vera didn't know about her brother's refusal to be part of the baby's care proceedings, *until* Channel 7 got involved. Isaac knew there was an adopted child looking for their mother. Somebody must have blabbed.'

To Peddyr's mind, this was an acceptable rationale for Vera's willingness to be interviewed by Konrad Neale – she was a woman seeking answers. A woman who had lost her baby to the care system, just as she had been. Sadly, it did not entirely explain her disappearance. He chided himself. 'Oh dear, I may have overstepped the mark when I suggested to Mr Harkness that Watson could have spirited Vera Hudson away and buried her body somewhere never to be found again.'

With those words, he stopped to kick at a frozen mole hill where Roger had taken an interest and was sniffing the ground. 'In my defence I should like to add that it was a reasonable assumption on my part,' he continued. 'On the face of it, kidnap and murder could have been a viable option for him to take... when you think about it. If Vera was about to expose family secrets or was trying to ruin his reputation publicly through Konrad Neale, Austin Harkness could have decided to take pre-emptive action. He knew about the *This is your Life* surprise as early as New Year's Day and Vera disappeared after that, just over a week or so later... Just a thought,' he said shrugging.

'I smell a rat.'

'So do I but the question is, who is the rat?' He glanced down at Roger who was trotting along at the brisk pace set by Connie. 'You any good at sniffing out rats, Roger?'

Stepping over a semi-frozen puddle Connie growled in frustration at having to lift her skirt. 'Grrrrr, this long winter skirt was a bad idea. Oh, sorry, Roger. I didn't mean to scare you,' she said, rubbing at his ears in apology for the noise she made. 'Poor thing. Shall we head back to the car? Even you look cold.'

Peddyr was breathing deeply, striding out as they talked. 'Goodness knows where Vera is. If she *is* alive, she could be staying nearby somewhere, stalking her brother, seeking a chance to strike. Look around you, Lao Po. Fields everywhere, woods, a ruddy great river. Plenty of places to dump a body.' He stared at the ominous skies for a second. 'Pressure may be the best way forward,' he said. 'Personally, I'm looking forward to tomorrow. Isaac may have to succumb to interrogation methods not seen in these parts for many a year if we are to get answers. Whether he has rehearsed his lines well enough to back up what his parents have told us, we shall have to wait and see.'

'Why make us wait until Tuesday before we can meet with Isaac?' Connie asked, more out of irritation at the lack of progress than annoyance. 'It's a strange day to have as your day off, don't you think?'

The beef sandwiches and coffee from a flask sufficed as lunch and, with a few hours to spend making the most of their road trip, they embarked on a tour, first heading to the airship hangars at Cardington before driving on to the village of Arlesey at Connie's behest. 'I'm becoming obsessed by the place,' she admitted. 'Fairfield Hospital used to be the old Three Counties Asylum built in the Victorian era. Some people say the place is haunted by the ghosts of tortured souls who died within its walls. There's even a memorial to past patients and staff who worked there.'

'And what are you hoping to find?'

'Someone in the village who may have worked at the hospital before it closed or at least knows of someone who did. Someone who knows the story of Verity Hudson and her baby. We can't access childcare social services records, and Cara can't get access to her complete files because they've been deemed too psychologically damaging, which means she has little idea about her mother's psychiatric history. Given what we heard from Austin, and the fact that it ties in with what we know of Verity Hudson's unwholesome character traits, she could be dangerous. Poor Cara, fancy having to be faced with the possibility of a psychopathic mother who had psychotic tendencies when pregnant.'

The first shop they came to in the village was Burton's Convenience Store which sold groceries and everyday items with most of the available space dedicated to a sizeable off-licence. An elderly man in a beige woollen cardigan was at the till and was very willing but unable to help in Connie's quest for names. He introduced himself as the proprietor, a Mr Amos Burton. 'Me and the wife were due to retire but I haven't got the hang of it yet. Prefer to keep active,' he said rubbing at gnarled arthritic fingers.

His daughter-in-law, who appeared from a door to the rear of the counter, was more knowledgeable when it came to the history of the old hospital site. A badge bore her name in bold black type. Melinda. 'There's a book called *A Place in the Country*, you can order it online,' she suggested, sweeping a floppy fringe from mascara-caked eyes. 'Your best bet is to contact the authors. If I remember rightly, at least one of them used to work there. It's worth a try. But if you're looking for a hospital administrator, we might know of someone.' She turned back to her father-in-law who was handing change to a lady in a thick coat wearing earmuffs.

Assuming she couldn't hear him, Amos Burton was shouting at the lady customer, mouthing his words in an exaggerated fashion. 'That's three pounds fourteen change, Mrs Templeton. Good day to you.'

'Dad, what was the name of the woman who was here overseeing the hospital closure back in the nineties? The one who used to come in complaining about underage drinkers. Up herself. Moved to some posh place with her husband. What was his name?'

After some deep thinking and rubbing of his chin, her father-in-law brightened at a sudden recollection. 'Derek Flowers. And anyway, they weren't underage drinkers. It was our Terry and his mates hanging around the shop after school. I told her that at the time.'

'Derek Flowers? Are you sure? Who the hell is Derek Flowers? Shout up the stairs, see if Mum can remember.' Despite protests from Connie that they needn't disturb other family members on the off chance they could help, there was no stopping the enthusiasm.

'Derek Flowers... or p'raps it was Dennis Flowers...' Mr Burton mumbled as he pulled at the door Melinda had emerged from a minute or so beforehand. 'Maggie? Can you hear me, my duck?' Much to Connie's relief, the high-volume conversation was short-lived. 'She says his name was definitely Derek Flowers. The wife was a bossy woman, but we can't remember if we ever knew her well enough to be on first name terms. He was an accountant, worked in international shipping. Used to come along to the local football matches. Never saw *her* there. Too busy telling everyone how important she was, I suppose.'

Peddyr's words of thanks were showered on the shop keepers as he grabbed Connie's hand and dragged her to the door, clutching the paper and magazine she had bought and paid for.

'What's your hurry?' she demanded of him as he bundled her unceremoniously towards the car.

'Which way to the hospital grounds?' he asked. 'I need a pee. Too much coffee.' He checked the sat nav and turned the car around, heading back onto the A507, by-passing the village centre, and heading for Fairfield Park. 'Eliot Road takes us to the cemetery, there should be a convenient bush or tree somewhere; kills two birds with one stone,' he said, accelerating rapidly towards the next roundabout.

'Two cemeteries in one day,' Connie said, mocking. 'Lucky me.'

'Dead lucky.'

UNPLEASANT FINDINGS

*O*nce more, Cara listened intently to the audio file sent to her from Rory at Channel 7. Evidently Vera Hudson had declined to answer the question thrown at her by Konrad Neale. The question about children. 'You haven't turned that bleedin' thing back on, have you?' she demanded, and her voice got much louder as if she had leaned in too close to the microphone.

'You disreputable rogue, Konrad,' Cara said to herself. The camera had never been switched on, but the sound recording had continued without Vera's knowledge. What came next, therefore, was raw, unadulterated, and not accidental. Konrad Neale's reputation for using underhand strategies preceded him and for once Cara approved.

'Who told you I had children?' Vera asked. Her hoarse smoker's voice rising.

'Nobody, it's why I'm asking. I'm interested. Do you have children?'

'If I did have, I wouldn't be telling the likes of you about it. I won't be having you getting personal just because you're Billy Big Bollocks. It don't wash with me. Stick to what we agreed.'

Head cupped in her hands, elbows on her desk, Cara listened harder as the sounds of rustling clothes and harsh coughing could be heard. After a few long seconds, Konrad made his play.

'Out of personal interest, Mrs Hudson, how much money did Isaac Harkness pay you for this?'

'You've got a fucking nerve.'

'How right you are, Mrs H. We are similar creatures you and I, and it takes a conniving bastard to know one. Let me put it this way… You were miraculously discovered in a council property in a small town nobody's ever heard of. After a lifetime you are persuaded to be reunited with a brother you claim to despise for abandoning you. I'm amazed, nay flabbergasted, that you never sought him out before now to give you a financial boost, shall we say.'

'Piss off.'

'You've been written out of his biography all together. I know this because I was threatened with the sack and legal action if I didn't adhere to the script written especially for the programme. I can't believe Channel 7 thought they were going to wheel you out at the end of a live show as the emotional crescendo to a load of tripe about your brother's fantastic life story. I say fantastic because most of it *is* fantasy. Nobody can be that nice? Can they?'

There was another dramatic pause before Konrad spoke again. 'Here's your chance to tell me your side of the story. We can make this happen. Whatever you are being offered by Junior Harkness… I'll double it. Me personally. I want your story. The real one. Give me facts and evidence and I will make it happen.'

Cara raised her hands to her cheeks and yelled at the laptop. 'Rory West, you sneaky little bastard!' She didn't know whether to laugh or stamp her feet in temper or cry at the blatant corruption on display. However it came about, by letting her hear this, Rory had made her an accessory and Konrad would be hounding her now because she already had a professional relationship with Isaac Harkness and knew as much as anyone about Vera Hudson. What Konrad Neale wouldn't do for an inside route to the Harkness family, didn't bear thinking about for too long.

'Fucking Ada!' Cara shouted out. 'If they find out I'm the child of Vera Hudson and related to Austin, Olivia and Isaac Harkness, the proverbial smelly stuff will hit the fan and create the most spectacular patterns on the walls of my life.'

The audio recording continued to play as Cara ranted. One phrase immediately stopped her dead. 'Due diligence,' Konrad Neale was saying. 'No money will find its way into your purse until I see proof. The executive producer may be willing to let it slide, but if you are who you say you are, I want proof.'

'You've had it,' Vera replied with a snarl. 'Copy of my birth certificate, household bills, Ray's death certificate. What more do you want? Blood?'

Cara could see it coming. Konrad's cajoling would be inevitable because he needed the Harkness side of the story, something the Quirks could provide but luckily Konrad didn't know she had anything to do with them. He didn't even know where she lived.

To achieve his aims though, he would badger Cara until she furnished him with more invaluable insights into the privileged world of Vera Hudson's brother... the real target in Konrad Neale's sights. He would be calling her any day now.

Previously she would have done as asked and agreed to Konrad's demands because he always paid well and because she gained great satisfaction from utilising her skills. However, this time it was about *her* life and not merely that of a newsworthy tycoon.

'Balls to you,' she said, standing up, reaching for a tissue from a box which lay beside her computer. The box was nearly empty.

Wiping angry tears from the corners of her eyes and flapping her hands to shake off the taint of bribery, she couldn't shift the feeling of betrayal that was weighing her down.

'You had me adopted out because all you care about is yourself, money, and who you can misuse to get hold of it. Konrad Neale is the same, only he does what he does in the name of journalism and spends it on luxury holidays and a fancy house in the country. What does your money go on, Vera? Booze and fags and a shitty little life doing sod all. I should thank you for what you did. Being adopted by the Laidlaws saved me from neglect and poverty. Just think… I could have joined you in your social underclass. Thank God I was adopted. Thank God!'

She looked up for no reason other than that was where heaven was supposed to be. 'That decision made me who I am today,' she said, and the rant stopped abruptly as Cara caught sight of herself in a distorted window reflection and questioned the person she saw there.

'Cara, pull yourself together. This is dragging you down, making you sad, and you're worth more than that. What is the point in having a career reliant on the likes of shifty showbiz types out to feather their own nests? Bev's right. I need to go home. Forget Vera Hudson, forget Isaac Harkness, forget Konrad Neale. Fuck the lot of them.'

Grabbing her mobile phone, she began to compose a text to her oldest friend. 'Enough is enough,' she said, directing her ire towards the two budgies. 'Yorkshire beckons, my little feathered friends. We begin flat hunting today. Maybe Skipton or Harrogate, Keighley, or Ilkley… somewhere dead posh. I could probably rent a whole house back home for a lot less than I pay here each month.'

Startled by the vibration of the phone in her hand she gasped and looked at the screen. 'Oh, thank Crippin for that. The voice of reason,' she said, pressing down with a fingertip to accept the call. 'Connie? I have something I need to send through to you straight away. You're not going to like it… but in the meantime, any news?'

Ending her involvement in the search for a missing woman, birth mother or not, was proving hard for Cara. First hurdle, and she had fallen flat on her face. She cursed her natural curiosity as she held the phone tight to her ear, keen for an update on the mystery.

* * *

*T*he headstone was impossible to read, covered in lichen and tilted at a slant. With a cold breeze blowing, Connie hugged her coat tight to her as she spoke to Cara. 'We have some news, but nothing concrete,' she replied, stamping her feet to keep warm. 'We met Mr and Mrs Harkness in their substantial mansion. All very lah-di-dah. And I'm now standing in the grounds of the hospital where you were born.'

'Oh! What are you doing there?'

'Waiting for Peddyr to have a piddle behind a tree. He doesn't care where he pees. Says he can't possibly think straight with a full bladder. Anyway, I was just checking in. Did you catch the BBC Valley Radio show this morning?'

'Yes, I did.' Cara perked up. 'The story about the pride march was brilliant. You have to listen to it if you get chance. Download the app on your phone. Don't miss it. Honestly, it totally took my mind off the mess I've made of my life. Christine Fowler got carpeted. Slated. She'll never get re-elected after what she said. I think BBC Valley Radio is continuing the theme this afternoon. I might have another listen in.'

From behind Connie, Peddyr approached, double-checking he had zipped up his fly. 'Do you want to go? You must be bursting by now. The tree is free,' he said gesturing in the general direction of the scattered headstones.

The call to Cara ended in polite goodbyes and a promise to

check in with each other later that evening. Connie smiled. 'As a matter of fact, I could do with relieving the pressure on my own bladder. However, you'll not catch me in the middle of winter in a cemetery, with my knickers down.'

'Ah, those were the days,' he replied with a grin. 'I suppose we could find the nearest service station...'

'Too right we will. There's one near the A1 junction. Not far, according to good old Google. Then we should head off to the B&B to defrost and debrief. You ought to check in with Bernie and break the news.'

'Which bit?' Peddyr asked as they trudged back to the car to be greeted by a wagging Roger with his nose pressed against a steamy window. 'The good news that we have been formally engaged by Mr Harkness to find Vera Hudson or the bad news that until today we were pawns in a game being played by Mr Harkness to defend his privacy. Insulting, if you ask me, and downright dubious.' He pulled open the driver's door and wafted the air. 'Pooeee. The smell of wet dog.'

Sniffing the air and quickly pinching her nostrils with one gloved hand, Connie said, 'Crikey, Roger. You do hum a bit.'

OUT OF SORTS

*W*hen Lois arrived home, she looked up to the third floor and waved at Cara before getting out of her car; a weekday security habit they had fallen into. A godsend for Lois, who was always comforted by the sight of Cara's face at the window returning her greeting. Knowing she had someone looking out for her made Lois feel slightly less fearful after the chaos and near rioting the previous night. She needed all the security she could get when faced with a lonely walk from her car to the safety of the building, especially when Dan wasn't around.

It wasn't her imagination running away with her, with the dark mornings and sunless winter afternoons taking their toll; the added anxiety came whenever she faced the possibility of bumping into a neighbour. She didn't trust any of them, apart from Cara who seemed to be struggling too. The usual smile was missing. It had begun to fade rapidly in the past week or so, which could not be purely because Pilates was on hold.

Cara tried to put on a resolute face, but something wasn't right.

Instead of heading directly into her flat, Lois knocked at her neighbour's door. 'Thought I'd pop my head in and say hello to you and the budgies. How are they doing?' Grey smudges under the eyes hinted at Cara's lack of sleep, and sadness showed itself in her weak smile and the absence of a reply. 'You been cooped up in here all day?' Lois asked, scoping the room, the scattered paperwork on the desk and the box of tissues to hand by the keyboard. 'What do you say to a brisk walk into town and supper at the carvery place. They're open on a Monday and they're cheap. Good idea?'

'That would probably be nothing short of a life saver,' Cara replied nodding. 'Shower first?'

By six thirty that evening the two friends were heading out of the main entrance to Brookside's left wing and across the car park. 'Through't ginnel?' Cara asked.

Lois grinned at her. 'Or should that be snicket?'

'Better than calling it a plain old alleyway,' Cara replied. 'How boring is that…'

The alleyway was dimly lit and, despite cutting off the corner, they didn't risk it.

'Apparently the company doing the boiler refit at the hall haven't even started yet,' Lois said with a breathy sigh. 'There was a mention about it on Facebook from Pristine Christine. Have you heard anything from Hazel?'

A glance ahead to make sure the pavement was clear, and the pair soon scooted through to Station Road, peeking into the lounge window of number ten, home of Sharon Osborne the Second. Lights were blazing and, as the curtains were not fully closed, Sharon could be seen sitting with Tracey Dart drinking from mugs, nattering animatedly, a scruffy dog curled up asleep at their feet. 'At least Kyle looks happy,' Cara whispered. 'Let's hope Tracey has the guts to head for a women's refuge. She can't stay there, when the police let him out, Jed will come knocking soon enough and drag her back home. Literally and probably by her hair.'

Lois gave her friend an admiring look. 'The dog is called Kyle? I never knew that. Amazing, you pick up on everything.'

'I don't,' Cara said. 'Far from it in fact. Vera Hudson has gone missing, and I didn't notice until it was too late.'

'Too late for what?' Lois asked, somewhat puzzled by the strange statement. 'What could you have done?'

The route took them past the Memorial Hall, and they were both keen to see if the workmen had made a start that day. The hall was in darkness but as they drew closer a car pulled into the car park with a purr.

'So, you've heard nothing from Hazel to say the hall will be closed for longer than originally planned?' Lois asked, picking up on the previous subject again.

'No, but she did say the contractors needed a couple of weeks to do the work, so, God knows how long before it's up and running,' Cara replied. Her eyes remained on the car in the car park. 'I think it's the photographic society who meet on the third Monday of the month. Normally it would start in half an hour...' She and Lois stopped and waited for the driver to step out of the vehicle. 'It's closed,' Cara shouted. 'All classes are cancelled for—'

'Oh, it's Christine,' Lois stated on seeing who the driver was. 'Has she got another new car?'

'Everything alright?' Cara called out to a smartly dressed Christine, who was marching with purpose towards the hall entrance. Her neatly curled hair bounced with each stride of her high-heeled leather boots.

'No doubt I shall find out very soon,' she replied with exaggerated exasperation. 'The surveyor's office called. He has asked to meet me here to discuss a hiccup. One simply has to credit the man for his limitless excuses for not getting on with the job.' With a dismissive wave, Christine Fowler turned away and unlocked the hall entrance door with a rattle. Lois could hear the alarm beeping as Christine punched in the numbers to disable it.

* * *

*T*he carvery was at The Red Lion. Nothing fancy, but nevertheless the building was warm and unassuming; a nice enough place for Lois and Cara to chat, eat and drink. The Red Lion had the type of set up that would ensure dinner could be achieved in record time, given that they and another two tables were the only customers. A grand total of eight people had ventured out for food.

Incidental music tinkled in the background as they settled at a table in a corner and a uniformed server plodded her way to the table, electronic order pad at the ready. 'Rotisserie chicken or roast pork on a Monday,' the sullen waitress announced. 'Not much choice, but not many customers, not in January. Too cold and nobody's got no money.'

Lois cringed at the use of the double negative and sloppy diction. She couldn't help herself. Earlier she had shouted at the television when the continuity announcer had failed to pronounce his words with care. 'T H is not the same as V,' she had yelled. 'The word is "weather", not "wevver". How many more times!'

At the table, Cara caught her expression and was grinning down at the menu, deliberately avoiding her gaze.

'Starters?' the waitress asked, with her Bosworth accent mangling the word in her mouth. Lois almost slumped despairingly in the chair but managed to hold back from comment.

'Not tonight, thank you. We'll just help ourselves to the carvery. Maybe pudding.'

'Want drinks, do you?'

'Aye, if you can manage that on a Monday, in January,' Cara chipped in. 'Pint of lemonade for me. Lois?'

'Same, please.' Lois held up her knife and said, 'Could I have a clean one of these as well? This one is grubby.'

With a sharp tut, the girl shrugged, took the knife, and walked off, leaving the two bemused customers grinning at each other across the table. 'She'll go far,' Lois commented, before changing the subject and enquiring about Cara's day. 'You must be knackered. I know I am,' she said, wondering why her neighbour was unaccountably quiet. 'Is that why you're down in the dumps?' she ventured, straightening the placemat, and repositioning the cutlery to her satisfaction.

Engrossed in her ritualistic tidying, Lois hadn't been ready for Cara's life story. At first, it came as a much-abridged version, accompanied by eye-dabbing and nose-wiping. When Cara reached the part about being born in a psychiatric hospital and discovering what a reprehensible person her birth mother was, Lois reached into her bag for a packet of folded tissues which she handed to her friend without the need to interrupt her.

Cara couldn't seem to staunch the tears and her own tissues had become sodden and useless. Hands clasped in her lap, her words spilled out in a torrent, sobs punctuating the punchy sentences.

'So, in short, I came to Bosworth to find my mother. I don't like what I find. I'm in the shit for lying to Isaac Harkness who turns out is my cousin, and if I don't walk away from the mess I've made, I'll be dragged through the courts with Konrad Neale for invasion of privacy or defamation of character, or worse.'

She paused to blow her nose again. 'When Isaac did manage to meet up with Vera, he had to use bribery to get her to do what he wanted simply to impress his father. I used him to get to her, he used me to get a deal with a TV company, she used Channel 7 to get more money, and then Konrad Neale steps in and offers even more cash for the real story.' The tirade ended abruptly as a thought seemed to occur to Cara. 'What if Vera turns up dead and they think I did it?'

At last Lois felt she had been given permission to respond.

'No wonder you're out of sorts,' she said, stretching across the table to touch her friend's hand. 'Tell you what, let's finish this and order the puddings. My brain needs sugar. Now then, where is that dopey girl? If I order now, we may see an ice cream without too much delay.'

In truth she needed time to work out what best to say in the circumstances. Since meeting and befriending Cara, she never would have guessed such a complex history would have brought them together.

The ins and outs of the sorry tale were completed over dinner, and with Cara unburdened, the words flowed more easily.

'You make a good listener,' she said to Lois.

'You are a great storyteller.'

'If only it was a work of fiction, eh?'

STIRRINGS

*P*eddyr was heartened to see road signs for Marston Moreteyne. He'd had enough of driving through the murk of a dim January afternoon, with a head full of uncertainties. 'What we are left with, Lao Po, is nothing but a pile of unanswered questions at our feet,' he said.

'And a smelly wet dog in the back seat,' Connie replied. 'Neither are very palatable.'

'And nor is the news that a certain E J Cooper reported Verity Hudson as a missing person twenty-eight years ago. E J Cooper,' he repeated for his own benefit. 'Someone who resides in the small town of Rushden, in a house previously rented by a Mrs Verity Hudson before she went missing the first time. How's that for unpalatable? And Rushden is horribly close to the village of Sharnbrook where Austin Harkness happens to own a mansion.'

While his wife had made use of the toilet facilities at the service station, Peddyr had been back in touch with Sergeant Kevin Spratt and unearthed a new puzzle for P.Q. Investigations to get their heads round over supper. 'The woman who reported Verity Hudson as a missing person was called Elizabeth Cooper,'

Kevin had said. 'She was a lodger, or a friend. The report doesn't give a great deal of detail but does mention that Verity Hudson had been in psychiatric care the previous year and was still on the road to recovery.'

'Does the report give any other contact details for this Elizabeth Cooper? Previous known addresses? Telephone numbers? Anything?'

'No. Just that she had taken on some sort of caring and support role and was worried about Verity Hudson's state of mind. Full name, Elizabeth Jane Cooper, the address is the same as for Verity herself.'

'Elizabeth Jane Cooper? E J Cooper. You're sure?'

'In black and white. Right in front of me.'

Peddyr didn't doubt Kevin's word. He doubted his own judgement. The letter that he had found in Vera Hudson's flat had been addressed to an E J Cooper. He had handed that letter to Esther Cooper, making a basic straightforward assumption for which he now berated himself.

'Kevin. Can you do me a favour and find out the full name of Esther Cooper of 13 Browns Court. I may have an unusual coincidence on my hands, or failing that, a piece of the puzzle I can't yet explain.'

* * *

'Where do we start to unpick this?' Connie asked. '18 Browns Court was home to Verity Anne Hudson. E J Cooper lives in Verity Hudson's old house and a letter addressed to someone of the same initials is sent to 18 Browns Court, Bosworth Bishops. If Esther Cooper's middle name is Helen, then it could be a simple typo. H is next to J on the qwerty keyboard.'

Obliged to follow the instructions from Sat-Nav-Suzie, Peddyr made a left turn. 'Buggered if I can make any sense of it,' he said, unable to come to any satisfactory answer. 'Vera disappears from her home in Rushden nigh on three decades ago, Elizabeth Cooper – who said she was a friend staying there on a temporary basis – reports her missing but remains in the house taking on the tenancy. And she's still there according to the local council.'

He cursed under his breath, deeply regretting his actions regarding the letter he'd found with Vera Hudson's unopened post. 'Fuck it. I wish I'd opened the damned letter now... I wonder if the delightful Esther Cooper of Bosworth Bishops will let me have sight of it. Maybe if it wasn't for her, she'll let me have it back. Too many Coopers in the world, that's the trouble.' A sly grin crossed his face. 'Surely she must hoard post as well as all the other crap in that flat of hers. If she hands it back, it will be one less piece of worthless crud for her to find room for.'

Connie pointed towards the windscreen at the sight of a brightly illuminated brick farmhouse. 'There it is. Home sweet home, Roger. The best little bed and breakfast in the area according to TripAdvisor.'

* * *

*E*nsconced in their spacious room, showered, and changed, Peddyr sat in an armchair waiting for Connie to finish drying her hair.

Having listened to the audio evidence sent to them from Cara, in which Vera spoke to Konrad Neale, he opened his notebook. It helped him to think, to form a chronology of events. He had barely scanned his bullet points when he stabbed a meaty finger at the open page. 'There's a fair chance that Elizabeth Jane Cooper knows about Verity Hudson's past life, so we should take the opportunity to speak with her.' He shot a look at Connie who was watching him via the reflection in the mirror on the dressing table, and he made a fist pump motion. 'Rushden bright and early,' he said.

Flicking the controls, Connie turned off the hairdryer to hear him. 'What?'

'We are making a visit to Rushden tomorrow, first thing. With luck we will catch them out and Vera will be miraculously discovered staying with her old friend Elizabeth Cooper. Just like we thought. She upped and left because it got too hot. Too messy. She took the money and skedaddled, knowing there was more coming her way from that slimy git Konrad Neale. She's gone into hiding before spilling her guts to the press and earning a fortune.' He clapped his hands. 'They are in cahoots.'

Connie made a face in the mirror that he knew well. Her "scrunched-up nose" expression. A tempering of his enthusiasm would shortly follow; it always did. Sure enough, she turned to face him and released a gentle sigh. 'Can it be that simple?' she asked.

'Kevin seemed to think it was worth getting in touch with Elizabeth Cooper on the basis that she knew Vera years ago and cared enough to report her missing, but he didn't know about the letter I found in Vera's flat until I told him over the phone this afternoon, while you were… inconvenienced.'

'Very witty, Lao Gong,' Connie said with a giggle.

Peddyr tapped the side of his head. 'Upstairs for thinking, downstairs for dancing,' he replied smiling broadly, congratulating himself silently for the sharpness of his mind after such a long day. 'I'll drop Kevin a message, tell him not to bother asking for an officer to go round to Elizabeth's address. We'll do the honours.' A low gurgle emanated from his stomach. 'Come on, time for food. Are we alright leaving Roger here?'

The local village pub usually served food on a Monday evening but had experienced a flood, knocking the kitchen out of action for at least a week, they were told when they had telephoned to enquire earlier. Therefore they had decided to aim for the nearest pub chain for the predictable cheap drinks and beige grub. On arrival at the farmhouse, when Connie had mentioned to their hosts the problem of seeking out an evening meal with a dog in tow, very quickly a solution was offered.

'Dog sitting is all part of the service,' came the reply. 'He can curl up by the fire with us until you return.'

Guilt about leaving a stinky wet dog with such generous people had compelled Connie to give Roger a bath and she had dried him off with an old towel they had in the car. Before either she or Peddyr could make use of the bathroom, she scrubbed the place clean to hide the evidence of a makeshift poodle parlour.

'I'll drive,' Connie said as they waved goodbye and left a wagging fragrant Roger with two new admirers.

Peddyr had taken her offer for granted. It wasn't far, he fancied a pint and Connie rarely touched alcohol. 'Only if you desist from doing your impersonation of a rally driver. The roads are greasy.'

Once inside the car, Connie linked her phone with the audio system, set the sat nav and repositioned the seat. A familiar voice came over the speakers as Peddyr clicked his seatbelt into place. Talbot Howkins, presenter with BBC Valley Radio was introducing a guest to his programme. 'Ahh,' said Peddyr. 'You found it then. Christine Fowl-Mouth spouting off on the radio this morning. I've been looking forward to this.'

He and Connie fell silent as Christine Fowler's credentials were shared across the airwaves. 'Town councillor for the last twelve years, Mrs Fowler has gained a reputation for speaking her mind. Those of you on social media will know she isn't afraid to stir the pot.'

Pulling into a parking bay some fifteen minutes later, Peddyr puffed out his cheeks. 'She hung herself with that comment about homosexuality being an insult to God.' He stared at Connie whose eyebrows had disappeared beneath her glossy fringe in shock. 'Every member of the gay community will be baying for her blood.'

'That's her career over,' Connie agreed. 'You can't say things like that in this day and age. You're bad enough at times.'

'Such as?'

'Such as asking Alleyn and Joe who is going to throw the bouquet at their wedding' – she tutted – 'but that's you. *She's* a public figure. What was she thinking?' Locking the car door with the remote key, she caught her husband's eye. 'Spouting her full CV was boastful, but to hear her say she was solely responsible for coordinating the search for Vera Hudson was ludicrous. And being so personal about the woman. There was no need for that.'

Peddyr considered Connie's observations and recalled Christine Fowler's description of Vera Hudson. They were alarmingly barbed words for someone who only saw Vera from a distance in church on a Sunday. Putting on a starchy voice he said, 'Whoever she is, Mrs Vera Hudson has lived a shameful life. She made little contribution to society and yet here we are, leaving no stone unturned in our search for her,' he repeated aloud, mimicking Christine Fowler's clipped and snobbish tones. 'When we get back home, we need to speak to Lady Fowl-Mouth.'

He pulled open the door to the pub to allow Connie to enter.

As she passed by, she said, 'What was it Pamela Watts overheard in church?'

Peddyr grabbed at her arm. 'Connie Quirk, you are a wonder.' He approached a tall desk in the shape of a lectern and asked the woman there for a table for two. Holding tight to Connie's hand he almost skipped his way through the restaurant, taking his seat but not looking at the menu. He was too wired.

'Lao Po,' he said, earnestly. His thoughts tumbled out with such a rush he could barely keep up with them. 'The man in the shop in Arlesey today mentioned the name Derek Flowers. Derek Flowers must be Des Fowler. Christine's husband. Christine knows about Vera because Christine worked at the hospital. Fairfield Hospital. You heard her just now. On the radio. According to her, she single-handedly applied the Community Care Act in the 1990s helping with the closure of a large psychiatric institution in favour of group homes and…' He made a rolling motion with his hands and fast forwarded the conversation. 'Christine knows more than most about Vera Hudson.' Resting his case, he leaned back in the chair and picked up the menu. 'That was no friendly neighbour who informed Isaac Harkness of Vera's whereabouts. It was Lady Fowl-Mouth. I wonder what she's really up to.'

'And she hasn't said a word to the police…' Connie said, her face mirroring that of her husband's.

CURIOSITY

*H*aving confessed all to Lois in the Red Lion, Cara suddenly felt tired. Very tired. 'Shall we pay at the bar?' she suggested. 'By the time our dynamic waitress gets the message that we wish to settle up, they'll be serving breakfast.' They split the bill and briskly made their way home along well-lit streets. It was around a quarter to eight when they turned into Memorial Road, which suited them both.

'I'm ripe for an early night,' said Lois. 'Let's just hope that bloody low-life Jed hasn't been let out of jail.' She looked across at Cara, their arms linked at the elbow. 'If you are moving back to Yorkshire, I think I'll be on my way too. I can't stay in Brookside without you as my angel to make sure I'm safe of an evening. And God knows what goes on in the summer months. Can you imagine?'

'Maybe you and Dan could shack up together. Or is it too soon?'

'Way too soon,' Lois replied with a purposeful shudder. 'No. I'll find somewhere less drug fuelled to live, somewhere closer to the school. My pay should cover it and I'm getting rid of the car. Compromise to the rescue.'

'Oh, 'eck,' Cara said as they spotted a van parked outside the entrance door to the Wigmore Memorial Hall. 'Bet the poor bloke is getting a rare ear-bashing from our Christine.'

'And the door to the hall has been left open... careless,' noted Lois.

Cara faltered. 'That's too good an opportunity to miss. Let's go and listen in.'

Lois didn't possess Cara's innate sense of curiosity and baulked at the idea, until she found herself standing alone on the pavement watching Cara's back disappear inside the entrance, lit only by a green glow from the fire exit signs. 'Wait for me,' she stage-whispered, scurrying to catch up.

In spite of her haste, Cara applied some caution as she approached the double swing doors to the main hall. It was possible that there would be more than two people involved in the maintenance contract meeting which sounded well underway in the hall. With a hooked finger she beckoned for Lois to join her in the kitchen, where the roller shutter to a large serving hatch provided a much better listening post than lurking outside the hefty hall doors.

Christine Fowler's voice carried clearly. 'I've just spent the last half an hour going over this with you and your lackey. You must be satisfied by now that I know what I'm talking about. Let me make this clear. I don't want your money, I'm not in the business of being bribed. I want facts and I want to hear them from you.'

Cara and Lois exchanged puzzled looks and shrugged at each other. In her head Cara was filling in gaps. Was there a local authority scandal at play here? Were the contractors trying to pay her a sweetener? She hunkered down in the semi-darkness. Lois remained in the doorway, checking the entrance every few seconds and silently beseeching Cara to come out of the kitchen.

A man's voice, bordering on intimidating, came from somewhere just the other side of the shutter. It made Lois flinch. 'Then why not go straight to the police?'

'Because I've absolutely no proof,' Christine answered.

A heartless laugh escaped from the man. 'You wanted a confession – is that it?'

'I wanted to make it apparent to all concerned that someone was perpetrating a very brazen deception. I also expected you to expose yourself as the liar you are. Our business is over. I will be reporting the facts as I see them to the police. You are right, I should have done that in the first place.'

Lois appeared at Cara's shoulder and tugged at her sleeve, pointing to the doorway where an emerald glow spilled across the flooring. Cara gave a thumbs-up and they both slunk away as quietly as they could. It sounded as if the conversation in the hall was coming to an end. Christine had concluded her meeting and, if the two girls didn't decamp in a hurry, then they were in danger of being caught.

Leaving the hall sedately, so as not to draw attention to their uninvited intrusion into Christine Fowler's negotiations on behalf of the local council, Lois and Cara crossed the road before glancing back.

The interior light of another vehicle caught Cara's eye before the sound of shoes on tarmac alerted her to the presence of someone else parked up next to Christine's Range Rover. As the girls watched on, two shadowy figures could be seen striding slowly into the gloom of the hall entrance.

'Christine has called for back-up,' Cara announced. 'Not that she needs it.'

'I didn't even notice the other cars in the car park until that one opened the driver's door just now,' Lois said in a forced whisper. 'Imagine if they'd walked in on us behaving like a couple of burglars.'

Once at a safe distance from the hall, Cara and Lois stopped to gather themselves. 'That was close,' Lois said with a nervous laugh. 'I haven't done anything that daft since I was at uni. Can you imagine how embarrassing that would have been if we'd been spotted? We didn't even have good reason to be there.'

They walked on and thought nothing more of it until the following morning.

FOUND

*T*he car sped along the A6, Peddyr at the wheel once more. Beside him Connie sighed. 'I feel like we are retracing our steps, Lao Gong. I've just seen the sign for Sharn-brook back there.'

'I said it was close.' He tapped his fingers on the steering wheel in time with the music on the radio. 'Keep a note of how long it takes to drive from here to Rushden, and have a search for bus timetables, if you wouldn't mind. If Vera is in Rush-den...' he let the thought trail off. Connie wouldn't need an explanation.

'Pemberton Street,' he said, reminding himself of where they were headed. 'I'm going to park up the road where there happens to be a classic motorbike dealer. Can't hurt to see what he's got in stock while we're here. A little shufti through the window won't kill me.'

'But I will if you buy another motorbike,' his wife snapped back with a cheeky smile. He was teasing and she knew it.

On the street view of the online map, Peddyr had got the measure of the area they were about to visit. Narrow streets with terraced housing, mostly late-Victorian two-up two-down, with street parking at a premium; they would make use of Roger and walk the pavements.

Their timetable had been squeezed, mostly because of the substantial and delicious breakfast served at the farm that morning, and as a result they missed the rush hour. In fact, after the leisurely morning and a walk around the farm with Roger, it was nearing ten o'clock before they left Marston Moreteyne. They would have to speed up their enquiries at 12 Pemberton Street if they were to be on time for the appointment with Isaac Harkness scheduled for two o'clock. At almost an hour away, if the traffic was in their favour, they didn't have too much leeway.

'At least we won't have to stop for lunch,' Connie remarked with a dramatic groan and a rub of her abdomen. 'I'm stuffed to the gunwales.'

The area was much as Peddyr had expected, a busy part of town peppered with traffic lights and congested junctions. A littering of independent businesses was to be found either side of the main road, from the inventively named Rush-tan tanning salon, to various fast food takeaway shops appealing to the palate of the late-night drinkers in nearby pubs. With the recent arrival of the new shopping centre a few miles away, Rushden had gained a reputation as somewhere for the retail-hungry to go. However, losing out to the shopping centre, the area around Pemberton Street had signs of decline as far as Peddyr could see, especially when the drabness of the streets was accentuated by a mid-winter pessimism.

'No messing, straight to the point,' he said, knocking on the door of number twelve, Connie just behind him holding Roger's lead. Direct from the pavement she peered in at the front room window.

'More dead pot plants in there than I have at home,' she commented. 'I guess Miss Cooper is a busy wo—'

The door rattled open to reveal a squat man in his late forties, dressed in a brown suit, a knitted jumper beneath the jacket and an orange tie. With his neatly combed hair smeared to his head, he reminded Peddyr of Hitler without a moustache. Unblinking, the man stood stiffly poised, eyes switching between Peddyr and Connie. 'Yes?'

Puzzled, Peddyr stepped back to double-check he had the right house number. 'I do beg your pardon,' he said. 'We were hoping to speak to Elizabeth Cooper. Do you know anyone by that name?'

'Yes, I do.'

'Does she live here?'

'No. She's my landlady,' the man replied in a robotic fashion. His expression at first passive, turned to one of anxiety when Elizabeth Cooper's name was mentioned, until he noticed Roger wagging his tail expectantly, and only then did the man appear reassured enough to continue the conversation. 'My name is Vaughan Probert. I am pleased to meet you.'

The way he forced the greeting was enough of a giveaway for Peddyr, who didn't need Connie to tell him that this man found social interactions to be a painful experience. He determined to be brief and direct. 'Is Elizabeth Cooper here?'

'No, she is not here.'

'Do you know where she is?'

'No, I do not know where she is at this precise moment.'

Peddyr realised that he would have to be more specific about what he asked and how he asked it.

'Is she at work?'

'Yes. She is away on business.' He looked again at Roger and at Connie. 'Is this about Council Tax?' he asked, pausing only long enough to answer his own question. 'No, I think it is not. The dog would indicate that this is a social visit.' Vaughan Probert was processing the scene before him and doing so in a monotone.

'Does anyone else live here with you?' Connie asked.

'No, I live here. I also work from home.'

'What work do you do?'

'I'm an accounts analyst. I see patterns in numbers. Neuro-typicals don't possess such a skill.'

Peddyr smiled to himself. He had expected to find an unpleasant, manipulative, and obstreperous Vera Hudson hiding away with her friend Elizabeth Cooper; instead, he had been met by one of life's innocents. Connie had clearly arrived at the same conclusion, and she was keen to press home the advantage.

'In which case, Mr Probert, you may be just the man we need. We are looking for Miss Elizabeth Cooper in relation to a missing person. We hoped she could help us, but you may hold the answers. You may see a pattern where we can't. Can we come inside the house?'

'Do you have any form of identification with you?' Vaughan asked, holding out a soft-skinned hand. From her shoulder bag, Connie pulled a business card for P.Q. Investigations while Peddyr flicked open his wallet to find his driving licence.

'You are not the police.'

'No, we're not the police,' Peddyr confirmed, 'but we are here with the consent of Sergeant Kevin Spratt from our local police missing persons unit. I'm sure he would be only too glad to speak to you on the phone to confirm this if you wish.'

'I think you are genuine, because scammers wouldn't have a dog with them,' Vaughan announced, stepping back to allow them into the hallway.

With some guilt Peddyr agreed with Vaughan's assessment. 'Quite true,' he said, knowing full well that a conman worth his salt would use any old trick to gain access to a vulnerable person's home. And without a doubt, Vaughan Probert was a vulnerable individual.

'I like animals,' Vaughan continued. 'I have a cat, but she has been keeping Miss Cooper company. The cat is not here so the dog may come in. What is his name?'

'Roger,' Connie replied. Smiling at Peddyr as Vaughan patted the dog on the head, his palm rigid.

All three remained wedged awkwardly in the small hallway until Connie suggested a move to a larger room.

'You are obviously capable with figures,' she said, following the peculiar man into a sparsely furnished front room.

This was the place where Vaughan Probert's pot plants came to die, Peddyr decided. There were several brittle and brown examples of deceased houseplants on the windowsill, hosting spiders' webs and dead flies. The walls of the room were covered in *Star Wars* posters and the many shelving units were home to various scale models of spacecraft, including a sizeable Death Star. Against an internal wall was a long desk and a computer, above which hung a replica of Darth Vader's helmet.

'Do you manage Miss Elizabeth Cooper's accounts for her?' Connie asked. Her eyes had fixed upon several cardboard boxes on the carpet, the slender files inside them piled neatly.

Peddyr almost gasped at Connie's ingenious approach; their normal questioning style would have been useless in the face of such concrete thinking. When Vaughan labelled others as being neuro-typical, he placed himself in the alternative category. He was intelligent, gifted perhaps, and very likely on the autistic spectrum; a place where black and white rarely merged to become grey. Unambiguous questions were in order, not a meandering discussion about Ewoks and the world according to Yoda.

'She makes use of my services,' Vaughan said. 'A simple task of balancing income and expenditure. Tax calculations, account reconciliation.'

'Can you tell us whether the name Verity Hudson appears anywhere in the accounts?' It was a wild punt and one which Peddyr did not expect to pay off. He wasn't even sure why it had sprung to mind as an idea, but before it formed fully it was out of his mouth.

'Yes, I can tell you.'

Vaughan had answered the question he had been asked, and Peddyr was duly embarrassed by the simple mistake he had made.

'Does Mrs Verity Hudson's name appear in the accounts?'

'Yes, it does.'

This was going to be much harder than Peddyr realised, so he deferred to his wife with a flick of a hand.

'Is Verity Hudson a tenant too?' she asked. 'Does she reside in a property owned by Miss Elizabeth Cooper?'

'No, she is not a tenant like me, she is Miss Elizabeth Cooper's business partner.'

'You know her?'

'No, I have never seen Mrs Verity Anne Hudson.'

The formality meant that neither Peddyr nor Connie were required to clarify the subject of their inquiries. Vaughan Probert was very precise. 'Mrs Verity Anne Hudson currently resides in Browns Court, Bosworth Bishops, a town on the borders of Oxfordshire and Gloucestershire. She moved there on the eighth of July last year.'

'Would you have records of any other places where she has lived previously?'

'Yes. They are all carefully documented.'

'Any pattern?' Connie asked.

'Yes. Regular payments. A three-year pattern of new tenancy agreements. Mrs Verity Hudson takes the tenancy of a property to check suitability for other tenants. Miss Elizabeth Cooper also sometimes visits her and stays with her. My mother tells me that this would indicate a lesbian relationship. I agree. The properties rented by Mrs Verity Anne Hudson have only one bedroom.'

Peddyr tried to focus on what this would mean in the neuro-typical world, in Vera Hudson's world. Nobody had mentioned seeing a visitor at 18 Browns Court, let alone a partner.

Next to him, Connie tensed.

'So, Mr Probert, you are a man who sees patterns. Do you see any patterns when it comes to the accounts that you manage for Miss Elizabeth Cooper?' she enquired.

'I always see patterns in numbers, Mrs Connie Quirk. Spending patterns would support my mother's theory. Domestic bills for this property are paid by Miss Elizabeth Cooper—'

'Even though they are incurred by you?' Peddyr queried, interrupting.

'This is her main business address. She makes use of the computer and I deal with the bank accounts. I'm a lodger – all bills included except food. I buy my own and Mother helps me to label it.' He pointed to where the kitchen would be at the back of the small property, and his arm remained raised for longer than was necessary. He lowered it again as he returned to the question. 'Domestic bills for Mrs Verity Hudson are paid by her.'

'Where does her income derive from?' Connie asked, a thoughtful expression crossing her face.

'She is on benefit payments.'

'But she is a business partner, you said.'

'Miss Elizabeth Cooper says Mrs Verity Hudson is her business partner. Mother tells me it is a lie. She says it is a polite way to say they are lesbian lovers. Mother says Mrs Verity Hudson is a dirty business partner. It's a joke,' he explained without so much of a shimmy from his lips. 'I don't understand jokes.'

Peddyr felt a tingle weave its way up the back of his neck. A major piece of the puzzle had just fallen into place. He reached inside his coat pocket and produced the photograph of Vera Hudson, the same one that he had shown to her neighbours in Bosworth Bishops, the photograph provided by Isaac Harkness. 'Do you know this person?'

'Yes,' said Vaughan with a deep nod.

'Who is it?' Peddyr added.

'Miss Elizabeth Cooper. Everyone calls her Liz. She dislikes the name Elizabeth.'

Peddyr channelled his emotions into something appropriate for the setting. If his hunch was a good one, Vaughan Probert had been well and truly taken advantage of. 'Correct,' he said, forcing a warm smile of encouragement. 'And the last thing we need from you is a list of the properties she rents out.'

Vaughan stared back at him. 'She rents two properties out. This one to me and one to Mr Pavel Pivac. She has her own home in the next street – 3 Montague Street.'

Connie was onto something. Peddyr had watched her face for so many years he could read it. 'How many business partners does Miss Cooper have?' she asked.

'Two others. Mr Mohammed Khan and Mr Pavel Pivac. Mr Pivac provides estate management services.'

Connie stood. 'Thank you, Mr Probert. You have been very helpful. One last thing. When Miss Cooper makes a visit, do you stay in the house to assist her with business matters?'

Vaughan Probert shrank visibly. 'No, I go to visit Mother. I stay with her to give peace and quiet to Miss Elizabeth Cooper. She says I give her a headache.'

Peddyr couldn't let that be the last question, his head was reeling, and he had to know more. 'When is Miss Cooper coming here next?'

'She said she would call in on her return this morning.' Vaughan looked at the computer to check the time and began wringing his hands together.

'And when did she leave home on this business trip?' Peddyr asked.

'She said she went yesterday to tidy up pressing matters with Mrs Verity Hudson and to bring my cat back. While she is away, she will call in to Oxford to see how Mr Pivac is doing with repairs to another house.'

Peddyr held back a smile. If his theory was right, he and

Connie had uncovered a serious web of deceit involving benefit fraud on a grand scale. Vaughan Probert was unwittingly laying out the business model for them without knowing the seriousness of his involvement in robbing the public purse.

All the information they needed was in the room in which they now stood, and they had no legal way to access it.

'How would you get from Bosworth Bishops back to here?' Peddyr asked, hoping to receive an accurate time of Elizabeth Cooper's arrival.

'By train to Oxford then to Northampton where I would catch the bus near the railway station,' Vaughan replied somewhat puzzled. 'The X47 from Northampton will be at the Waitrose stop in three minutes.'

'Will Miss Cooper walk from there?'

'No, she has a van.'

Connie stifled a snigger and whispered to Peddyr, 'Well, you did ask ...'

'She will be here any time soon and I must leave before she arrives. I have to arrange to take these to the dump.' He nodded to the boxes, something akin to fear flashing across his face. 'But they are too heavy. She said I must destroy them today. Without fail.' He hopped from foot to foot, arms flapping at his sides and herded them into the hallway. 'You must go now. I'm not really allowed visitors apart from Mother. Thank you.'

In the doorway, he reached down and stroked Roger. 'You are very friendly. I like you.' Without waving or exchanging farewells, Vaughan Probert opened the door wide and stood back against the wall.

32

RUSH HOUR CHAOS

*C*ara woke with a start. She had been sleeping so soundly that the message alert from her phone had roused her when her alarm had failed to do so an hour earlier. She stretched and yawned, feeling more refreshed than she had for several weeks. She reached for her mobile to find she had missed a call from Bev and that Lois had sent an early WhatsApp message.

Another reason to move. Memorial Road was closed first thing. Accident probably. Police car blocking the way, so I had to take the long way round and I was nearly late.

Poor old Lois, Cara thought, she was always pathologically early for everything, believing lateness to be a sign of inefficiency and bad manners. Cara pinged a brief reply of sympathy and a couple of smiley emojis before getting out of bed and rushing into the lounge to open her office for the day.

'Morning my little feathered friends,' she said as she removed the cover from the budgie cage. 'How are you both today?' Over their pleasant chirps of greeting, the sound of sirens prompted her to turn on the radio before she sloped off to the bathroom for a rapid shower.

The voice of the BBC Valley Radio traffic announcer wafted from the Bluetooth speaker, too quiet to hear above the noise of cascading water. She allowed herself a certain level of smugness at not needing to worry about traffic jams and roadworks. The distinct advantage to working from home was the avoidance of commuter stress. The local news, fifteen minutes later, was part way through when Cara emerged fully dressed for the day ahead and there was mention of a police incident on Memorial Road requiring traffic to be diverted. Lois had been right about the Tuesday traffic chaos.

Jimmy and Rab McTartan were hopping about on their perch, vying for attention. She usually let them fly about for a while in the mornings as she prepared breakfast and they were letting her know this was expected today, late or not. Windows firmly closed, they had enough freedom to fly throughout the flat, but rarely chose to. Instead, they fluttered across the lounge; Jimmy liked to potter around on Cara's desk, whereas Rab preferred the windowsill.

'All quiet in the Gaza Strip?' Cara asked the bird when she too peered through the window. 'Nah then, there's a thing…' she said, spying Tracey Dart and her dog Kyle on a lead pulling her along. She looked to be having some difficulty, because behind her a large suitcase on wheels was wobbling side to side. Cara watched on as Tracey Dart cut through the alleyway and turned right towards the railway station, pausing only to wave at someone and right her suitcase again.

'Good for you,' she said. 'Better off without the bastard.'

The first business phone call of the day broke the optimistic mood and soon enough it was mid-morning before she had chance to take a break from the flood of emails, payroll queries and policy updates she was asked to attend to. 'Time for a brew,' she said to the budgies who were safely back in their cage watching her every move. 'Then I'm off to the shop to re-stock your favourite snacks,' she said. She felt lighter and brighter and shared this with Bev who phoned while Cara was pouring milk into her mug.

'… And I'm coming home,' she said. 'There's nothing and nobody here for me, except Lois and we've not known each other too long.' The squeals from Bev were a delight to hear and Cara laughed along with her old friend, caught up in the excitement of the pending reunion. 'If you can put up with me and a couple of budgies, I'll start flat hunting when I'm back, there's no easy way to look at properties from here.'

'What about your *other* search?' Bev asked, diplomatically avoiding the word mother.

'I don't want to pursue it. I've found out what sort of person she is, and I don't have any desire to be part of her life. I'm going to disappear, just like she has. I'm done with the lot of them.'

'What about work?'

'I can keep on my virtual office clients, but as for the research work… Konrad Neale will set me another task sooner or later, I suppose, but until then he'll have to whistle for his supper about Vera Hudson. If she's dead, then he'll have a great story anyway. Bollocks to him, bollocks to them all. I'll get another research job in Leeds for ITV.' Cara glanced around her. 'Tell you what, I'll hand in my written notice to the property management bloke today. One month, Bev and I'll be home. My new sofa, if it ever arrives, and everything I don't need can go into storage for a few weeks. I can work from your spare room until I get a place to call home. Is that alright? Are you sure?'

Cara was ready for some exercise and fresh air. She forced herself to ignore the fact that a light drizzle had settled in for the day and pulled on her boots remembering to tuck the letter of notice to quit her tenancy into her pocket. She coiled a scarf round her neck and grinned. It would be at least one overcoat colder back home, she reminded herself. Time to toughen up again.

The footpath that meandered behind Brookside, following the edge of the fields, was a useful shortcut so she followed it until it branched, then cut through into a close of modern detached houses and from there on to Memorial Road where her way was barred by red and white plastic barricades and several police officers positioned to deal with pedestrians and drivers alike.

'Sorry, Miss. Not today I'm afraid. Where are you headed?'

'The pet shop on The Parade,' Cara answered while stealing furtive glances over the officer's shoulder. 'What's up?' she asked, pulling at the brim of her hood, shaking off droplets of rain. 'Did something happen at the hall?' Then she spied the crime scene tape and batted away her next thought.

The officer aimed a hand over her shoulder. 'If you retrace your steps, then turn right, the path brings you out some two hundred yards beyond the Parade. Just double back and you'll find it.'

'I was here last night,' Cara blurted out.

'Oh? What time would that have been?'

'Went past a few minutes gone half six and back again around eight.'

'See anything out of the ordinary?'

'Not really. We saw Christine Fowler, the local councillor… you know. Me and my friend do Pilates with her twice a week in there.' She glanced at the hall, emphasising her point.

'You spoke to her last night?'

'Aye, a few words… in passing like.'

The officer turned his head towards the hall and shouted to a fellow officer who was standing at the entrance doors. 'Frankie, get Inspector Webster out here. I think he should speak to this young lady. Make sure he brings a brolly.'

33

A SHOCKER

*B*ack in the car once more, Peddyr stared into the rear-view mirror, not speaking while the car warmed up and the windscreen demisted. Connie kept her eye on the roads and pavements behind them by using the wing mirror which her husband had remotely tilted to a suitable angle.

'Genius idea of yours,' Peddyr said, grinning at his wife. 'Shame you had to lie.' In the boot of the car were four boxes of files, once destined for the dump. Roger was now confined to a nest of rugs and towels on part of the back seat, the rest taken up by overnight bags and coats. Connie had offered, very kindly, to shred the contents for Vaughan who readily agreed. He took Connie at her word.

'Unless she knows a different route, she should drive right up behind us,' Peddyr announced some thirty minutes later. He raised his phone and touched the camera icon. 'I want proof.'

'Your proof is here,' remarked Connie, eyes locked onto the mirror. 'She's driving a dark grey people-carrier and is about to park where those traffic cones are. I'm pretty sure it's her, although she's wrapped up like the Michelin man.'

The clouds of confusion had increased when Peddyr showed

Vaughan the photo of Vera Hudson and it was playing on his mind. Was Liz Cooper passing herself off as Verity Anne Hudson, or was it the other way round? Either way, Sergeant Kevin Spratt would have himself a field day with what they had been told by Vaughan Probert – a man who was too trusting for his own good.

'The pressing business matters Vaughan mentioned must be connected to Vera Hudson's disappearance. But why the mad dash to Bosworth?' Peddyr mused, checking out the scene in his mirror. 'This is going to be tricky,' he said. 'I might try the direct approach. You stay here. I'll ask her if she knows what time the motorbike place opens.' He looked towards the unlit window display to their left. 'You try to get some photos out the back window and I'll see if I can take a selfie or something.' He would work it out on the hoof.

Pulling on his tweed cap he stepped out of the car and sauntered towards the frontage of Northants Classic Motorbikes. He cupped his hands against the window and made a show of looking about before pretending to spy Elizabeth Cooper who he hailed just as she opened the driver's door and stepped out.

He went for his favourite Irish accent. 'Excuse me there, Miss. Can you tell me what time this here motorbike shop opens?' He raised his phone. 'It says nine thirty on the website but...' He paused, shrugged at her, and took a sneaky wild shot of the woman without looking at his phone. The chances were slim that he had captured anything of her face, but it was worth trying.

She scowled at him. 'Who cares?'

'Well now, that would be me... I've come an awful long way.'

'Can't help you. Couldn't give a shit one way or the other. All bikers are wankers.' With that she sneered and broke eye contact. She slid open the side door to her vehicle and retrieved a pet carrier which she placed on the pavement while she pulled a large bunch of keys from her pocket.

'Thanks anyway,' Peddyr shouted after her.

'Yeah, fuck off.'

He stood at the corner and watched as she pushed at the front door to number twelve, risking another photograph or two, ensuring he took one of the car number plate once she was out of sight. He heard her shouting out as she entered the house. 'Vaughan, you weirdo, you'd better not be in here...' The door slammed shut and the knocker resting above the letterbox rattled loudly as Peddyr returned to his car a wiser man.

Connie was on her phone when he sidled back into the driver's seat, having divested himself of his coat once more. 'Jiminy Cricket!' she said, throwing her husband a look of alarm. 'Are you sure?' She pulled the phone away from her face and covered the mouthpiece with one hand. 'It's Bernie...'

Peddyr wasn't surprised. He'd ignored the vibration from his silenced phone only moments ago and had planned to return the call at a time less fraught with action. 'Urgent then?' he said.

She passed her phone to him, her eyes full of disbelief. 'He can tell you.'

'Hope you're sitting down, old bean.' At the end of the phone Peddyr heard the deep sigh from Bernie. 'Christine Fowler has been found hanging by her neck from a rope. Police are at the scene. Your friend Cara Laidlaw is here at the police station.'

'Why? What did *she* do?'

'At this point in time she and her friend Lois Finnegan are the last known people to have spoken to Councillor Christine Fowler. It's all rather a pickle, I'm afraid.'

The news was so unexpected that Peddyr took a second or two to compose himself. Allowing time for the story to unfold, he reserved comment as Bernard Kershaw shared the fact that he had drawn the proverbial short straw the previous night. The duty solicitor had succumbed to a bout of gastro-enteritis which had felled his whole family, and Bernard had been wheeled out of semi-retirement to cover any callouts as a favour to the chief constable and the other partners in the law firm of Bagshot & Laker.

'I blame the schools,' Bernard announced, as he rattled off the train of events which had led him to the police station that morning. 'There's a nasty bug doing the rounds and children spread it like wildfire. Grubby little creatures.'

Peddyr screwed up his eyes at Connie, mouthing the word 'grumpy'.

According to Bernard, the contractors tasked with replacing the heating system in Wigmore Hall had arrived at seven thirty that morning and although they were expecting to be met by the caretaker, they found the hall door to be unlocked. When they entered, there was Mrs Fowler in a crumpled heap, length of rope around her neck, chair toppled dramatically at her feet. They called the police.

'And why were you summoned to the nick? Who required *your* attendance?' Peddyr asked. The answer could not have been predicted.

'A delightful young person by the name of Jody Oakden, who prefers to be identified as female but is still genitalia intactus as a male. She was arrested on suspicion of threats to kill under the Offences Against the Person Act after posting on Facebook in retaliation to Mrs Christine Fowler's public condemnation of all things non-binary.'

Momentarily taken aback at his good friend's mastery of gender issues, Peddyr straightened. '… Because Christine was found dangling from a ceiling…?' Peddyr pulled at his left earlobe. Something didn't make sense. 'Are they certain Christine Fowler took her own life?'

The laughter from Bernard seemed inappropriate given the topic up for discussion, it was loud enough for Roger the dog to prick up his ears.

'That, my friend,' Bernard said, with his rumbling voice still carrying an edge of amusement, 'is why you are so reliable as an investigator. It looked like suicide, but the information coming in from all quarters, including that of Mr Fowler would indicate otherwise.'

'She wouldn't be the sort to go quietly,' Peddyr conceded.

'That's just it, old fruit. She wasn't dangling, probably never did dangle. Initially that's what was assumed but, from what I can glean, the scene was badly staged to *look* like a hanging. If my sources are correct, Mrs Christine Fowler was tied at the throat and strangled after putting up a splendid fight for her life.'

'I told you that woman would not go down without a battle.'

'Indeed not,' Bernard replied vehemently. 'The police have arrested Jody in response to the comments made on social media which were very direct and threatening. Even if it had been suicide, the police would have been lambasted for not making an arrest on those grounds alone.'

From what Bernard had learnt about the investigation so far, Desmond Fowler had been adamant: his wife had received a call from the surveyor's office asking to discuss a potential snag in the plans. She left home at about seven fifteen in the evening telling her husband that she had arranged to meet the surveyor himself and one of the engineers at the hall at seven thirty.

'Did they meet with her?' Peddyr asked.

'It appears not. Rather peculiarly,' Bernard added, 'nobody at the surveyors' office knew anything about the arrangements. A call was not made to Christine Fowler from their offices yesterday. My magnificent ears have been to the ground all morning on this one.'

'Haven't they just.' Peddyr looked across at Connie who was listening in as best she could. 'And why didn't Mr Fowler go looking for his wife when she didn't come home last night?' he queried.

'In short, old bean; alcohol and lack of enthusiasm. She phoned to say she was delayed. He had a nightcap and went to bed, grateful for free use of the TV remote control. By all accounts, she often stayed out late and therefore he didn't raise the alarm because he wasn't alarmed. In fact, her body had already been found by the time he tried to phone to see where she had got to. Goodness knows where her phone is. It wasn't at the scene. Poor chap had a terrible shock when he was told what had happened, but he insisted that there was no way on God's green earth that his wife would have taken her own life. And I believe him.'

After a short discussion, Peddyr pulled together an action plan with Connie nodding along in agreement.

'I say we still meet up with Isaac Harkness, then hightail it back to Bosworth. Something tells me this incident is well and truly linked with the disappearance of Vera Hudson who we may or may not have found. We have a bucketful of news to convey to the police on that front. Who's the SIO on Christine's suspicious death? There's a vehicle registration number they may want to check out.'

He frowned as his friend spilled forth the unwelcome news.

'DI Webster – your favourite. Blame the children. Half the police station staff are off with projectile vomiting and—'

Sagging over the steering wheel, Peddyr exhaled loudly. 'Enough with the gory details. Please tell me DS Helen Forstall is still in rude health and on the case too. I can't face having to deal with that pillock Webster without a referee present at all times.'

Joining him in his exasperation, Connie released a long sigh. 'Oh, no. Not old Whiffy-Breath Webster. Why haven't they moved him somewhere he can do less damage?' She looked despairingly at Peddyr. 'I can almost smell the halitosis from here.'

'Actually, I think the dog just farted.'

AN ALLY IN THE HOOD

*C*ara had never been questioned by police before and had only once set foot inside a police station to hand in a purse she'd found on the bus when she was a teenager. She knew she was there to help, and yet nerves were making themselves known as her thoughts turned immediately to her own duplicity. She had moved to Bosworth Bishops to spy on the woman she believed was her birth mother. That woman had now vanished, and she still hadn't told the police the truth. She wasn't purely a neighbour who happened to notice that Vera Hudson rarely went out, was hardly ever seen in public places, wasn't liked by the neighbours, and kept a light on day and night.

A series of thoughts occurred; by involving Channel 7 had she been the catalyst to her own mother's demise? Had the police found Vera's body in Wigmore Memorial Hall? Had Christine Fowler got something to do with it?

Within the claustrophobic interview room, she held herself stiffly in the chair, feeling her heartbeat pounding in her chest. The Detective Inspector had asked her to give a written statement about her sighting of Christine Fowler the night before.

The police wouldn't disclose any more other than to say there had been an incident, but the reaction, the crime scene lockdown, and the serious faces, hinted at something more sinister. This was an incident involving a death.

DS Helen Forstall seemed infinitely more primed for action than her superior officer. Once Cara had repeated what she'd told to the policemen at the barrier, the inspector had merely palmed her off to the nearest police vehicle and instructed his sergeant to 'Do the necessary.'

'I'm glad to get out of the rain,' the DS said as she settled into her chair to record Cara's words. She referred to her notes and popped a coated lozenge into her mouth. 'New Year's resolution,' she said with a self-deprecating smile. 'Time to give up the cancer sticks. Can't say I'm finding it easy, and this gum tastes disgusting... but hey-ho, at least I don't smell of fags anymore.' She paused to give Cara a reassuring look. 'So, you are Cara Laidlaw of 30 Browns Court, Bosworth Bishops. Lots of Bs in that address.'

'I live in the new flats, in Brookside,' Cara replied, instantly wishing to distance herself from the likes of the people who lived opposite. With that thought came the next one. 'Is Jethro Dart still safely in a cell? I wouldn't want to bump into him.'

'Try not to worry. You're safe here,' the officer replied, without answering the question. 'Now take me back to last night. You said you were with your neighbour Lois Finnegan.'

'Aye, she lives at number twenty-nine. You can ask her as well.'

'We already have an officer taking her statement. The pair of you could be our best chance of piecing together what may have happened and when.'

Cara repeated what she had already told to DI Webster, but this time her account was checked and double-checked. How did she know what time it was that they witnessed Mrs Fowler draw into the car park at the Wigmore Memorial Hall? What did

Mrs Fowler say exactly? And importantly, how would Cara describe Mrs Fowler's mood?

'She was her normal self. Officious, busy, bustling and with a cutting wit. She doesn't suffer fools gladly. She was pretending to be annoyed about having to meet a bloke about the repairs to the hall.'

'Pretending?'

'Aye, you know. Making out it was all very inconvenient while actually loving the fact that she was in demand, that she held the power to decide what happened. I could see she was looking forward to a showdown and being formidable. It's how she is.'

'What was she wearing when you saw her?'

Cara thought back, retrieving the pictures from her memory, and placing them in the present. 'The orange lighting plays havoc with the colours, but she was well insulated against the cold. Leather gloves, long dark wool coat, lighter coloured cashmere pashmina round her neck as always. High heeled leather boots to the knee. No hat.'

'No hat?'

'Her hair was immaculate. It's why we call her Pristine Christine. She's one of those women who must take hours to get ready before they set foot out the front door. Never to be seen crumpled or stained. Expensively dressed whatever she wore and always neat to the point of ridiculous.'

'And when you walked back home that same way what did you see?'

Cara recalled the scene without having to think too hard about it. 'Christine's car was in the same place. There was another vehicle there, a van. Like a VW transporter but not. Black probably, although as I said, with the lighting it could just as easily have been blue or green. Who knows?'

'Number plate?'

Cara shrugged. 'Sorry. Never thought it would matter... But

I think I may have seen that van parked there before. Then again, I suppose that's possible if it belonged to the surveyor bloke. He must have been there a few times.' She wracked her brains to think when this might have been but came up short. 'I could be wrong about that.'

'Any signwriting on the side of the van?'

'Not that I saw.'

'Did you see anyone else?'

'Not a soul at that point. The place was quiet. A light on somewhere inside, but nobody else was in the car park.'

The questioning took a turn for the serious when Cara admitted what she and Lois had done later.

'You went inside the hall?'

'Only as far as the entrance where the kitchen and toilets are, we never went inside the hall itself.'

'Why?'

'Just being nosy. I know it sounds stupid, but we were simply being childish. The entrance door had been left open... not that it explains what we did. It was one of those impulsive... silly. Daft.'

Flustered, Cara could hear herself stumbling through her confession. 'We left as soon as we realised the meeting was about to finish.'

'How many people at this meeting?'

'We heard one man's voice, quite posh, although Christine referred to someone else. A "lackey", she said. Could have been anyone, she can be quite rude at times.'

Overall, the rest of the questioning didn't take long, and Cara told DS Forstall every detail she could recall. Soon enough Cara was on her way back home empty handed. No treat for the budgies. No letter delivered to the letting agency. No way of knowing what had gone on at the hall. The one small consolation was the absence of rain falling from the skies above.

As she rounded the corner into Browns Court, somewhat

distracted by her thoughts, she stepped off the pavement to allow room for Marie Delgado to pass by with Petunia on a lead. Marie had previously limited her interactions to a brief acknowledgement, but never a friendly chat, so when Cara paused only to raise a smile out of habit, a conversation wasn't what she expected.

'Busy day round here,' Marie said, catching Cara off guard. She stopped, one foot on the kerb the other in the gutter.

'Is it?'

'Tracey's legged it. About time, if you ask me. That druggy wanker Jed is on remand. Good thing too and good riddance, I say.'

'Aye, I watched her go…'

'Tracey? Yes, I saw her too. What a relief… But did you see who took Vera's cat?'

'What?'

'Jody and Taylor were out looking for it last night, in their fluffy slippers, lord love us. No sign of the bloody thing. Esther at number thirteen reckons she saw someone scoop it up and walk off down the road with it under their arm, but you can't trust a word she says. Then half a dozen coppers turned up hours ago and arrested Jody and Taylor. That's how I know about Jed. One of them let it slip when Jody took a swing at the smallest one. Never trust a tranny with a broken nose, that's what I say.'

Cara rubbed at her forehead. 'Let me get this straight. Someone catnapped Vera's cat. Vera Hudson from number eighteen – the lady who's missing?'

'That's right.'

'And Jody and Taylor from number fourteen, who may be transgender but who almost certainly dress as females even though they're not, have been feeding the cat and were concerned enough to be out looking for it last night?'

'It wasn't to be found round here, so they changed into court shoes and puffer jackets, as you do, and went off up the road with a torch.'

'What time was this?'

'Gone eight o'clock, maybe half past at a push.'

'Then, a while ago... today... they get arrested?'

'That's right. But what for, I ask you? Scrabbling around under bushes with a torch? Must have looked suspicious right enough. Or was it to do with the slanging match on the radio yesterday about Christine Fowler, or the mud-flinging on Facebook?'

Cara couldn't help what she was thinking. *Did this have anything to do with the incident at Wigmore Memorial Hall?*

Meanwhile, Marie lit a cigarette as Petunia shivered at her feet. 'Who knows? And anyway, where were you when today's excitement was going on? You're always in your flat, nosing out the window.'

Internally Cara smiled. Apparently, between her and Marie Delgado not much went on in the cul-de-sac that wasn't noticed. 'I work from home.'

'I know. I've seen you. You and that teacher watch out for each other. So you should. There are some rough types in Browns Court. Jed is the worst. Hope he never comes back. Nor her at number eighteen. Didn't see too much of *her* comings and goings, mind you. She slipped out through the fence, so I had to rely on Gavin, the bloke what lives on top of her at number seventeen. He's good at keeping an eye out.'

'What fence did she slip out of?'

'The one to the side of her place. Behind the communal washing lines. The fence that separates Browns Court from the driveway of the dentist surgery next door. They've got a big car park at the back what they rent out to rail commuters for loads of money. You must know the dentists – Jed done them over last year with his midget mate.' She held her palm parallel to the ground indicating a person the size of a small child.

'Oh, the short-arse in the red tracksuit.'

'That's him. They got themselves arrested for attempted burglary. Something to do with the drugs they have locked up in there.' Marie waved her cigarette around in the air, head tipped back. 'Still, what would you know, you've only been here five minutes.'

'Can you show me how she got through the fence?'

'Walk this way… come on Petunia, the lady wants to see a fence with a gap in it. Takes all sorts…'

35

HEAVE AND RETCH

*I*saac Harkness lived on the outskirts of Leighton Buzzard in a place that went by the name of Heath and Reach. 'Sounds like a comedy duo, Heave and Retch, only classier,' Peddyr remarked as they passed the road sign and navigated the winding narrow tree-lined lanes. He wasn't surprised to see a scattering of substantial detached houses set back from the road, nor that most had gate security. 'Here we are,' he announced, pulling into the opening to a long drive flanked with a small cluster of rhododendrons and pines trees, presumably to provide privacy. An elderly man in tatty boots, an old tweed jacket, and thick leather gloves, tended a smoky bonfire. He poked at the embers with a pitchfork.

Drawing up, Peddyr pressed the button to wind down the window. In a conscious decision he replaced his natural accent with one more likely to be found in the Home Counties. 'Hello there. Is this the right place to find Mr and Mrs Harkness?'

The man leant on the handle of his pitchfork and peered into the car with rheumy eyes, reddened from the smoke. 'What address were you looking for? The name of the place is as plain as day...'

'I was expecting an intercom and some security gates. Everyone else has them on this road. Thought I'd made a mistake,' Peddyr added.

'Don't tell me – you'll be looking to buy. Londoners with cash to spare. I should have known. You'll be the first of many, I suppose,' the man went on. 'There'll be a for sale sign going up soon I shouldn't wonder.'

With a brief glance across at Connie to prepare her, Peddyr turned back to the groundsman. 'Your talents are wasted. What gave us away? Mr—?'

'George, the name's George. Oh, it wasn't you. I've been expecting it. Divorce is on the cards. He's in a right old two and eight. Hasn't been to the office since Christmas. Working from home he said.' The man rolled his eyes and made a lacklustre stab at the damp bonfire. 'Her ladyship has been away without him; I've been ordered to tidy up the grounds. His wife's car is in one of the garages, like it should be, coz she's flown somewhere foreign. Never takes the car to an airport, she don't. But his company car, that black Mercedes thing, must have gone some time yesterday. It weren't here this morning. It all adds up. I'd say there are signs of imminent disaster for himself. I dare say that's why his mummy turned up yesterday too. Weird bunch, the upper class...' He lifted his head and looked along the drive on which stood a Mercedes A class, parked outside the house. Tucked to one side of a row of garages, built in the style of a mews, was a pick-up truck that had seen better days.

'If we do like the look of the place, would you stay on as gardener, George?' Connie asked in her best telephone voice. 'If you don't mind, I'll take a photo of the side of your van. That way we have your contact details.'

'Go ahead. No skin off my potato.'

* * *

*A*s they rolled towards the house, Connie asked, 'Shall we play guess the number of bedrooms again?' She stared about her at the neat gardens, tennis court and a three-story Victorian house complete with decorative red brickwork, ornate gable trim, and bay windows. She swivelled in her seat. 'Sorry, Roger. We won't be long. Snuggle down for a while, then we'll be on our way back to normality in no time.'

'What do we know of his home situation?' Peddyr asked, stretching across to the passenger side and slipping his notebook from the glove compartment into his pocket.

'Isaac Harkness. Only child. Public school educated, like his father. Married into money—'

'Like his father.'

'Wife is Natalie Fortesque of the famous hotel chain family. If the glossy magazines are right, she wears the trousers. Isaac is managing director at Harkness Healthcare who have their head offices up the road in Milton Keynes. Two children, both at boarding school. The couple holiday abroad several times a year where they hob-nob with the ostentatious set in Monaco, Le Mans and anywhere else fast cars can be found.'

Peddyr nodded to the Mercedes parked in front of them. 'If he's a flashy car man, then I'd be surprised if that car belongs to him.'

'The spare Aston will be locked away in the double garage,' Connie said playfully, reaching for the door handle. 'Let's see what we make of him. I'm expecting a chinless wonder type. Bound to be out-and-out Phwaa-Phwaas.'

They waited on the doorstep, only the sound of George's bonfire-stoking keeping them company. 'No butler then...' Peddyr said, poking at the brass doorbell for the third time. 'Ah ha! Movement.'

A shadowy figure approached, the outline indistinct through the stained glass of the panelled door.

'Christ all bloody mighty, George! I said I'd pay you on Friday. What the hell do you want?'

The door was yanked wide to reveal a barefooted man, in a crumpled T-shirt and a pair of navy-blue tracksuit bottoms. His sandy coloured hair had yet to see a comb that day and he rubbed at his eyes as if he had just woken up.

'Rough night, Mr Harkness?' Peddyr asked.

'What bloody business is it of yours? Who the hell are you?'

In the awkward pause that followed, Isaac Harkness stared his visitors up and down and glanced suspiciously at their car. His distraction was absolute until Connie stepped forward proffering a dainty hand.

'You should be expecting us. Connie and Peddyr Quirk. Your father has asked us to help trace the whereabouts of a Mrs Vera Hudson. His sister. Your aunt.'

As an automatic response, Isaac shook Connie's hand, but his face had betrayed him. He had forgotten the arrangements made with Bernard Kershaw. Either that or he didn't know what day he was on.

'I... I'm terribly sorry. This isn't the best time,' he said, moving his hand back to the edge of the door, intent on closing it inch by inch. 'Another day perhaps.'

A woman's voice reached them from behind him. 'Tell George to bugger off and keep the noise down. I've got a stinking headache.'

'Oh, your mother's here,' Connie piped up, taking another small step towards the threshold. 'I met her yesterday. She can vouch for us. And we have come a long way to speak with you,' she added, forcing Isaac Harkness to retreat. He shouted back over his shoulder.

'It's not George, Mother. It's the people... the private detective people. The ones from Bosworth.' He turned back to face the Quirks. 'Sorry. What were your names again?'

Although she was well out of sight, Peddyr heard the panic in Olivia Harkness's voice.

'Give me a couple of minutes,' she yelled. 'Visitors... Oh Lordy, look at the time...'

Isaac escorted his guests into a spacious gleaming entrance hall where they were shown an uncomfortable bench seat and asked to wait.

'I need to pull on a jumper and find my slippers,' Isaac muttered, appearing flustered.

'No problem,' Peddyr said, 'take as long as you need. We understand that this is a difficult time for the family.'

'Yes. I'm afraid we rather overcompensated with alcohol last night. It has been a stressful time. Mother came over to give me some moral support.'

Alone together, Peddyr and Connie exchanged looks which said, *What's really going on here?* 'Play it cool and ignorant,' Peddyr whispered to his wife. 'Keep your eyes and ears open. Young Isaac was all too keen to pick up on an excuse for the state the pair of them are in.'

'Message received and understood,' she replied.

Like a pair of undersized giraffes, they extended their necks to pick up on the frantic whisperings coming from a nearby room. Snippets of the conversation came to them, and they remained statue-like to avoid missing a vital piece of information.

'How could you forget?'

'Well... in the circumstances it wasn't uppermost in my mind, Mother.'

'Shit, shit, shit...'

'What should we say?'

'About what?'

'If they ask what we were doing last night?'

'Just say we cracked a bottle, and I stayed the night rather than drink and drive. It's true, isn't it?'

36

CARS

*T*he damask-draped sitting room had been made use of as a safe place to talk, Peddyr guessed. Although the kitchen would have been his preference, he doubted they would be given the chance to glimpse the empty bottles and dirty wine glasses likely to be found there. Peddyr recognised a couple of hangovers when he saw them. Isaac's eyes were bloodshot, his hands tremulous and his pallid face hinted at an unsettled stomach. Isaac paced the room as Connie and Peddyr entered, called in by his mother.

She had recently added lipstick in an overt attempt to hide the visible excesses of the previous night. 'Mr and Mrs Quirk.' She caught Peddyr's eye. 'We haven't had the pleasure, Mr Quirk. You met with my husband.'

'Peddyr.' Hands were duly extended and shaken. 'Firm grip,' he said with admiration.

'Thoroughbred horses,' Olivia replied. 'Unusual name, Peddyr.'

'Manx.'

On hearing this, Isaac stopped his pacing. 'Into motorbikes?'

'Wouldn't be without them,' Peddyr replied, sharing a conspiratorial grin with his wife.

Isaac and Olivia Harkness were playing for time. Not wanting a difficult conversation about their current state of poor health and hygiene, they were seeking alternative subjects for discussion. Despite the hour, neither had dressed for the day, indicating that something significant had taken place the night before. Embarrassingly, the results had been seen by two relative strangers. A social faux pas on their part, Peddyr noted.

'I'm into cars,' Isaac said. 'Couple of beauties in the garage if you'd care to see them?'

'I'd love to.'

Connie was again left with Olivia Harkness while Peddyr ventured outside with Isaac to discuss torque, thrust and handling. With that completed, he delved straight into the purpose of the visit.

'When did your mother first know about your efforts to locate Vera Hudson?'

Isaac swallowed hard before answering. The distraction of the chat about cars had side-tracked him long enough to disarm him, and Peddyr's direct question had him stuttering again.

'I... I mentioned it to Mother as soon as I'd located Mrs Hudson in Bosworth Bishops. We had a tip off.'

'We?'

'Yes, me and the research team at Channel 7. We baited a few hooks on social media and landed a winner. Mother didn't think I stood a chance, but I proved her wrong for a change.'

'When did you tell her that you'd met with Mrs Hudson?'

'The day after I met the dreadful woman for... for the first time. I couldn't keep it to myself any longer.'

'You never mentioned this to anyone else? Only your mother. Not even your wife?'

Isaac tutted dramatically as he leaned gently against the bonnet of his prized Ford GT 40, hugging himself to keep warm.

'Especially not Natalie. She would have told our friends Sophia and Luke, they would have told Sebastian and Marcus, and before you know it my father would have found out. Mother wasn't convinced it was a good idea at first, but she said I should try to meet with Vera again, get to know her better, find out all about her.' He cleared his throat. 'And most importantly, to make sure there were no nasty surprises in store before it went public. You know how obsessed my father is with privacy. Mother had her suspicions. Thought the woman was a chancer.'

Already the united front presented by Austin and Olivia was crumbling. Isaac was telling a very different story to the one his parents had shared with Peddyr and Connie the previous day. He was about to launch into more valuable revelations when the automatic door to the garage began to rise.

'You really must see the beast,' Olivia was saying to Connie. 'Men assume we aren't interested but how wrong can they be?'

Connie's face carried her apology to Peddyr as she said, 'Actually I've never raced, I just like speed.'

With their arrival Peddyr was forced to change tack. 'So, tell me, what is it you do in your role at Harkness Healthcare, Mr Harkness? It probably doesn't involve big engines and high-octane thrills, I would imagine.'

'Sometimes it does. Very loosely,' Isaac replied getting to his feet. 'As well as the overall private health care contracts, I've spent most of my adult life managing the private ambulance service. Some of the vehicles in the fleet have a surprising turn of speed.'

In his peripheral vision, Peddyr noticed Olivia Harkness had frozen, her jaw slack, her eyes sending out a warning to her son. Somehow, he was treading a risky path by following the topic of vehicles. Something Connie had picked up on.

'And which of these do you get to drive into the office every day?' she asked, openly admiring the two cars in the garage.

Prompted by his mother's discomfort, Isaac too seemed to

become more tense at this straightforward question about car ownership. 'I have use of a company vehicle. It's not here today.'

'At the garage for a service,' Olivia interjected, rather too rapidly. She moved forward, spreading her arms apart. 'Like what you see here?'

'Is this a Dodge Charger?' Connie enquired with childlike enthusiasm. 'I'd love to hear it start up… can we?'

Peddyr could have kissed her. Quite clearly Isaac's company car wasn't at the garage for a service and even if it was, in his position he would have had free use of several others. It was important, therefore, for Peddyr and Connie to brush over this slip up and pretend they hadn't noticed the clumsy lie. Unfortunately for him, the lie had been made all the more obvious because Isaac's face had blanched to the degree that he was in danger of vomiting on the garage floor.

'No loud engines today,' Isaac said, placing a hand to his temple. 'Don't think my head could take it. How about a cup of coffee, Mother? We'll go back inside, it's bloody cold out here anyway.'

With Olivia out of the way for a few minutes, Connie trotting after her, Peddyr had to be brief.

'Tell me why you think your aunt was hardly mentioned in the Harkness household.'

'Don't you know the story?'

'I know only what I've been told. I'd like to hear what you think. You met Vera; she must have given you her side of the story. In fact, you could be the only person to have had a conversation with her about such private matters.'

Isaac let out a low groan. 'I wasn't the only one. I think Konrad Neale met with her briefly. Didn't get to do any filming though. She wasn't happy to show her face. We were working on that when my father found out. I only met her once. It wasn't the most productive of meetings. She said her parents – my real blood grandparents, come to think of it – committed suicide.

She and my father were taken into care. She didn't do so well, ended up a hippy or a new age traveller or something. Married a man older than her. He died; she lost the plot. Ended up in a mental hospital.' Closing his eyes briefly, he thought about this for a moment. 'Father did alright though.'

'Yes. Public school educated. That was a lucky break.'

'He made the grade for a scholarship because Grandpa Harkness was headmaster there, which may have swung it. Father made good, married Mother. Her parents, known to you as Lord and Lady Derwent, invested in his business ideas and we all ended up rich.'

'And nobody talked about your aunt?'

'Nobody. I knew she existed and that her name was Verity, but they said she went missing years ago and was probably dead. As you would expect, Father kept any mention of a sister out of the press.'

There was a crashing sound which shortly preceded Connie who entered the sitting room where Peddyr and Isaac were continuing their chat. She was carrying a tray filled with mugs and a cafetière, a glass of water and a pack of paracetamol. 'Your mother is on the hunt for some biscuits. She'll be along in a moment or two. Sounds like she's had a case of butter fingers.' She placed the drinks on a table and took a seat next to her husband as Isaac grabbed for the water and a cure for his headache.

'I met Watson yesterday,' Connie said to Isaac. 'Don't *you* have security, or a butler?'

Isaac tilted back his head to swallow down the tablets. 'Natalie forbids it. We have cameras and we lock the gates at night, but nothing like that. There's George the groundsman, a couple of cleaners, and Charmaine the private chef for dinner parties but other than that we don't have live-in staff, not since the children left for school. No need for an au pair these days.'

'Have your parents always had a Watson?' Peddyr enquired, picking up on what Connie was getting at.

'Yes. Ever since my parents moved to the Ouse Valley when they were first married. Grandpa Derwent insisted. Bevan was the one I remember most. He guarded Mother like she was a princess and treated me in the same overprotective way. Bevan lived forever or seemed to anyway... In a home now, poor old sod. One of our private residential nursing homes, of course. Only the best for Bevan. A reward for years of faithful service.'

Clever, clever, Connie, thought Peddyr. Watson knew everything going on in the Harkness household. He was fiercely loyal and likely to be impenetrable as far as divulging information went. Especially if Peddyr's hunch about him was correct. But an elderly faithful retainer could be more open to revealing hitherto undisclosed secrets, so long as his memory remained intact.

'Funny how they only ever have a surname,' Peddyr said.

'Bet his name was Eric,' Connie added. 'Eric Bevan.'

'Wrong, I'm afraid,' replied Isaac, throwing her a patronising look. 'It was Chester. Chester Bevan. After him came Fisher, then Haywood and now Watson and his gang. Super-efficient and highly discreet. More like personal bodyguards these days.'

Head down, pouring milk into his coffee, Peddyr smiled to himself. Connie was as sharp as ever. She had played it just right. Not revealing what they knew, not asking probing questions about why Isaac had paid Vera Hudson for her time. She had done as instructed and in doing so had liberated the full name of the man who could answer important questions about the Harkness family.

WHO DID WHAT?

'What's the skeet? What went on with you and Olivia Harkness in the kitchen, Lao Po?' Peddyr enquired, once they were back on the road to Bosworth Bishops. The first few minutes of the journey had been made in silence, the only noise being a gentle panting from Roger on the back seat.

'Can we stop somewhere?' Connie asked. 'I need to get my head together. Everything is happening so fast.'

Turning left at a sign for a country park, Peddyr nodded in understanding. 'Good idea. I feel like we need to debrief in walking boots and fresh air. And the little fella in the back could probably do with a run about.'

The day seemed less grey as they took the marked footpath towards the woods and followed the circular trail as outlined on a board in the car park. Peddyr turned to his wife who was deep in thought. 'So, what did you say to Olivia Harkness in the kitchen?'

'I asked if she thought Verity Hudson was dead.'

'And?'

'She said she had no idea. Then turned her back on me.'

'No opinion at all? From a woman like that?'

'She wouldn't be pushed into saying much more. Just that we were wasting our time.'

* * *

*C*onnie had watched Olivia very carefully as she set about making coffee in Isaac's kitchen. She had trouble locating the cups and resorted to opening several cupboards before she found the necessary items. Connie had helped in the search for teaspoons. All the units were glossy, and every appliance was integrated, making location of the milk more of a challenge than it should have been.

'Not a frequent visitor then?' Connie had enquired at the time.

'Natalie and I don't always see eye to eye about the grandchildren,' Olivia had replied.

When Isaac and Peddyr had traipsed out to the garage to look at expensive cars, they had stuck to safe and generalised chit-chat but before long Olivia insisted that they too should cast an eye over the very sought-after vehicles in Isaac's possession. Connie was in no position to argue, and she had no intention of doing so because the contrast in Olivia's behaviour from the day before had struck her immediately. The woman could barely concentrate on civilities. It was as if she couldn't bear for Isaac to be left alone. Connie needed to know why.

Immediately before the direct question about Vera Hudson being alive or dead, the tea tray had been hastily loaded.

'Here, take this through. Don't hang about, Isaac is in dire need of painkillers.'

The way she was spoken to would ordinarily have earned a scowl at the very least, but Connie's response was a lesson in self-control as she tried to drag out the conversation for as long as possible, to give Peddyr a few minutes more alone with Isaac.

Instead of a rebuke for being spoken to like a servant, Connie said, 'Do you think Vera Hudson could be dead?'

The plan to buy time for Peddyr backfired. Instead of answering, Olivia reached into a tall kitchen unit, facing away from Connie, snubbing her. She then fell silent, unnecessarily shifting bottles and jars on metal racking, tutting loudly.

When Connie failed to move, she said, 'You and your husband are wasting your time.'

'Can you be sure about that?'

'Yes. No. Pretty sure. The woman is probably dead in a ditch somewhere, who knows...' She stepped to one side, visibly trembling, and avoided looking at Connie. 'Now that's enough with the questions. Do get on before the coffee goes cold. I'm sure I'll find some biscuits somewhere in this ludicrous kitchen.'

* * *

'*T*he woman was a bag of nerves. Nothing like as confident as she was yesterday,' Connie said in response to Peddyr. 'Whatever they were up to last night, it had shaken them both rigid.'

'So, they took to alcohol to calm the nerves.'

'Undoubtedly. And it has something to do with Isaac's company car. From what I could see, a large bottle of brandy had been demolished and several bottles of red wine by the looks of things. No wonder they were both suffering.'

She plodded along the muddy track, caught up in her thoughts, not paying too much attention to her surroundings. Peddyr on the other hand was staring up through the trees, willing the sun to break through. 'We're not righteous enough, that's the trouble, Lao Po.'

'Speak for yourself.'

'I was—' Peddyr stopped suddenly. 'I was speaking for myself... but who was Olivia speaking for? She definitely knows something. Is she covering up for her son, I wonder?' As was his way when he needed to think, he paused to lean against a tall pine tree and watch Roger charging from rabbit hole to fox hole in a frenzied search for something to chase. 'Isaac told his mother ages ago about his search for Vera Hudson and yet we are led to believe that she never mentioned it to Austin. Somehow, he finds out on New Year's Day and Isaac then contacts Vera Hudson to tell her the game is up because Austin knows about the so-called birthday surprise; one that Isaac has coughed up a considerable wedge of cash for her to attend. In record time, Channel 7 are threatened with legal action if they proceed with the programme as planned. A much sweeter version of Austin's childhood is created, but before negotiations proceed too far, low and behold... Vera vanishes.'

Connie held up her hand. 'No Vera, no emotional reunion. Austin puts on the distraught estranged brother act and ties Olivia and Isaac into the agreed story behind why his sister disowned him and vice versa.'

'Good. We're getting somewhere. Olivia is protecting her son from the wrath of his father. Austin protects himself and his reputation from being dragged through the media mud. Equilibrium restored.'

Connie sighed loudly. 'And then there's Vera. She escapes with the money. Has she been living under the assumed name of Elizabeth Cooper all this time, alternating it with her own to avoid detection?'

'Which is why the Harkness clan think she's probably dead.'

'And it would explain why Austin would go along pretending to care enough about his sister, until he can get control of the situation. He could have paid Vera to disappear. It could even be blackmail on her part.' Connie turned on her heels. 'We need to get back to Bosworth, pronto. We must give those boxes to DI Webster. Bad breath or not, he needs to be told and so does Kevin Spratt and Bernie, and I want to speak to Monica, and someone's got to tell Cara.' She set off at a brisk pace, leaving Peddyr to stumble after her while attaching the dog to its lead.

'Tell Cara what?'

'There's good reason why Monica's report is so fascinating. Why Fairfield Hospital holds my attention.' She held her hands out. 'Car keys.'

'You're driving?'

'I'm driving, so hang on to your hat, mister. I feel the need for speed.'

'But why?'

'Because you have yet to read Monica's report thoroughly enough. You are missing a few vital clues to this puzzle. Ones that Christine Fowler also knew.'

Peddyr made it to the car in time to kiss his wife firmly on the lips before she took up position in the driving seat.

'What was that for?' she asked.

'For telling me what has been staring us in the face all along.'

She adjusted the seat and the mirror as he climbed into the car beside her. 'What?'

'We have been deliberately manoeuvred away from Bosworth Bishops. Austin Harkness has had us checked out. Watson and his troupe of security spooks know what I used to do for a living. They needed us out of the way, hence the incredibly unlikely offer of a visit to Harkness Hall and a Tuesday meeting with Isaac. You were right. Nobody in his position would have a Tuesday off when he can take any old long weekend he likes.' He paused only to take a breath. 'And it's been bugging me. I'm sure Watson has crossed my path before. If my memory serves me correctly, he did not pass muster.'

'You mean he failed the course?'

Connie and Bernard Kershaw were the only people in Peddyr's private life who knew his full and truthful service history. His son Alleyn had no doubt used his position in the civil service to find this out for himself but had never mentioned it. He wouldn't. He too was bound by several layers of the Official Secrets Act.

Since setting up P.Q. Investigations, the accepted history of duty had always sufficed. Ex-policeman: true; Ex-Royal Protection Squad: true; Security Consultant: true. All true, even his role in an advisory capacity for film and television. But what wasn't made public were the skills at the heart of his career and the role that had led to him becoming a valuable asset to the police services, wherever he was stationed. To this day, his consultation work continued. Despite taking official early retirement as a serving officer, Peddyr remained as an instructor and an adjudicator when it came to deciding who else could make the grade as a police service negotiator – from suicide to hostage negotiations, to terrorist threat and criminal crises, Peddyr was the man in demand to train others because he was considered up there among the best there had ever been. Even the military thought so.

Now he had shared his suspicions with Connie, convinced that Watson had come his way before and had failed the course, like many ex-servicemen who joined the police. Many were too keen for a fight. 'If I'd been called John Smith, this wouldn't have happened,' he announced as Connie checked in with Sat-Nav-Suzie and entered the fastest route home.

By the second page of Monica's assignment into the case of a woman she called Julia, Peddyr was hooked. He read on avidly, absorbing the details, fitting the facts together. Monica had determined that Verity Hudson had every right to be hysterical, angry, violent, distraught, and utterly bereft. She had remained under a section of the Mental Health Act while the authorities made decisions about what was to happen to her child. Her only child. The baby had been taken into emergency care as soon as she was born. Her birth had been registered by a stranger, an administrator from Fairfield hospital. If he was right, Peddyr thought this was likely to be Christine Fowler.

'Is this why Christine was killed?' he asked of Connie. 'Did Vera Hudson, AKA Liz Cooper move to a town where she was confronted by her past and then take her revenge last night? We know she was there. She went to fetch her cat… or was that an excuse, an alibi should she need one.'

'Hang on… one minute you're suggesting that Austin Harkness makes sure we are out of town so he can confront Christine Fowler about her part in Vera's disappearance, now you're wondering if Vera killed Christine.'

'Both have good motives, both have the opportunity, and given Vera's propensity to violence and Austin's use of Watson to do his dirty work for him… they are both in the frame.'

'I can't see that Austin would stoop to murder. If he was found out, that would ruin him. Why not Jody and Taylor, in revenge for homophobic attacks, like your friend DI Webster thinks?'

'No way. They might break a fingernail in the process.'

'Peddyr!'

'Sorry.' Peddyr grimaced. He had gone too far again. 'Actually, there's no reason why Webster can't be right with his thinking, which means there are far too many possible suspects all waiting for forensics to place them at the scene or not.'

DEADLY SERIOUS

*L*ois let herself into her flat, wiping her shoes on the mat six times before removing them. The shocking news being talked about in the staff room that day had been hard enough to assimilate but when the police turned up at the school, asking to speak to her, she'd near on had a panic attack. Something dreadful had happened at Wigmore Memorial Hall; she could tell by the tone of the questions put to her and the inability of the officers to allay her fears. By the time they had finished with her she was all jelly legs and dry mouth. In a fit of uncharacteristic kindness, the head teacher sent her home early, which inevitably led to several suspicious looks from her contemporaries as she walked unsteadily to her car.

To make matters worse, once she had arrived back in Browns Court, the habitual wave to Cara's window hadn't happened. She was sure to be there at this time of day, Lois thought. But number thirty was in darkness, no sign of the constant light from a computer screen or an Anglepoise lamp. Nothing.

Lois's imagination went straight into overdrive. *Where was*

Cara? Had she bailed out and left for Yorkshire in a panic? Had she gone missing too?

Rather than make a dash for it to the main entrance of Brookside, she remained in the car to phone Cara and ease her worried mind. No answer. Rattled, she phoned Dan and he stayed on the line until she was safely on the stairs, trying to calm her when she could get no answer to Cara's doorbell.

'Steady on. If she's out, she's out. She may well be at the police station or something. There's bound to be a logical explanation.' That made perfect sense; Cara would be giving a statement to the police, that was why she wasn't in. 'Go home, get a hot drink inside you with plenty of sugar and I'll come to see you straight after work. I'll try to finish early.'

Knowing he would be on his way over later that evening, she breathed a long sigh of relief as she put the key in the lock of her front door. 'Thank you, Dan. Don't know what I would have done if you hadn't been there for me.'

'Aye, and you can thank me later. I'll take a big fat snog as payment.'

'Deal.'

With the recent unsettling events happening all around her, the well-intentioned ground rules about him visiting Wednesdays and weekends only had smartly gone out of the window. Dan had come good again.

* * *

*C*oat and gloves neatly stowed in the hallway closet, Lois checked her phone once more. A message from Cara had arrived.

I can see your light is on. I'm outside. Look towards the dentist surgery next door.

'Thank goodness.' In stockinged feet, Lois flicked on more lights before heading to the French windows and peeking through the blind into the murk of the dull fading day. Mostly shielded from view by a ship-lap wooden fence and a line of sycamore trees that provided a sacrificial strip between Browns Court and the neighbouring plot, Lois could just about make out two people and a dog, leaning towards the fencing. She waited for them to straighten before attempting to wave at Cara who thoughtfully waved back as soon as she caught sight of her. She then pointed wildly to let Lois know she would be making a visit as soon as she was done.

Lois gave an exaggerated okay gesture and made her way to the kitchen. Kettle on, she sank gratefully onto the sofa before tuning into the local news via an app on her phone. The talk was of little else but Memorial Road.

'Two arrests have been made in connection with the incident,' the announcer was saying. 'Local sources believe this may relate to yesterday's objections to a Pride march in the town planned for the summer.'

Lois got to her feet again. 'Then it *must* be to do with Christine Fowler,' she said. *What was keeping Cara?* she wondered and took another peek through the vertical blinds. This time her attention was taken by the arrival of a police van which parked outside number fourteen. Cara had spotted it too and, with the person Lois now recognised as Skinny Marie from number twelve, she was trotting back through the alleyway. Instead of heading to Brookside, Cara remained with Marie and her dog as they unlocked the front door to Marie's downstairs flat.

Before long another text arrived from Cara.

Keep the coffee hot, I'll be there soon. Have prime spot to see what the police are up to. Men in white have just entered the home of The Bosworth Influencers. It's all happening here today.

The police van was blocking the way, meaning Lois didn't have a clear view of the comings and goings. She relied heavily on Cara who sent photos as proof over the next hour, after which she returned to Brookside.

'I got bored, and besides with all the piggin' fag smoke I was starting to resemble a kipper. Look at the state of my eyes.' Without needing permission, she used Lois's bathroom to freshen up. 'I still stink,' she said as she emerged pulling at her jumper. 'My coat will need airing for the next fortnight.' She gave Lois a hug. 'You look shocking. PC Plod tell you something I don't know?'

'It's what they didn't tell me that's got me all of a quiver,' Lois replied, hands clamped to a mug of coffee. 'Yours is on the side in the kitchen.'

Once Cara had settled beside her on the sofa, legs crossed, Lois broached the subject of their neighbours Jody and Taylor. 'Do you think they did it?'

'Did what?'

'Well, that's just it. I don't actually know. Yesterday, they were more vile to Christine on Facebook than ever before. There was a frenzy in the local media about what she said.' She blew at the contents of her mug before taking a dainty sip. 'Has Christine Fowler been assaulted do you think? Or worse... has Vera from number eighteen been found... dead. Maybe Christine and the man she was talking to discovered her in a cupboard or—' A hand shot to her mouth as she realised her insensitivity. Despite the in-depth conversation the night before, it still hadn't sunk in that Vera Hudson was Cara's birth mother. Someone she had sought out. Someone she could call family. Someone who had turned out to be extremely unpleasant. What turmoil her new-found friend must be in now, she realised.

Regrets tumbled from her tongue, embarrassment showing in her cheeks.

'No need to say sorry. It's what everyone's thinking. And given that the police have just removed Vera's shopping trolley from the boys' flat, I'd say they are in a whole heap of manure.'

Unable to quell the myriad of questions rolling around in her head, Lois gabbled on. 'But how are you feeling? I mean, what if Jody and Taylor killed Vera because of the cat, or because she was more homophobic than Christine, or something, and now you'll never get to know why you were adopted.' She reached out to touch Cara gently on the shoulder, not knowing how to bring comfort.

'Good God, woman. Slow down.' A brave-faced smile came from Cara. 'If she's dead, then so be it. It's bad, it's sad, but I don't belong in her world or the Harknesses'. I have to put aside hopes and childish dreams about a sweet mother in desperate straits giving up her child for a better life. This *is* my life. Mustn't waste it on wishes, eh?' She shrugged into her coffee. 'I'm alright. Really. I've switched off from it.'

'And what if something bad happened to Christine? We were there...' This thought had been bothering Lois. 'The other people who turned up when we were leaving the hall; maybe they weren't there to support Christine. What if we left and *then* something happened? We could have saved her.'

'Is that right, Wonder Woman? From now on I think you should stick to watching musicals or romantic comedies,' Cara replied, looking askance at Lois. 'What has come over you?'

Lois could feel the tension release itself as she laughed. 'This bloody place, I suspect. Honestly... drug dealers, missing women, domestic violence, internet trolls, prostitution and now who knows what else.'

UPDATES

*H*aving declined to link his phone to the in-car system, fearing that Connie's concentration would waver, Peddyr turned down the volume on the radio the moment Bernard Kershaw called from the police station in Bosworth.

'How's the journey home?' Bernard enquired.

In the main Connie wasn't breaking any rules of the road but she was on the limit and enjoying the distraction. By this time, the radio was tuned to a station playing 80s tracks which resulted in an extended session of car karaoke between phone calls.

'Noisy and entertaining,' Peddyr responded. 'And when she thinks she can get away with it, Connie engages rally driver mode. *Her* mode, not that of the car, you understand. How's your day turning out?'

Bernard grumbled in annoyance. 'I can't wait to get home for a proper cup of tea from a china cup. This plastic nonsense should be banned. Apart from that minor and middle-class inconvenience, I have news for you, old bean.' Peddyr could visualise the scene. Bernie was hanging around waiting for his client to be called in for more questioning. He would be making use of this time by earwigging and chatting to the civilian staff who were less likely to think through what they disclosed. 'Vera Hudson's pensioner trolley has been liberated from the home of Jody Oakden and Timothy Taylor. It was full of cat food,' Bernard said.

'How is that news?'

'Webster thinks it implicates the pair in the disappearance of Vera Hudson. He's sent a full forensics team back to the flat to rip up the floorboards. So to speak.' There was a shuffling sound and muffled voices could be heard requesting Bernard's presence in interview room three. 'Must dash. Before I go... the latest on the number plate you gave me is negligible. Registered to an Elizabeth Jane Cooper, Northamptonshire. You got that spot on. But another witness to last night gave a partial plate and better description. One of the vehicles is a top of the range Mercedes saloon, the van was also identified as a Mercedes Vito. The place was full of the darn things.'

'Try company vehicles registered to Harkness Healthcare. On second thoughts, I'll pass on the details when I get there. We have a few boxes to drop off at the nick. I'll explain later. Have fun.'

'Fun? Oh, very funny. Cheerio and tell Mrs Q to take it steady.'

With another hour to go before they reached sight of home, Peddyr decided to call Sergeant Kevin Spratt. 'He'll have a better idea what to make of this than DI Duncan Webster,' he said to Connie as he scrolled through his contacts on his mobile.

Before he had chance to press the green button, a call came through to Connie's phone which was linked to the car system. 'It's Cara,' she said. 'Take the call but don't say too much. Not a word about Liz Cooper, or Christine Fowler's demise.'

'Hi Cara, it's Peddyr here. Connie's driving at the moment.' He had swiftly picked up Connie's handset and diverted the call from car to phone. He disliked the thought of her private conversation being broadcast as they drove through the outskirts of Thame, muffled though it might be.

'I'm glad you're on your way back,' she said. 'All sorts of shenanigans going on hereabouts.'

'So we understand.'

'I got called in to the police station.'

'Yes. Knew that. You were a witness to something fairly serious.'

'Jody and—'

'Yes, that too.'

'Chuffin Ada. Is there anything you don't know? What about the gap in the fence that Vera Hudson used to slip out of Browns Court when she felt like it?'

Peddyr sat more upright and held on to his seat belt as Connie took a bend a tad too fast in his estimation. He scowled at her, and she eased off the accelerator. 'Now then, you've got me there. Tell all.'

He settled back into his seat as Cara told him about her close inspection of the fence with Marie Delgado and how, later, when she had left Lois to her own devices, she had been unable to settle. On a whim, she went to the dentist surgery on Station Road and entered. Fully prepared with ID and household bills, she asked to register.

'Very sensible, but...' With little time to spare, Peddyr had planned to make better use of this news rather than to hold a discussion about NHS dentists.

'I thought so, but while I was there, I asked about whether the missing lady had been a patient. No, they said. Nobody by the name of Vera Hudson was registered with the surgery, but they had seen the local news, knew all about her disappearance and mentioned that she looked just like a lady who rented a car parking space from them. Here's the thing... I think Vera Hudson had a car but was using another name.'

Even though he knew she couldn't hear the full conversation, Peddyr automatically risked a right eyebrow raise in Connie's direction. 'Did they tell the police?'

'No. The woman on reception said there were loads of middle-aged ladies who looked that miserable. She wouldn't give me this woman's name, but she did say that the parking space was in almost constant use until the week beginning the thirteenth. To their knowledge, the space hasn't been used since, even though it has been paid for until the end of March.'

'And they really didn't think to tell the police? What a caring thoughtful bunch they are. Out of interest, what stops someone else parking in these rented spaces?'

'Retractable bollards with a key.'

If he hadn't been holding Connie's phone, he would have rubbed his hands together with glee. 'Great sleuthing, Cara. Leave it with me. I'm just about to speak to Sergeant Kevin Spratt, I'm sure he'll contact the surgery for the vehicle details. This could be really helpful. Well done. We'll be in touch soon.'

He ended the call and turned in his seat. 'Retractable bollards.'

'Same to you,' his wife replied.

Information was arriving at such a rate of knots, Peddyr hardly had time to write it all down. Luckily, on this occasion, he was finally able to get through to Sergeant Kevin Spratt without being diverted to an answerphone. Having established that Kevin was at his desk, Peddyr said, 'I've been trying to get hold of you since we visited Rushden. I hope you have a pen to hand, there's loads to tell.'

'Ditto,' came the reply. 'You know about Christine Fowler?'

'That she was found dead in suspicious circumstances. Yes. I know the news. I've got a solicitor on the inside...'

There was a gentle chuckle from Kevin in appreciation. 'So you have, I'd forgotten about that. Anyway, did you also know that many years ago, Mrs Fowler held a very responsible position—'

'At Fairfield Mental Hospital in the 1990s? Yes. I knew that too. How did *you* find out?'

'I have just spent quite some time with Desmond Fowler. The grieving husband is also a man on a mission. By rights what he handed me should have gone straight to DI Webster, but Mr Fowler seemed to think it could help in our search for Vera Hudson.'

What Desmond Fowler had found at home had not come as a complete shock to him. Apparently, Christine had always harboured guilt about the case of a woman at Fairfield Hospital who had given birth there because no suitable bed could be found elsewhere. Blaming herself, she had gone so far as to contact the unit to where the patient was subsequently discharged. In addition, she involved herself in the social services child protection case where she somehow wangled a forwarding address, allowing her to keep tabs on what happened to the woman, until that woman mysteriously went missing. That woman was Verity Hudson.

The morning of his wife's supposed suicide, Desmond Fowler went in search of proof that her state of mind was far from unstable. In doing so he had found a document on Christine's laptop and printed a copy off, knowing it was linked to the disappearance of Vera Hudson.

'You just have to see this,' Kevin said in hushed tones. 'It's dynamite.'

'Does it mention Elizabeth Cooper by any chance?'

'Yes, it says she's named in a letter sent from Verity Hudson to Christine Fowler dated the day we think she disappeared the first time around – all those years ago. If we could get our hands on that letter, the one from Verity Hudson to Christine… we'd have something which puts this misper case in an entirely different light. Unfortunately, Mr Fowler says there are no signs of any such a letter or anything else pertaining to it. Looks like she destroyed them some years ago.'

'Bugger.'

'Yes. Bugger indeed. By the way, I got your brief email to say you'd been to Elizabeth Cooper's address, but the phone messages you've left me since then are too cryptic, I'm afraid. What the hell is going on?'

The drive from Rushden to Heath and Reach had been taken up with several calls, mostly unsuccessful ones, in an effort to update Kevin on the findings at Pemberton Street. Now he had him as a captive audience Peddyr could at last reveal his findings. 'We saw a woman calling herself Liz Cooper at the address you gave us. However, according to the photograph taken by Isaac Harkness of his aunt, she is either the twin sister of Vera Hudson or she *is* Vera Hudson.'

'Come again?'

The full explanation from Peddyr took up a considerable amount of time and the journey home seemed quicker because of it. There were several breaks in the chat while Kevin galvanised action from colleagues; one was ordered to contact the dental surgery on Station Road before they closed. Another he tasked with asking local authority housing providers to search out the list of names Peddyr gave him.

'In short, my friend, the mystery is solved. Vera Hudson is no longer missing. We have a woman who may or may not be Vera Hudson, calling herself Liz Cooper. This woman, in all likelihood, is defrauding the taxpayer by subletting council properties and taking advantage of rich tossers like Isaac Harkness, as well as vulnerable individuals who can't see her for what she is. We are told she was also in Bosworth Bishops last night in or around the time of Christine Fowler's death. I'll leave that with you and see you later. We'll drop off the boxes of evidence, CID may want a peek at them.'

He was about to hang up on a bewildered Kevin Spratt when

he remembered to call in another favour. 'Given that Christine's death could be firmly linked to Vera Hudson, any chance you can blag information from Harkness Healthcare about what company cars are registered at their head office? Mercedes, that sort of level, and for good measure ask for details of any shiny black private ambulances, the sort used for discreet removal of the deceased.'

Connie was due to work her magic to discover what deluxe Buckinghamshire care home had the pleasure of Chester Bevan's company. They wouldn't need Kevin's help for that task, even so Peddyr felt sorry for the man, he was going to have his work cut out trying to prove the real identity of the missing woman. As Peddyr rang off, he heard Kevin bark out another order, demanding a further PNC check on Elizabeth Jane Cooper.

40

WHO IS MISSING?

'*R*oger and I are going for a stroll in the park, then we shall unpack, sort out the washing and check the state of my amaryllis,' Connie said, dragging her overnight bag from the back seat. 'After that I'll make a start on calls to residential care homes and Christine Fowler's hairdresser because they know everything. Perhaps you could check in with Monica. I hope she's had some luck with that psychiatric unit in Northampton.'

Peddyr slipped from the passenger seat and prepared to take over as driver. With one foot on the door sill, he glanced at his watch. 'Christine Fowler's hairdresser… Now that is a mighty idea. I bet Webster won't think of that as a line of inquiry. I'll see you sometime later.'

Connie tilted her head to accept the kiss he puckered up for. 'Tell you what,' she said. 'If it can be proven that Liz Cooper is posing as Vera Hudson and not the other way around, it leaves us with a serious problem.'

'Which is?'

'There has been no sign of Verity Hudson for nigh on three

decades, and there's no registration of her death. Meaning that she really did vanish, just not as recently as we first thought.'

The look from her husband was one Connie knew well. His thoughts were running along the same lines. 'I'll get you a copy of Christine's document from Kevin Spratt. From what he said, it sounded like some sort of running diary or chronology. We'll take a look at it later, over a bucket of homemade soup. I'll pick up a crusty loaf on my way home. And I suggest we arrange to meet up with Bernie tomorrow in his office for a pow-wow.'

'A pow-wow. Now there's an expression I haven't heard in a while.'

* * *

*T*he kitchen was much as she'd left it early on Monday morning, as was the rest of the house, save for the mat at the base of the stairs which led to reception. The main entrance to P.Q. Investigations had its door on Dyer Street and one of Connie's many daily tasks was retrieving the post. Today there seemed more than was usual for a Tuesday. A large Manilla envelope, handwritten, demanded to be opened first. The bills could wait. Connie trotted up the stairs, Roger at her heels, and she placed the pile of post on the neat reception desk. One glance at her domain told her all was in order. A swift slip of a paper knife and the contents of the large envelope were freed.

'Oh, my goodness,' Connie exclaimed, a hand flying out for the phone on the desk. She dialled Peddyr who she knew was most likely to be still on his way to the police station. 'Lao Gong? The reason Desmond Fowler couldn't find any letters relating to Verity Hudson squirrelled away by Christine in *his* home is because they are in *our* home. Christine sent them to us for safe keeping and to help in... and I quote, "Exposing the woman posing as Vera Hudson. She's an out-and-out fraud.

Here is the proof. I am unable to present this to the police as it may compromise my position on the town council and besmirch my good name in the town. I'm therefore engaging your confidential services, for which I will pay the necessary. The Harkness family should be made aware that someone is posing as Vera Hudson with the intention of obtaining money by deception. Her disappearance may be due to my direct challenge to her to prove who she was. Please correspond by post only to my home address. No phone contact, no fax, no email."'

'Christ in a leotard! When was that posted?'

'Friday... Our first official day on the case. It wasn't here on Saturday, there's no post on a Sunday... and we've been away since.'

'Did you check the post on Monday morning?'

'It doesn't arrive until gone 10.30, Lao Gong.'

'I knew that... silly me for asking, Lao Po. Sorry, I wasn't doubting you, I've just had trouble working out why she would put her faith in us.'

Connie sighed. 'Integrity, honesty and a reputation for both. She knew we would do the right thing. Besides, she wasn't reporting a major crime as such, merely a suspicion that there was an intent to defraud the Harknesses by a woman she believed to be posing as Vera Hudson. I think...' She shook the papers in her hand. 'Crikey, even I'm getting befuddled by it all. I'll read this through thoroughly, match it against Monica's written assignment and see what we are left with. The police can tackle things from the angle of benefit fraud based on the paperwork in the car and the information they already have about Elizabeth Cooper and the woman known as Vera Hudson.'

'The question still stands, Lao Po. Where is the missing woman by the name of Vera or Verity Hudson who is related to Austin Harkness? We carry on our search, right?'

It was agreed between them that their remit had yet to be

fulfilled, galvanising Connie into a tornado of activity. 'Sorry Roger. Slight delay. I must read this file before we go for a spin round the park. Won't be long.'

Her notepad was in front of her, the dog beside her at her feet, under Peddyr's desk. The list of dates and important facts was not an extensive one, but it was damning. The date of Verity Hudson's admission to Fairfield Hospital, the date her child was born, the attending doctor and midwife, were recorded. As were the actions of social services, the registration of the birth carried out by Christine herself, the date Verity was transferred to a local unit near her home in Northamptonshire and dates when letters were sent by Christine to Verity. What Connie gleaned from the records kept by Christine was that the letters themselves must have been handwritten, with no copies made of the ones sent by Christine. Therefore, Connie rifled through the replies from Verity and sank back in Peddyr's captain's chair as the possibilities thundered into her head.

'Oh Christine, did someone kill you because of this? Who else would know you had done these things?' She added notes and tapped the pen rapidly like a drumstick. 'So, Christine wrote to Austin to ask for his help, did he reply?' She fingered the final letter sent from Verity Hudson to Christine Fowler. The words on the page led her to one conclusion. 'Peddyr needs to read this.'

Impatient for his return, Connie sent him a text before seeking out Roger's lead. 'I made a promise and I keep my promises where I can. To the park and some thinking space,' she said to the excitable dog, now turning circles and wagging his tail. It was then she remembered to call Fiona McFarland, Bernard Kershaw's secretary, to arrange a pow-wow. This was never a chore when Fiona's reassuring tones were such a calming tonic to the ears.

'Well now, so lovely to hear from you, Connie. Any luck in locating the missing lady?' She didn't pause long enough for a reply and came across as unusually flustered in Connie's opinion. 'I only mention it because Mr Harkness has been making inquiries by telephone today. He was rather abrasive I'm afraid to say and has asked Bernard to call him. However, I have deliberately delayed him as Bernard wants the chance to speak with the two of you first.'

'Good. Peddyr has requested a meeting as soon as Bernie can fit us in. He did think tomorrow would be the best bet, but lots of new information has come to light and we perhaps need to bring things forward. Although having said that, Peddyr is at the police station and I'm not entirely certain when he'll be free.'

'Freed? Has he been arrested?'

With a short laugh, Connie corrected herself. 'Bad choice of words, Fiona. I do apologise. He's supplying them with evidence in connection to our missing lady. It's not certain how long he will need to be there answering any questions they may have for him.' She relaxed her shoulders and took a deep breath. 'It's been a busy few days. Shall we meet first thing in the morning. Say eight o'clock if Bernie can manage that?'

Arrangements in place, Connie apologised to Roger once more before finally heading out of the door with a torch in one hand, Roger's lead in the other. The park was well lit along the main footpaths, but despite this, the winter darkness seemed to shroud the wooded areas and Connie felt slightly safer with a hefty torch to hand for any would-be muggers. As it was, she only met other dog walkers out for their nightly stroll. All of them greeted her warmly, making comments about the cold weather and the evenings getting shorter.

She wondered what had got under Austin Harkness's skin. Was it their visit to see Isaac? Surely not. They were invited. It had been arranged. Perhaps it was the questions they had asked or what they had witnessed. Was it linked to Christine Fowler's death somehow? Her mind whirred endlessly as she made her way back to the gate which opened out onto Dyer Street where she caught sight of Peddyr ambling towards her.

'I assumed this was where you'd be. Solved the case yet?' he asked with a lopsided grin.

'Fat chance. I think we are back to square one. Verity Hudson is missing, although having read the letters from her to Christine, I think she killed herself and I think she made her brother aware of why she took her own life. She made sure Christine Fowler knew... all the facts are on your desk.'

'Not quite all. I had a call from Monica. She twisted a few arms and accessed archive records which confirm that an Elizabeth Jane Cooper was an inpatient at the same time as Verity Anne Hudson at an adult psychiatric facility in Northamptonshire. They were both moved on to a group home and from there Verity managed her own council tenancy.'

Connie handed Roger's lead to her husband while she fumbled for a tissue. 'Runny nose. Hope I'm not going down with something.' After a blow and a wipe, she asked, 'What was she in hospital for? Elizabeth Cooper? What was her diagnosis?'

Peddyr grinned and a cloud of winter breath escaped as he puffed out his approval. 'Straight to the nub of the matter. She has a diagnosis of—'

'I bet it's Borderline Personality Disorder,' Connie piped up, cutting him off.

'How the hell do you know that? And why did you bother asking me if you already knew the answer?'

'Monica and I had a chat about the Vera Hudson from Browns Court and her pattern of behaviours and that's what Monica concluded. She knows her stuff that woman. And she's definitely got a soft spot for Bernie.'

'Here we go again,' Peddyr mocked. 'By the way, did you get hold of him? When is the pow-wow? Please don't say it's this evening, I need food and warmth and to sit on my own sofa admiring what's left of your amaryllis.'

'It'll be all dried up. I haven't got that far down my list of things to do,' Connie replied as she stepped through the back door. 'Oh, Pedd… I need to tell Cara. Please read those letters while I make us some supper. They are heart-breaking and she needs to know what really happened.'

'I'm heading that way at top speed. Need to check the hand-writing against the sample we pulled out of those files. I should hold fire on speaking to Cara until we get something back from the police. I'll tell you all about it over a thick slice of crusty bread in a few minutes. I didn't forget to buy a loaf; my stomach wouldn't let me.'

41

NEEDLE IN A HAYSTACK

*P*eddyr's visit to Bosworth Police Station had been less time consuming than he'd anticipated. Out of respect for his rank, rather than the man himself, he asked to speak to DI Duncan Webster, intent on handing over all relevant information on Liz Cooper. Between them, Kevin Spratt, Vaughan Probert, Monica Morris, Desmond Fowler and his wife Christine had come good with enough detail for Peddyr to be satisfied that Liz Cooper *was* posing as the woman known as Vera Hudson. He could say with some certainty that Liz would have had access to personal identification relating to Verity Anne Hudson, enabling her to make use of such documents to set up tenancy agreements in Verity's name, to live as her and to pocket the benefits that she would have been entitled to and many she was not. Finally, in his own mind, he concluded that Verity Anne Hudson was dead.

There was work for Kevin Spratt on this matter, so while he waited for someone to put in an appearance and collect the boxes of account files, Peddyr and Kevin held an impromptu meeting in a side room away from the front desk.

Kevin had brought with him a few printed pages. He handed

Peddyr one from the top of the small pile before taking a seat at the table, opposite Peddyr.

'Your photography skills need some work,' Kevin said with a wry smile. 'This snap of Elizabeth Cooper is badly on the wonk. However, it is clear enough as far as facial recognition goes and we've matched the face to the name. She's known to Northamptonshire Constabulary. Your Liz Cooper has made a nuisance of herself for many years and as far as they are concerned this is your woman. Elizabeth Jane Cooper. Nice work. Your job is done.'

'Not quite. We still need to find out what happened to the *real* Vera Hudson. The one who preferred to be called Verity, her *real* name. Desmond Fowler came up trumps with that document, and my wife has the rest of the evidence. As soon as we collate it, I'll get it to you. Verity Hudson is still a misper after all.' He handed the printed photograph back to Kevin before asking, 'How many unidentified bodies are on the national books these days?' Pausing for the answer, he took a sip from a wishy-washy coffee courtesy of Kevin and a vending machine.

'The UK figures for the year are published each March, but last year's figures for England and Wales stand at 628 bodies unidentified, and 127 sets of partial remains.'

'Fancy keeping those figures in your head. I don't know whether to be *im*pressed or *de*pressed. Either way, as Verity Anne Hudson wasn't declared dead, she remains as a missing person from years ago. Is there a way of accounting for bodies that relate to persons reported missing in 1992?'

'I'll get right on it, but don't hold your breath.'

'Wouldn't dream of it, there's enough death around these parts without me adding to the total.'

The door opened without a preceding knock to warn them of the intrusion. Duncan Webster, chest puffed out with self-importance, stepped through the doorway, disapproval stamped on his features.

'You have time for a cosy chat and a coffee, Sergeant? You lot are obviously overstaffed. Now then, Mr Quirk, I'm reliably informed that you have evidence relating to the suspicious death I'm investigating. Please don't tell me you think it relates to your missing person case. Such speculation isn't helpful.'

'I'm not one for speculation, Inspector. What I bring you are facts and evidence, what you choose to do with them is your call. CID investigations into benefit fraud can be incredibly time consuming, so I can only hope that my wife and I have saved you some man hours. Sergeant Spratt has been able to confirm the identity of the perpetrator. He'll furnish you with all the details of the case because yes, it relates directly to the missing persons case, which in turn is linked directly to the death of Christine Fowler.' He held up one hand to stem the interruption on Webster's lips. 'Yes, I know that is confidential information, but there we go. I wouldn't be much of an investigator if I didn't have my sources.'

Duncan Webster murmured his displeasure, folding his arms as he leaned his back against the wall to stare down at the two men. 'Your interference will only serve to muddy the waters. I have two individuals under investigation for that particular crime and while my team is open to consideration of new evidence, if it is pertinent, I fail to see what benefit fraud could have to do with it.'

'In which case I shall ensure this information is handed to DS Helen Forstall. Perhaps she has better eyesight.' The word "blinkers" popped into Peddyr's head, shortly followed by the words "incompetent" and "pratt". He held Webster's gaze until the man caved in and turned back to the doorway.

'I'll see she liaises with you, Sergeant. You can explain this tenuous link to her when she has time to spare.'

'Thank you, sir. I look forward to it.' Kevin Spratt had sounded sincere enough, but Webster had caught the inference.

'No need to be insolent, Sergeant. Your career isn't exactly an inspiration.'

'But his diligence is, Inspector,' Peddyr chimed in. 'Without his level of dedication, we would not have exposed such a serious fraud case.' He nodded to the boxes in the corner of the room. 'Tens of thousands of pounds. Taxpayers' money. Money that could have contributed to the policing budget. Just a thought. Think of the kudos. A murder, a missing persons case and a fraud case all wrapped into one. Lots of handshakes and congratulations to the senior officer and the team who can pull that off. Don't you think?'

Webster paused in the doorway. 'As I said not a moment ago, Mr Quirk, let the professionals take over. I'll send DS Forstall along right way.'

The door had barely closed after the DI before Kevin Spratt uncharacteristically verbalised his thoughts. 'If he gets any further up his own arse, he'll turn inside out.' He looked across at Peddyr who was shaking his head in despair. 'And how come you always stay as cool as a cucumber,' Kevin asked. 'How is it you know precisely what to say to make him do what needs to be done? And... thanks for the vote of confidence, appreciated.'

'Deserved. You are a credit to the service and he's nothing but a fucking liability. Luckily, Helen Forstall is a good copper, and I'm sure she'll get this moving, which means that Liz Cooper will get what's coming to her. The next job is to find out what happened to Verity Hudson. If Helen Forstall is as quick as I think she is, she'll be wondering if Liz killed Verity. In those boxes over there, are samples of Liz Cooper's handwriting. It won't take long to compare them. I'll know as soon as I get home. I'll ring you if that looks like a possibility.'

Kevin's mouth had dropped open.

'Fuck a duck. It never occurred to me,' he announced. 'Of course... Liz Cooper reported Verity Hudson missing. Who's to say she didn't make her disappear? Who's to say she didn't write those replies to Christine Fowler pretending to be Verity Hudson?'

Peddyr gave him a thumbs-up. 'You're getting it. And how about the fact that Liz Cooper was back in Bosworth Bishops on Monday evening at around the time Christine Fowler was killed. And how about the fact that Christine had challenged her and had uncovered her deception. If you were facing prison for major fraud, would you kill to prevent that happening? You would if you were a raving psychopath. It's just one possibility, Sergeant.'

Kevin stared across the table, unable to speak as Peddyr continued. 'Webster has two individuals under investigation who have a motive for killing Christine Fowler, and at the same time he is running around like the proverbial headless chicken, checking partial number plates and jumping to conclusions.'

A gentle knock at the door was followed by Helen Forstall whose face lit up at the sight of Peddyr and Kevin. 'Thank fuck for that,' she said. 'Peddyr Quirk to the rescue. Please tell me you have what I think you have.'

'He does,' said Kevin Spratt, breathy with excitement. 'And the way things are looking, he may just have the bloody case tied up altogether.'

INSIDE HEADS

*P*eddyr held the letters written by Verity Hudson in chronological order. There were five in all. He read through them noting that the shaky spider-like scrawl seemed to stem from the emotions of the writer; someone wracked with despair at the loss of their child, someone fuming at the injustice of her life. That remained the case until the last letter where he immediately recognised that the letters were formed with more control as the emotions of the writer had become detached. 'Oh dear, oh dear…' exclaimed Peddyr.

Kevin Spratt answered his mobile almost immediately. 'Well?'

'Is Helen Forstall up to speed yet?'

'Not quite. What's the news on the handwriting?'

'It's nothing like that of Liz Cooper. I have to assume it's Verity's writing on all the letters we have here. In the last one she outlines her intention to kill herself because nobody ever took her side. Nobody listened to her when she was telling the truth about the abuse she suffered at the hands of her brother, and she wanted to die because she had given up hope of ever finding her baby. But, I must say, when I compared the two sets of handwriting, the way certain letters are formed would suggest that Liz Cooper is left-handed, so get Helen to check the knots on the noose.'

'The what?'

'The noose, tied to make it look like Christine Fowler hung herself. Left-handers make knots a funny way round. I'll check with Pamela Watts from the Knit and Natter group. I'll ask her if Liz was left-handed... only making sure to use Vera Hudson's name, of course.'

A sharp intake of breath reached his ear, making him stall in his thinking. 'Peddyr, I need to throw a major spanner in the works,' Kevin said, interrupting.

Peddyr paused and reset. The tone, the rate, the volume of his speech, and the words used by Kevin had his full attention. 'Go ahead, I'm listening.'

'Helen Forstall has been very generous sharing certain matters of intelligence that you may find interesting. At Wigmore Hall on Monday night several people were present. An unknown male was overheard talking to Christine inside the hall by Cara Laidlaw and her neighbour Lois Finnegan. Two more people, a male and an older female were spotted entering the hall before that male left. Your request for details about company cars belonging to Harkness Healthcare came up trumps and it is highly probable that a black Mercedes saloon known to be used by a certain Isaac Harkness was present in the car park at the time, as well as a dark van as yet not identified. Although that vehicle is not thought to bear the number plate of the waggon belonging to Liz Cooper aka Vera Hudson. Is this ringing any bells with you?'

'Big Ben is going off,' Peddyr replied. 'Any forensic evidence from inside the hall itself?'

'Tons of the bloody stuff, I'm told.'

He threw a few suggestions Kevin's way, who in response

readily handed over his phone to DS Helen Forstall who had been standing close by for just such an eventuality.

'Ah, Helen, can you make an early meeting at the offices of Bagshot & Laker? This could take forever unless—'

'We combine forces,' she added, finishing his sentence for him. 'But isn't Bernard Kershaw working for Austin Harkness? Isn't there a potential conflict of interest?'

Peddyr thought for a second before declaring that, as Bernard had been instructed to locate Vera Hudson based on the photo provided, and this had been achieved to a greater degree, his task had been effectively completed and Mr Harkness would be billed for the time spent. 'We can safely and truthfully tell him that his sister remains missing as of nearly thirty years ago and that the woman more recently going by that name was not in fact his sister so he can merrily sue Channel 7 for the distress caused, etcetera. Does that suit?'

He smiled at the laughter coming from the phone and predicted that it was going to be an extremely interesting pow-wow. 'Great. See you in the morning then.'

* * *

*F*eet up in front of the fire, Peddyr trawled through the pages of his notebook and glanced at the time-line made by Connie earlier. 'You know what's so frustrating? Not having any idea whether or not Liz Cooper knew that Verity was corresponding with Christine Fowler. My hypothesis that Liz killed Verity doesn't hold water without facts to back it up. But there is something just as important to be gleaned from those letters she sent to Christine. Austin made out that Verity was the problem child, and he used her mental breakdown in the wake of her husband's death as a weapon against her. Before that, she was making her way in life but when Ray Hudson died, she fell apart and there was nobody to help her until Christine stepped in to right a wrong.'

'Sad,' said Connie, sitting curled up at one end of the sofa, peeling a satsuma and placing the peel in a neat tower on the small plate resting on the upholstered arm at her side. 'Not one person believed her story. Not social services, not mental health services, nobody until Monica wrote about her and raised the possibility.'

'But who read that assignment except some corduroy-clad university lecturer who gave her higher marks for use of research references to back up her assertions. It was Christine who tried to help Verity find the baby taken from her.'

With a gentle thud, the plate and satsuma peelings landed on the floor. Connie had knocked them flying. 'Think like Christine,' she urged. 'Imagine you are her at the time Verity gives birth in a hospital for psychiatric patients. You hold a senior position, you and the resident consultant agreed to the admission of the patient, despite it being less than appropriate, so long as social services are alerted. The baby arrives early. Panic stations. The patient is under a section and not in a fit state to care for the child. You do the necessary and register the birth while social services provide emergency care for the newborn, thus setting in motion child protection strategies and risk assessments and a whole heap of trouble for Verity.'

'I get where you are going with this,' Peddyr replied, scribbling in his notebook. 'Verity went through the care system, her parents topped themselves because they were accused of child neglect or worse, Austin has always laid the blame at the feet of his younger sister. He thrived in the system, she barely survived. What does that tell us?'

Connie got to her feet, walking and talking back and forth in front of the glowing fire. Roger watched her from his bed, his head following her every move, his tail wagging slowly. 'Social services have the records which detail the Thorn family case, and they are not accessible. We don't know what they know. Verity doesn't know. Cara doesn't know. Verity's voice was not heard when she was placed in care. She was a traumatised child, behavioural problems would have been present, I would say. It would be expected. She's labelled as disturbed.'

'That's what Austin would have everyone believe.'

'So why was he the favoured one? How come he was fostered without so much as a hiccup? How did he settle into a new life with a new family and blossom into this businessman extraordinaire?'

She fell silent for a matter of seconds before reaching down to clear the peel from the carpet and retrieve the plate. 'He's our rat.'

'He was Christine's rat too,' Peddyr said, tapping his pen to his temple. 'According to those letters, she had his contact details. I need to check something with Monica.' He pulled out his phone and called her.

'Mon? Quick Mental Health Act question. If Christine Fowler was the Mental Health Act Administrator when Verity Hudson was detained on a section, and social services had provided details of a brother… would that brother be deemed to be the Nearest Relative under the Act? In other words, would Christine have known his contact details?'

When the answer came, he flicked his eyes to Connie and nodded just once. 'That's what I thought. You taught me well during our little foray into the world of psychiatry together last year. Thank you and sorry to disturb you. Oh, hang on. I have another query. How would you describe someone who didn't seem to be impacted when they say they were the victim of sustained bullying and psychological abuse? Someone who sailed through their time in the care system, someone who settled into a—' He stopped to listen then nodded again. 'Yes, I am talking about Austin Harkness. Yes, I do suspect you were right about Verity. Yes, I am suggesting he was the abuser and I

think Christine Fowler suspected it too. And before you ask…
We have no idea who killed Christine. There are a number of
viable possibilities.'

'What did she say?' asked Connie when Peddyr ended the
call. 'About Austin Harkness.'

'She told me to check out narcissistic personality disorder as
a possible starting point. Manipulation has always been his forte
and there's no-one as important as Austin in Austin's world. She
said to "think Konrad Neale only more polished and accom-
plished".'

Connie grinned. 'I think she may be right.'

Monica had supplied Peddyr with a better definition than
he'd hoped for. His one meeting with the man at the centre of
the Harkness empire had left him perturbed and riled because
he'd instinctively recognised the skill with which Austin had
attempted to influence the decision making. The expectation
that Peddyr would do as instructed had been plain. 'I must have
pissed him right off when he didn't get the reaction he needed
from me. Oh dear, what a bloody shame.'

43

THE POW-WOW

*T*he pow-wow began shakily. Bernard was raring to get started at eight on the dot, but Helen Forstall had yet to arrive. 'Where is the blasted woman?' he demanded, scuttling to his desk to take up position behind it, adjusting his braces. 'Please don't tell me she's gone off sick with the rest of them. We will begin without her in five minutes. Fiona is rustling up some tea and crumpets.' He looked at Peddyr reprovingly. 'Couldn't you have dressed more appropriately?'

'Forgive me. There was no frost this morning and the forecast is good. I'm heading for a secret bike blast after this. While Connie's away she can't nag me for risking it, but I tell you what, fella, I'm fair sweating in these trousers.' He had liberated his winter bike gear from their designated storage cupboard as soon as Connie had left home in the car. She assumed he would be walking to the meeting. Fiona had supplied the flip chart for him, so he only needed his notebook. However, the main roads would meet his need for a spin, and he couldn't resist.

'On your head be it,' said Bernard. 'We will inevitably miss Connie's contribution, but I do agree that her plan of action should take priority. I hope you've done your homework though, because a certain Austin Harkness is already on the warpath.'

'Why, what's his beef?' Peddyr asked. 'The bloody woman has been found, she's not his sister. End of.' Taking up a fat-nibbed pen and smoothing the flip chart paper he wrote out a series of names in clusters as he listened to Bernard's explanation. By the time he'd finished, his efforts looked less like a spider gram and more like a sprawling mind map.

'Police have been making inquiries about Harkness company vehicles and he's not a happy bunny.'

'Not my problem,' Peddyr commented flatly.

'He is accusing you of being over-enthusiastic in your dealings with his wife and son.'

'Nonsense. I was as nice as pie. Should have applied more pressure like I planned, but circumstances caught us on the hop.'

'He wants you off the case.'

'Good. I agree. As soon as we find out what happened to his real sister, I'll tot up our time and bill you.'

Bernard rubbed at his ample jowls with both palms. 'I'll be glad to see the back of him too. He can use his own lawyers from now on. The man hasn't changed.'

'What was he like at school? You never did say.'

'The headmaster's son. What would you expect? He demanded respect and he got it without the need to bully or cajole. He was charming, charismatic, athletic, and bright. Couldn't stand the bloke. He was the sort to dob you in and walk away rubbing his hands with satisfaction at a job well done.' The phone on his desk rang. It was Fiona. 'Send them in.'

'Them?' asked Peddyr.

'DS Forstall and sidekick. Fiona is increasing the numbers of cups and saucers as we speak. She's a marvel.'

Before Peddyr had chance to ask for clarification about the so-called sidekick, the door opened to reveal Helen Forstall and Kevin Spratt. 'Guess who got roped in to a murder investigation?' Kevin was shaking his head ruefully as he spoke, holding the door open for Helen to enter ahead of him. 'I suppose I have you to blame for this, Mr Quirk. Thanks a bunch.'

Helen was smiling weakly. 'Sorry we're late, Mr Kershaw. DI Webster is throwing everything at Christine Fowler's case because the DCI was swayed by his argument that the misper, a benefit fraud, and Christine's death, are linked. Who'd have thunk it?' She tilted her head in Peddyr's direction. 'Still, at least she's on board now.'

Webster had taken the credit when it was not due. However, in doing so, the convoluted case had been given the priority it deserved and with DCI Mshana in charge, there would be a decent SIO to oversee the investigation into Christine Fowler's untimely death. Peddyr wasn't unhappy about that, nor was he disappointed with the news that Kevin was part of the wider investigating team.

'Don't stand on ceremony, come in. Take a seat. Refreshments are on the way. Peddyr, if you would,' Bernard said, a finger aimed at his friend. 'No time to hang about.'

Kevin Spratt was slow to make his way to a chair, appearing somewhat awestruck on entering the well-appointed office. He stood for a while taking in the wood panelled walls, the expensive Persian rug, and the walnut veneer of Bernard's desk. From his position next to the flip chart, Peddyr welcomed the pair. 'Great to have you here for this, Kevin. You know all the finer details better than I. And, Helen, lovely to see you looking so bright-eyed. How long since you gave up smoking?'

Stunned, she hovered above the chair she was about to sit upon to stare at him in amazement before completing her short journey. 'How on earth could you know that?'

'I noticed it yesterday. No smell of fags. Today you have gum to chew. Keep it up, it suits you better. Now then. To business.'

Poking at the paper with the chunky felt pen, he indicated the names he had written. 'A quick recap, just to make certain we haven't missed anything. Vera Hudson turns out to be a fearsome old bag by the name of Elizabeth Cooper. Liz to anyone she knows. I would say close friends, but I don't think she has any. Anyhow, she was posing as the long-lost and estranged sister of Austin Harkness because that opportunity presented itself courtesy of Isaac Harkness and his search for an aunt he'd never met. Everyone keeping up so far?'

He rattled off the information about the life history of Elizabeth Cooper and Verity Hudson and the Harkness family, without need to refer to notes. At this juncture, Kevin produced a plastic evidence bag from his pocket. 'Last night, I made a late visit to Esther Cooper of 13 Browns Court and retrieved that letter of yours, Mr Quirk.' He waved the bag in the air. 'Thought it could be of help in linking the two women.'

'And she found it? In that appalling flat of hers?'

'The place did pong a bit and the mess inside was like a Grand Canyon of litter, but she knew exactly where the letter was. It wasn't for her, she said. And being a hoarder, she'd kept the envelope too.' Plainly pleased with himself he handed the bag to the DS. 'E J Cooper is the name on the envelope. The covering letter inside is addressed to a Verity Anne Hudson and outlines monetary matters relating to a former tenancy. The letter comes from an Elizabeth Cooper although that was typed and not signed. Whoever wrote it put the wrong name on the envelope. A straightforward error. Easily done.'

'Vaughan Probert, at a guess. Great with numbers, not brilliant at common sense.' Peddyr glanced at Bernard. 'The chap we met in Rushden. He's not a suspect but he is a victim. As I see it, there are links all over the place. However, it is not thought that Liz Cooper had any dealings directly with Austin Harkness that we know of. Moving on to the contents of letters sent to us at P.Q. Investigations by Christine Fowler...'

Bernard passed an envelope to Helen Forstall. 'Yours. We have taken copies. I'm sure you understand.'

'Those letters confirm a significant link between Christine Fowler and Verity Hudson and between Christine and Austin Harkness,' Peddyr explained. 'More recently, as Christine recorded on her laptop diary of events, she tried a two-pronged approach. As well as instructing us to prove Vera Hudson a fraud, she also contacted Olivia Harkness, seeking a meeting on the evening of Monday the twenty-second. Guess where... Now we really start to see the pieces slotting together nicely.'

Bernard heaved a sigh. 'What on earth did the woman think she was doing? If only she'd hand-delivered that envelope to you on Friday instead of posting it, you could have saved her life by warning her off. By taking control of the whole situation.'

The same thought had occurred to Peddyr. It was a simple decision that Christine had made. 'Perhaps she didn't want to be seen posting something through the door to a private investigation company.' Whatever her reason had been, it had cost her dear.

Peddyr resumed his presentation. 'One letter sent from a hopeless and disconsolate Verity to Christine suggests that she planned to take her own life but, as we all know, her body has never been found. The one person who can answer some very important questions about Verity's disappearance is Liz Cooper. She is back in Northamptonshire panicking about being caught for benefit fraud. Bearing in mind that she thinks hardcopy evidence has been destroyed, I'll warrant she will be getting rid of her computer, severing links with her tenants to whom she sub-lets, and doing her own disappearing act.'

Helen Forstall raised a hand. 'Actually, she won't. Northants have already detained her.'

Peddyr was dumbfounded. 'Why on earth would they do that at this early stage?'

'Webster,' Kevin said. 'Thinks he can break the world record for the fastest prosecution. He's expecting to charge her with everything from murder to motoring offences.'

There were half a dozen choice profanities making their way from Peddyr's brain towards his mouth, but in the nick of time he converted them to a simple, 'Okay, well, that's an optimistic start.'

'After what you told us, Liz Cooper became an instant suspect in the killing of Christine Fowler,' Kevin continued. 'And her waggon was caught on security camera at the dentist surgery car park on Monday night, confirming the sightings you reported to us. Arrived at eight, moved off less than fifteen minutes later.'

She had the opportunity, Peddyr realised, as well as the motive, and was capable of physical violence. A hot contender.

'Her car has been impounded by forensics and Liz Cooper is being questioned right now,' Helen said, picking up from her sergeant. 'It's why we were late. I had a high-speed chat with the arresting officer and he's on board with our need to treat her as a possible suspect in a murder inquiry, as well as being central to benefit fraud and a missing persons case. Quite the trio of charges there. Having spoken to DS Tony Di Angelo, I'd say there is scope for Northants to drop in a few questions about Verity's disappearance before our bumbling DI gatecrashes the interview. He's on his way there now. If Miss Cooper did kill Verity, we'll know soon enough. I'd give it another hour. Di Angelo was very much old school. No softly-softly from him.' She looked around the room and back at Peddyr. 'Other than that, it's out of my hands I'm afraid. Where's Connie?'

'She's on a mission.'

'Oh?'

Eyebrows were raised but Peddyr was not to be drawn. 'No need to fret. If it pans out, you'll hear from us.'

44

NUISANCE

*C*ara was up early on Wednesday morning with a determination to organise as much as she could in the way of work schedules and plans for a swift move back to Yorkshire. She had storage to find, removals to arrange, a sofa to redirect and two budgies to provide for. When her mobile rang, she wasn't surprised to receive a call from Connie Quirk just before nine that morning, but she was intrigued by the questions asked of her.

'Last year, when you put out social media requests for information on Vera Hudson, were you and Isaac aware of the identity of the person who replied? Who was it that contacted you to give Vera's address?'

Cara remembered the call very vividly. It was the first inkling that her birth mother was still alive. News she had all but given up hope of receiving. 'I took the call on the work phone, but she never left her name, and the number was withheld.'

'Apart from it being a woman, what do you recall?'

'Well spoken, you know, received pronunciation towards the posh end of the spectrum. She didn't want to leave her details and declined to accept the tempting reward on offer. A tour of Channel 7 studios and the chance to meet Konrad Neale didn't appeal.'

'So, nobody at Channel 7 knew the caller's identity, not even you?'

'Nobody. Why do you ask?'

'Because we think it was Christine Fowler.'

Stunned, Cara cast her mind back to the call made months previously. The one call that had immediately led her to Bosworth Bishops and to Vera Hudson. 'It could have been. Aye. It could quite easily have been her voice now that you mention it.' She heard the sound of a car door closing. 'Are you on the road again?' she asked.

'Yes. I'm in sunny Aylesbury. Well... the outskirts of. Peddyr has entrusted me with an important job, and we hope soon to have some answers to give you about your birth mother. If you still want to hear them. Monica has much to tell you.'

That call haunted her for the rest of the day as did Konrad Neale. He wouldn't let up. The emails were easier to bat away with assertions that she was busy with other projects and would get back to him, but the calls from his office to her work phone and her personal line were driving her to distraction.

She relented just after two o'clock.

'Ah, Cara. At last. What took you so long? Been down the nick again? Helping the police with their inquiries? Another witness statement perhaps?' His sarcastic tones offended her ears, as did his way of boasting about how clever he had been. The old scoundrel was clearly up to his usual tricks: Scanning local news for titbits then smarming his way into the ego of some aspiring young journalist, persuading them to send him the latest updates. Spies in every police station. She'd fallen for it years ago, but these days she took the money and ignored the flattery. In return, Konrad had stopped dishing it out.

'You screwed this one up, didn't you?' he said with relish.

'What do you mean?'

'What were you up to, you naughty girl? Moving to live in the same town as Vera Hudson so you could stalk her. You never got close enough to find out the truth about her and her brother though, did you? Eh? Christine Fowler did. She knew exactly who Vera Hudson was.'

'Where did you hear that from?'

'A friend of a friend. Says it could be massive news when it breaks.'

Cara was dubious. It sounded very much as if Konrad was fishing. 'And why would this friend contact you?'

'He didn't. I sought him out. I had my suspicions when I interviewed the frosty Vera. You, dear girl, had unearthed more about her than she knew about herself. She wasn't as bright as you.'

Cara narrowed her eyes. Konrad was being nice to her. Dangerous territory was being entered because the infuriating man was only complimentary when he was after something.

'Are you saying she was a con artist?' Momentarily stunned by the fact that Konrad had taken so long to come to this conclusion and therefore must have recently found out something she didn't know about Vera Hudson, Cara began to justify her actions to him. 'But I searched the National Missing Person's Database. Verity Anne Hudson had gone missing in 1992, but she bubbled up again some years later. Finding a current address for her was the thing that was most difficult. Anyway, you saw her ID. She proved who she was.'

'That's right, Cara. I did see it, but she was a will o' the wisp, a phantom who appeared and disappeared. Hard to trace. Let me tell you, I accidentally took a couple of photographs without her knowledge. Put out feelers, pulled in favours until I had something to go on. And it has arrived.'

Cara's chest tightened, her heart rate accelerated alarmingly, and she began to tremble. 'Why are you telling me this?'

'Because I'm going to turn it into the best ever piece of TV investigative journalism and you're going to help me.'

'Am I?'

'Come, come, Cara. Don't toy with me. The newest series of *The Truth Behind the Lies* with me – Konrad Neale, will be awesome. The news is full of it. There's been a suspicious death. You were a witness. Christine Fowler was on BBC Valley Radio telling everyone she used to hold a vital administrative post at Fairfield Hospital in Bedfordshire where, according to the research notes you sent me, Verity Anne Hudson was detained on a Section 3.' He let out a victorious laugh. 'If that's not one hell of a story, then I don't know what is.'

Cara couldn't speak. She hadn't heard Christine mention any hospital by name on the radio. Even so, she hadn't put two and two together like Konrad had. Shaking her head, she couldn't quite believe what she had been told in the space of five hours. First Connie phones her to say it was Christine who furnished her with details of Vera Hudson's whereabouts, and now Konrad is telling her that Vera Hudson may not be Vera Hudson but someone pretending to be her, and that Christine Fowler had known this. It was staggering.

She'd told Isaac to check the woman out carefully before they took it further. Why hadn't he done a thorough job? Why hadn't she been more rigorous herself? Channel 7 had seen Vera's ID, and even the local authority had not doubted her identity when she took up her tenancy with them, but they should have done more. Matched against a sample from Isaac, a genetics test would have proved it.

Suddenly she understood.

'So… this person must have known the real Verity Hudson, stolen her identity, taken the risk of pretending to be a rich man's lost sister. She *was* a con-artist. No wonder she bailed out when she did. How much money did she get paid?'

'Who?'

'Vera Hudson. The woman you interviewed. The fake one. Isaac bribed her with money, and you did the same, I heard you on the recording you made when you interviewed her. It's important to know how much money she ran off with because that's what she's done.'

'I agree,' said Konrad. 'And she'd have been even richer if she had gone through with it.'

Cara held a hand to her forehead, trying to control her breathing. 'As far as I know, she didn't want anything to do with the show or with Austin Harkness until she was offered payment for her time. If she was bogus then that would fit. And if she was bribed to take part, that makes sense too. She got what she came for and she's gone.'

She heard Konrad release a long breath. 'And if Christine Fowler knew the real Verity Anne Hudson,' he said, 'she would have known the woman was a phoney. Are you seeing the connections yet?'

'Some of them.' Cara was being deliberately cagey, trying to force from Konrad what he knew without revealing her part in the Harkness family secrets. 'You think this imposter went into hiding and only came back to kill Christine because she knew too much?'

'Is that what the police think?'

'How should I know?'

'Didn't you ask them?'

'No, I did not. I told them what I'd seen and heard and that was all. It's not my place to ask who they think did the killing.'

'And what *did* you see and hear?'

Cara let out a disparaging laugh. 'Like a dog with a bone. Sorry, Konrad, I can't tell you in case it compromises a police investigation.' She cut him off and burst into tears.

45

A MAD DASH

*O*nce tea, coffee, and crumpets had been delivered by Fiona, the focus of the pow-wow turned to Christine Fowler's demise. 'If Christine wanted to expose Liz Cooper as a fraud, why did she do it through a Channel 7 researcher?' Bernard asked, as he leafed through a typed report provided through means of a voice dictation from Peddyr and the lightning-fast fingers of Fiona McFarland, who promised to have it completed and delivered with their refreshments. She really was a marvel.

'There was no crime to report to the police. Not one that Christine could prove. In her letter to me and Connie, instructing us to investigate—' Peddyr stopped himself mid-sentence. 'Jesus! She unmasked herself.'

'What do you mean?' Helen asked, leaning forward in her chair.

Analysing what had occurred to him, Peddyr slowed his thinking down. 'Last night, Connie said I should think like Christine Fowler, get inside her head. I did, I got into several heads last night. All of them pretty unpleasant.'

'Which may explain why you are a little crabby this morning, old bean,' Bernard chipped in.

'It may indeed, but it was worth it. This whole case is about what makes people tick. What makes certain people act in the way they do. Christine Fowler, Austin Harkness and Konrad Neale are similar creatures in many ways. Liz Cooper is a different animal altogether.

'If we think it through, Christine made an anonymous call hoping that the fake Vera would be exposed by doing so. But she can't resist the limelight, so she was on social media, local news, TV and radio as Councillor Christine Fowler, spouting off, asking the townsfolk to search for the missing woman. It was all for show because Christine couldn't help herself, she had already confronted the fake Vera to prove how powerful she could be. And it worked. Fake Vera buggered off.'

He threw out an arm, aiming it at the window. 'Hardly surprising when you consider that Liz Cooper had what she wanted; money from Isaac, money from Konrad Neale.' He faltered. 'Errr, don't ask me how I know that. Take my word for it. Both men bribed her, and I can provide the evidence, I simply cannot reveal my source.'

He coughed and carried on with his views about Liz Cooper. 'She was never going to go through with an appearance on a live TV show or being filmed or photographed at all because Austin would have known she wasn't Verity as soon as he clapped eyes on her close up.'

Helen Forstall was agreeing through use of a succession of rapid nods and encouraging hums, while jotting down reminders. She, Kevin, and Bernard remained quiet allowing Peddyr's thoughts to flow.

'I'm no psychologist, but even I can see that Austin Harkness revels in the attention and adulation he receives. He protects his privacy but courts publicity. There's little difference between him and Konrad Neale. Austin is more controlled and meticulous. Konrad Neale is a maverick, flawed, and makes poor judgement calls sometimes. He's a marmite man. Loves himself and doesn't care that some people dislike him intensely because attention from an audience satisfies his cravings.' Peddyr wafted his pen in the air, rocking on the balls of his feet.

'And then we go back to Christine's head. Christine had a high opinion of herself, but she had a heart, a sense of duty, and she felt guilt. Recognition was her motivator. Recognition for what she saw as doing good. Misguided or not, she generally lived up to her own high expectations.'

He ran his pen along her name written on the flip chart paper.

'The night she was killed, if Austin Harkness was there, then most likely Watson was at his side. The lackey.'

'Agreed,' said Helen. 'If only we could prove it.'

'But we do have a good chance of proving that Isaac and his mother were at the hall on Monday,' Kevin stated. 'And Desmond Fowler has given us evidence that the family were invited there by Christine. What we need to prove is who attended.'

Peddyr smiled encouragingly at the sergeant. 'You'll make a fine detective. We also have Liz Cooper in the area, and as unlikely as it may seem... two young men, who prefer to be identified as female, were out looking for Vera's cat that they had agreed to feed,' he said carefully, glancing at Bernard in acknowledgement of the need for gender sensitivities. 'Those two young people were arrested and questioned because of threats they made to Christine on social media. And not forgetting our two young ladies who gave witness statements.'

Peddyr had agonised for much of the night about whether to divulge the role Cara Laidlaw played in the whole story. In the end he and Connie agreed that her right to privacy should remain. She had no reason to kill Christine Fowler. In fact, she could have been the one person to tell Cara about her real mother.

'The question remains, who killed Mrs Christine Fowler?' Bernard asked. 'Forensics will take a while. Anything from your pathologist, DS Forstall?'

Referring to her own notes, Helen read out a summary of initial findings, but looked up when she came to the remarks about the noose. 'Not tied by a left-hander, Peddyr. The noose was expertly created, not a proper bona fide hangman's noose but a very effective slipknot, nevertheless. As you all know, initial examination shows that Christine did not have her neck broken by a long drop on a short rope. Our victim was strangled using her own pashmina then it seems the plan was to hang her to make it appear to be a suicide. The killer must have had a rope with them.'

'A tow rope?' Peddyr suggested. 'The sort most of us carry in the car?'

'It's being investigated. That answer could take a while. We are tracking down all the cars seen in the car park on Monday night. Then the forensic search begins again in earnest,' announced Kevin.

'Who among the possible suspects would have the strength to strangle her as well as the motivation to want Christine dead?' Helen pondered aloud.

Peddyr was the first to respond to her. 'Take it from me, Watson has the skills, the strength, and very little patience. If Austin Harkness had need to cover up his past and protect his image, his money, his power and status, he wouldn't hesitate to instruct Watson to carry out his orders and remove the threat. Understand the man and you understand the motive.' He was on a roll now, enjoying the ability to verbalise the thoughts that had become jumbled the previous night. He had untangled them, and it felt wonderful.

'Because of her dealings with Verity, Christine knew Austin Harkness for what he was, and she therefore had to be elimi-nated because her mouth had run away with her.' Peddyr tapped the board again. 'And what about Isaac's car. It wasn't at his home yesterday, but it was seen parked at the hall on Monday evening, so where has that gone to? Connie and I were out of the way, Christine had been on the radio shouting about Vera Hudson, goading Austin and Olivia into making a move. So, did Watson take the car and use it, intent on implicating Isaac in a crime? Steering any investigation away from Austin? Pardon the pun.'

Kevin and Helen exchanged knowing looks. 'We can answer that one,' Helen replied. 'We've found the black Mercedes usually driven by Isaac Harkness because it had been abandoned by the driver after being involved in a minor collision outside Oxford. It was still awaiting recovery and the PNC check from Oxford police gave us the edge with that one. However, we are struggling to identify the dark van. Harkness Healthcare have dozens of the damned things and, as of six o'clock this morning, nothing has been picked up on any cameras. So far, we have no real grounds to haul Austin Harkness in for questioning. However, Isaac Harkness is being spoken to again this morning. He hasn't been charged with anything at this point, but word is he's jittery. Tying himself up in knots. Oh, dear, it really is the morning for puns, isn't it,' she said, raising a hand in apology. 'Tasteless. Sorry.'

Bernard rose slowly from his seat and, with fists planted on the desk, he leaned heavily on his arms. 'That is one hell of an accusation, even coming from you, Peddyr. Austin Harkness and his son... implicated in murder? You can't be serious.'

'Oh, but I am. I'm not saying Austin killed her. No way would he do the job himself. Blood on his hands? Not on your Nelly. Having thrown that out there, it's down to the police to prove who killed her. Not my province these days.'

'And if the killer wasn't Watson, for argument's sake?' Kevin said. 'Liz Cooper? Olivia and Isaac?'

Peddyr took a moment. 'Liz Cooper would have no qualms

in throttling Christine with her own scarf, but she wouldn't have had the strength to haul her into the rafters. She may have killed her after Watson and the Harknesses had left. She'd simply given up trying to hoist her into the rafters.' He shrugged. 'It's possible.'

'Would Isaac Harkness have reason to kill Christine?' Kevin enquired.

'I doubt it. What would be his motive? To protect an emotionally corrupt father? … I'm not convinced. He's more of a sheep than a wolf. But Olivia … Now there's a potential suspect we haven't considered carefully enough.' When the thought arrived, it did so like a thump in the guts. Locking eyes with Helen Forstall, Peddyr asked, 'Did you pick up the silver Mercedes A class belonging to Olivia Harkness yet?'

'Not that I know of. Neither Olivia Harkness nor her car have been found. I'll check if any progress has been made on that one.'

'You're telling me that neither Austin nor Olivia Harkness's whereabouts are accounted for?' Without the need to pause, Peddyr rattled out some instructions, firmly, rapidly.

'I have to go after Connie. She shouldn't be on her own. Bernie, ask Fiona to call The Lawns Residential Nursing home in Aylesbury and leave a message for Connie to call me. I'll try her mobile. Helen, divert DI Webster from Northants. Tell him to meet me at The Lawns. Google the full address. I don't care how you do it, just get him to The Lawns to see a man called Chester Bevan and to keep Connie safe if he arrives before me.' He checked his watch. 'Bugger, bollocks and bum. She's probably already there.'

Helen and Kevin leapt from their seats. 'Who are we saving her from exactly?' Kevin asked.

Peddyr didn't reply straight away, dashing for the door to retrieve the rest of his bike gear from behind Fiona McFarland's office he paused to say, 'I'm not quite sure. Could be Austin,

Watson or Olivia… but there's a man at The Lawns who knows. We must get there before he is silenced, and I will be breaking the speed limit for the next hour or so. Thought you should know.'

46

THE LAWNS

'This is swanky,' Connie said as she pulled into a visitor parking space in front of The Lawns residential nursing home. Roger the dog was with her. It wasn't fair to leave him at home, and anyway she liked the company. He was more fun to talk to than Sat-Nav-Suzie. Connie read the advertising board which declared that Harkness Healthcare ensured their residents could want for nothing. *"More than a home from home"*, the strap line read.

She was a few minutes early so after letting Roger out of the car to stretch his legs on a lead with a circuit of the car park, she made a quick call to Cara to put her mind at rest. If someone was prepared to kill Christine Fowler to silence her, it was vital to know that her anonymous phone call about Vera Hudson had been just that. Peddyr had theorised that Christine had put herself in danger by interfering, instead of letting things take their natural course. And all things considered, it was hardly surprising that she had been so determined to expose the Harkness family to public scrutiny. But there was more to this story, Connie could feel it. It was time to find out.

'I'm here to see Mr Chester Bevan, I phoned yesterday to

arrange a visit,' Connie said to the smiling woman at a sliding window to a small reception office.

'My, he's never been so popular,' the woman replied baring her teeth with a smile wide enough to reveal a smear of lipstick across a top set of dentures. Her name was Sylvia Blast. 'Not to be confused with Sylvia Plath,' she added with a jarring laugh. Suddenly Connie was reminded of *Fawlty Towers*. Apart from the teeth, Sylvia was Sybil Fawlty to a tee.

'Mrs Harkness on Sunday, and now you, dear. He'll be thrilled. Take a seat, I'll be with you shortly.'

Twenty minutes later, following instructions, Connie handed over her mobile phone, asking why such precautions were necessary.

'Some of our residents are very vulnerable and we protect their privacy with care,' Sylvia said, snappily. 'No photographs without our express permission. Older people don't realise what can be gleaned from social media and scammers will take advantage if they can and you wouldn't believe what some visitors will try. But we have it covered.' Her eyes moved fleetingly to a screen showing CCTV pictures.

Connie was shocked to see how many cameras were in use. The screen was too far away to see what was being filmed, but evidently residents were in safe hands.

'Can you put your name, car registration, address and contact details in the visitors' book for our records. Time of visit nine twenty-five. Very punctual, Mrs Quirk.'

Connie had arranged a nine o'clock visit, but so far Sylvia had thwarted her efforts to see Chester Bevan on time.

'I'm not sure how long I'm going to be, so would you mind keeping a camera on my car. I'm looking after my son's dog and he's on the back seat. The dog, not my son.'

'Is he a well-behaved dog?'

'Impeccably.'

'Then bring him in. Our residents love to see a dog in the place. Mr Bevan would be delighted.'

'Are you sure?'

Sylvia had suddenly gone up in her estimation. It was a thoughtful gesture for all concerned. When she returned with Roger, she discarded her heavy winter coat and hat, hanging them on a row of pegs for just that purpose and she approached the office window again. Roger was an instant hit.

'What a little smasher,' Sylvia squealed as she leaned through the sliding window to get a better look. 'Adorable. This will be a treat. Mr Bevan's not been himself lately, perhaps this will cheer him up and if he can help with your missing lady, it will make him feel useful again. It may even return him to reality. Lately he's been telling all sorts of fanciful stories. Things we've never heard before. Anyway, I'll leave him to explain. Doreen will show you to his room. He was up half the night, but he's resting on his bed just now.'

The woman's diatribe flowed without a break and Connie didn't get chance to ask anything specific about the state of Chester Bevan's long-term memory. Neither could she see any reference to Olivia Harkness's visit on Sunday in the visitors' book, which was swiftly removed from her when she had completed the sections required.

Doreen described herself as a volunteer as she waddled along a carpeted corridor showing Connie the way, although at first Connie thought her to be one of the residents. 'I come in three times a week to read to them. Newspapers, books, magazine articles. They love it and I have a reason to get out of the house for a while. We did have a visit from a woman who brought her miniature pony in. They are thought to be therapeutic, you know, but it didn't do the carpets much good. Dogs are a favourite with the oldies though.' With a smile Doreen knocked gently on a door marked with Chester Bevan's name and cheerily asked the occupant if he was decent and ready for his visitor.

The room was far bigger than Connie had imagined. It was more like a studio flat, with an en suite bathroom, a kitchenette, dining table, and a lounge area leading to a curtained bed space where Chester Bevan was propped up on pillows. He appeared emaciated with papery skin, almost translucent, which looked to Connie as if it was about to disintegrate like a dried leaf. But when she approached with her notepad in her hands, she saw the glint in his eyes, an unnerving excitement of sorts.

'Come on in,' he said. His voice was soft and tremulous, each phrase and sentence a trial to produce between the puffing noises of his breathing. 'You and especially your canine companion are very welcome. I've been looking forward to this. I didn't think she'd do it.'

'Who?'

With every question came a delay in the reply, and each reply took considerable effort for Chester Bevan. He managed by using short sentences where he could and by pausing frequently to inhale.

'Mrs Harkness. I didn't think she would go to the police. I thought she'd keep it a secret. I'm glad. I want to give my statement. All of it. Unburden myself.'

With a sinking feeling Connie sat down on the upright chair positioned at an angle next to the bed, Roger settled at her feet. If he thought she was the police, Chester Bevan had not understood who she was and why she was there. 'I'm Connie. I'm here to ask you to help in the search for a missing lady. I'm not the police but I am working with them. I hope that's alright.'

'You write everything down. Share it with them. Write it all down. It's time.'

Time was the word. Even though this was going to be a long slow job, Connie was not going to hurry him along.

'The lady at reception said Mrs Harkness was here on Sunday evening. She told the staff she was worried about you.'

'Mrs Harkness told me I was coming unglued at the edges. I didn't think she believed me. She thought I was making it up.'

'What did you tell her, Mr Bevan?'

'Bevan, just Bevan.'

Connie wasn't expecting a deathbed confession, but in effect that was what she got. She thought she would have to coax information from Bevan, but he willingly gave up his secrets. One, slow, agonising breath at a time.

'So, Verity Hudson *did* visit the manor the year she was reported missing the first time. 1992.'

A very slight nod preceded the story and Bevan's breathing became more laboured. 'Mrs Harkness and young Isaac were away visiting Lord and Lady Derwent. I was in charge of the estate. Turns out I didn't do a very good job. I'd been digging a hole to bury one of young Isaac's pet sheep.'

'In the pet cemetery?' Connie asked.

'You know about that?'

'I've seen it. Very impressive.' She looked down to check that Roger wasn't listening. She didn't want him upset by talk of dead animals.

'It was one of the reasons for Isaac to visit his grandparents. I was given the job of burying the creature while they were gone, so that the boy didn't have to see. Mrs Harkness said she would arrange a headstone. Stupid idea really but every pet had a good send off. At lunchtime I thought to do an external inspection of the main house and there was a woman hanging from a tree. Noose round her neck. Dead as a dodo.'

'Did you know who it was?'

Bevan shook his head as best he could. Each movement seemed like a gargantuan task to him and whenever he moved, he flinched with the pain. 'Not until I went into the house to call the police. No mobile phones to speak of in those days. I found a letter, handwritten, shoved through the letterbox of the front door. Before that time, the postman would come to the house... but not then. Post went in the post box by the main gate. So, I knew it was by hand. I knew it was a letter from the woman hanging in the garden. When I read what she'd written, I couldn't call anyone.'

'But why?'

'It was my job, my life. I was there to protect the family. What she wrote would have destroyed them all if the police got hold of that letter or discovered who the girl was. Her story would have ruined them. You see, maybe six weeks or so before that, Mr Harkness had received a peculiar letter from some strange woman. Can't remember the name, but he showed me. The woman wrote about some terrible things, and she said the information had come from his sister. Never knew he had one until then. Mr Harkness was livid. He called his sister a liar. He said the woman who wrote the letter was a liar. That was when I was told to order a security gate and put the post box on the wall by the main entrance. He wanted everything. Cameras, alarms, more security staff.'

With Roger's dog lead hooked loosely over the arm of the chair, Connie was writing as fast as her cramping fingers would allow her. She wanted to capture every word just as it was being said. 'Why would he do such a drastic thing based on one letter?'

'Mr Harkness said his sister was a madwoman who'd been incarcerated on and off for years in various asylums. It was the reason he had changed his name and never spoken of her, he said. Reckoned she was paranoid and dangerous to boot.'

'Do you remember the date you found the woman dead in the grounds?'

He did. He said it without hesitation. 'I'll never forget it.'

With sorrow in her heart, Connie wrote the numbers down. One year to the day after Verity's baby had been born in Fairfield Hospital. Verity had given up hope and killed herself on her baby's first birthday.

'Do you remember the precise content of that letter? What was it in the letter which made him react so strongly to protect himself and his family?'

'The woman had written about how she was trying to assist Mr Harkness's sister to look for her child. She asked him to help. To make amends. The baby was called Caroline. Her name was Verity Hudson. So, you see, you can't still be looking for Verity Hudson. She died years ago.' His face contorted and he licked at dried lips. 'I still can't remember the name of the woman who wrote to Mr Harkness.'

'Never mind. I'm sure it will come back to you.'

Roger's ears pricked up as a woman's voice came from behind Connie. Engaged in listening and writing, she hadn't heard anyone enter the room. Taken aback at the sight of Olivia Harkness, Connie found herself apologising. 'Oh, I'm sorry. I was told you'd visited on Sunday. I didn't think—' The rest of the sentence was interrupted by Olivia, who in contrast to the last time she'd met her, was neatly dressed and groomed, almost serene in her manner.

'We meet again. Three times in one week, Mrs Quirk. I wasn't expecting to find you here.'

47

BEVAN

A cold wave of fear made its way along Connie's limbs and at first, she couldn't determine why that should be, but it was a reaction not to be ignored and it was being mirrored by Roger who was on alert. His tail was not wagging. 'We thought Bevan might have some useful insights and could help in our search for Verity Hudson,' she said. It was the first thing that popped into Connie's head to say, because it was true.

'And has he been helpful?'

'It appears you were right, Mrs Harkness. Isaac said you thought Vera Hudson might have been an imposter. That turns out to be the case I'm afraid, and now from what I hear, it sounds very much as if the real Verity Hudson took her own life some years ago.'

Bevan raised a stick-like arm. 'I buried her. I told nobody.'

Olivia Harkness entered the bed area, taking up position on the opposite side of the bed from Connie and Roger. She smiled down at Bevan as she reached out to smooth his wrinkled forehead. 'Poor soul. I can't think where this idea has come from. He keeps saying he kept a dreadful secret to himself. I have promised that if we find a body, we will make certain whoever it is receives a proper burial but I'm sure you can't have done such a thing, Bevan.'

'You knew this on Sunday?' No sooner had the question left her lips than Connie registered her mistake. In response, the glare from Olivia was unmistakable. Her eyes exuded hatred, the false smile belied her intentions.

'Mrs Quirk, I think you should leave now. Bevan hasn't been feeling very well. He needs his rest.'

'But—'

'I insist. Perhaps another time. Although I can't really see why you are here. Bevan has nothing more to contribute and your contract with this family has been terminated... Or didn't your husband tell you?'

Bevan tried to object but was silenced by Olivia who briefly placed a finger to his lips. 'Shush now, you'll exhaust yourself. I don't know precisely what Bevan has told you, Mrs Quirk, but I'm afraid whatever he said can't be fully relied upon. His age is catching up with him. Isn't it, Bevan?'

A statement, not a question. Bevan was being instructed to hold his tongue, but his agenda was obviously vital to him as he was unable to comply.

'There's nothing wrong with my brain, Mrs Harkness,' he gasped. 'And you said my wishes would be respected.'

She raised her hand to reveal a mobile phone, clutched tightly. 'That's why I'm here, Bevan. Look. I'll make a recording on my phone. So much easier than writing it down. Then I'll send it off to the police. Like I said.'

Outmanoeuvred, Connie was faced with no alternative but to leave. Olivia was making out that Bevan was of unsound mind, but Connie strongly thought otherwise. She would have to play along. 'Oh, I see. Yes. I'll go now. Well, it was a pleasure to meet you, Mr Bevan. I hope you get back to being your old self soon.'

Dallying outside the room with the dog, for as long as she

dared, she heard Olivia ask Bevan, 'Now where were we? Oh yes. We got as far as the sheep being thrown in the river. And the child? The baby. Caroline. Did the letter say what happened to her? Who adopted her?'

This was disquieting news. In the Orangery on Monday, Olivia had said that the baby's existence was known. But Olivia was trying to find out where that child may be now, as an adult.

Cara.

Cara was to be hunted.

What was it Peddyr had said? *'Someone's mopping up.'*

Isaac had a way of contacting Verity's daughter. However, for some reason Isaac had kept that secret to himself. He had lied to his parents about how the discovery of an aunt had come about and he hadn't told them of email correspondence with a cousin. A cousin whose name he didn't know. Connie prayed silently that he continued to hold his tongue.

Through the door, Bevan's voice was no more than a series of croaks now. It was almost impossible to pick up on his words. 'I don't know. It was in the letter. The suicide note.'

'And what happened to that letter?'

Connie had heard enough. Padding as fast as she could down the long corridor, the carpets muffling the sounds of her steps, Connie flew back to the reception office and banged on the glass.

'Are you done, dear?' said Sylvia approaching the hatch. 'You've been with him for quite some time. I'm sorry for the interruption, but Mrs Harkness didn't seem too pleased when she saw you were chatting to him.'

'Saw?'

'On the monitor. She's Mrs Olivia Harkness, dear, the family own this place. She came straight into the office, as she normally does, out of courtesy to say she was here again. She's so kind to that man.'

'She doesn't sign in?'

'The rules don't apply to her, dear. The same reason we don't switch on the cameras in his room when she visits.'

'You have cameras in the resident's rooms?'

'Yes. We can monitor for falls and ensure visitors and agency nurses are behaving themselves.'

'I don't think that's legal.'

'It is done with the signed permission of our residents, dear. All above board, Mrs Quirk.'

Connie was trying to make sense of what she had seen and heard, and with it came a dreadful sense of foreboding which mushroomed as the mystery unfolded in her head like shock-waves. Above all, she wished that Peddyr was with her. He would have known how to handle Olivia Harkness. At that moment Connie felt she had failed him. She looked down at Roger and up again at Sylvia. 'Have you switched the camera off yet?'

Sylvia flinched. 'Oh no, silly me. I got completely distracted by the telephone. There's a message for you. Hang on. Let me sort the camera out before I get myself the sack.'

On the computer screen Sylvia clicked the cursor over the required picture and it enlarged to full screen size. Before she had chance to take the next step to disable the camera, Connie shouted at her to stop what she was doing. Olivia Harkness could have been plumping up Bevan's pillows, but that's not what it looked like to Connie.

'Oh, no!' she cried with a gasp. 'I should never have left the room. Leave the camera running. Come with me,' she shouted at Sylvia. 'Hurry!'

Plainly shocked at the reaction, Sylvia failed to move, she just stared at Connie as if doubting her sanity. With no time to explain, Connie pivoted and made to run back to Bevan's room, and as she picked up speed across the hallway, Roger engaged in what he thought was a game and bounded along beside her. He barked as DI Duncan Webster appeared in front of them and

Connie, at full tilt, collided with him. Her shoulder made contact first and her head hit him in the chest. Stepping back, his shocked face displayed instant recognition. 'Mrs Quirk? What are you—?'

She righted herself and ran on as he called after her. 'Where is Mrs Olivia Harkness?' he demanded. 'I wish to inform her that her car is being impounded and I have questions for her to answer.'

'Then follow me and do it quickly,' Connie shouted back over her shoulder. 'I'll take you straight to her and get your handcuffs ready. I think she's about to kill a man.'

48

CONNIE HAS A FAN

*O*n arrival at The Lawns, Peddyr was met by a most incongruous sight. DI Duncan Webster was kissing the back of Connie's hand. This was so unexpected he nearly lost his balance as the bike slowed and he steered into a parking space. The car park was buzzing with activity. A flatbed truck rolled in behind Peddyr and was directed to where it could more easily load Olivia Harkness's Mercedes A class.

His relief at seeing Connie alive and well caught him out. He steadied himself, tightening the reins on his emotions; there was an audience to account for. He flipped up his visor and turned the engine off. The ritual of patting the petrol tank at the end of a journey was not forgotten either.

His wife had seen and heard his arrival and she excused herself from Webster's bizarre affections. 'I got your message, Lao Gong. Thanks.'

Hands on hips, Peddyr grinned. 'Explain yourself, woman.'

'I have been thanked for supporting DI Webster in his appre-hension of Olivia Harkness and for directing him to the CCTV footage as evidence of her intention to end the life of Chester Bevan.'

'You did all that?' Peddyr asked, taking off his crash helmet to hear her better.

'I did, Lao Gong.'

'Good job I tipped you off then.'

'It would have been if I'd received the message in time. No mobile phones allowed and by the time I got your message via the landline, I was just about to bury my head in Webster's chest. He'll have a bruise there I should think.'

Peddyr was used to Connie's tendency to talk in riddles at moments of high excitement, but this one had him flummoxed. 'I let you out of my sight for the morning and you fling yourself at a man you say you despise. That old chestnut...'

She hugged him as he stepped off the bike. 'And as soon as I leave home without you, you wrap your legs around one of the other loves of your life. I think that makes us even.'

'Not until you tell me what Bevan said. I hope we didn't go through this to find nothing out.'

She grinned up at him. 'Never fear. Stand by for a quick precis of events. And put your gloves back on or your hands will get cold.'

As she talked, Peddyr walked her back to their car and waved to Roger through the rear window. 'Verity Hudson went to the manor in 1992. She wrote a letter to say why and then managed to hang herself from a tree in the grounds. Goodness knows how she did it. Why not choose an overdose, or the river, or slashing her wrists? Hanging. Really unusual for a woman. Anyway, Bevan discovered her, then found the letter she had pushed through the letter box. When he read the contents, he didn't call the police, but covered up the death by burying her in the pet cemetery. He never told a soul until Sunday when he confessed all to Olivia because he knew he was dying.' She drew breath and grinned at Peddyr. 'That's the short version, but I didn't get all the answers because she interrupted.'

With a tilt of her head, Connie indicated across the car park where Olivia Harkness was being escorted into the rear seats of a police vehicle.

'Looks like her rights have been read to her. Why? Why did she do it?' Peddyr asked out loud.

Connie shrugged. 'To protect the good name of her husband and her own family, I guess. Like George the groundsman said, the upper class are a funny lot. The aristocracy even more so.'

Peddyr agreed with her assessment. 'They might have got away with Liz Cooper being exposed as a fraud. They could have expressed disgust at an attempt to gain money by deception. But,' he said, slapping his gloved hands together, 'Christine Fowler would not be silenced. Thanks to her and to Monica, we know that it was Austin who psychologically abused Verity as a child and not the other way round as he would have us believe. His sister's behavioural problems were in response to what he did on the sly to make her look bad and paint himself as the victim. At that age... I ask you.'

'Gaslighting?'

'I'd say he is a champion gaslighter. Anything to keep the attention on himself. A younger sibling was an insult to him, and his parents had no idea what he was up to. He even managed to make sure they were accused of the abuse he had inflicted. So mortified were they, that they took their own lives.'

'You're right, Pedd. Christine Fowler heard this direct from Verity when she was in hospital and in those letters we were sent. Monica also had it from the horse's mouth, so to speak. When Verity disappeared, the letters stopped. Christine assumed she'd done as she had threatened but could never prove it. She never forgot though, did she? When Liz Cooper trolled up pretending to be Verity Hudson, she was right on it. Once she started making waves, Austin and Olivia had a major problem on their hands.'

Peddyr looked past her shoulder. 'Watch out, Lao Po, your secret lover is on his way over to speak to us. No flirting now.

You'll only encourage him.' In jest Connie dug into him with her elbow and he feigned an injury. 'Alright there, Inspector?' he asked.

'Couldn't be better,' Webster replied, looking smug. 'The strategy employed by my team went to plan, I'm pleased to say. Fortunately, I was able to respond immediately as I was en route to Northampton. Busy few days ahead I suspect,' he drawled.

'I don't doubt it, Inspector. Do you need a statement from my wife?'

'We do indeed. She was most helpful.'

'Yes,' said Connie. 'It helps to recognise the difference between smothering and soothing.'

Peddyr sensed the full story from his wife would be entertaining. He looked forward to it.

'I'm off to Northampton now. Better late than never. Thanks for your help.'

'And forensics will be checking for horsehair on the rope used to set the scene in Christine Fowler's murder?' Peddyr couldn't let it go, he had to aim Webster in the right direction. It looked very likely that Olivia was the one who killed Christine. The strong arms of a rider, the availability of a rope, the need to keep family secrets. Secrets she had only discovered the day before. Liz Cooper's position as number one suspect had just been superseded.

'They check for everything, Mr Quirk. You should know that.'

'How is Chester Bevan?' Connie asked as Webster turned to go.

'Right as rain. He asked to speak with you when you can spare him some time, Mrs Quirk. Looks like you have a fan.'

This was great news to Peddyr's ears. They were to be given a second crack at interviewing Bevan. This time without interruption. He shouted to Webster who was on his way to his car.

'Is Bevan likely to see any other members of the Harkness family, or is he safe?'

With a rapid about-face, Webster retraced his steps and sidled up to Peddyr to whisper.

'And what makes you think to ask such a question?'

'They have to be involved because, even if you can't prove it just yet, it's a fair bet they were all together at the Wigmore Memorial Hall on Monday night. They couldn't resist an invitation from Christine Fowler who was trying to find out what happened to the real Verity Hudson. What she disclosed must have come as a shock for Isaac. So much so he pranged his car on the way home and had to be driven the rest of the way by his cold-hearted mother who then plied him with alcohol and bribes to keep him quiet.'

He had Webster's attention. The man was concentrating on every word he was saying.

'And you know this because?'

'Because we met with Isaac and his mother the following day and because Austin and Watson would not have been so careless as to plan to kill Christine on Monday night. Too many chances of being seen, vehicles being caught on cameras. Mr Harkness would have had something less predictable in mind. Therefore, Olivia strangled Christine – she had the strength and, being a horsewoman, she had ropes in her car. Also, she had very recently found out about Verity's death being covered up by Bevan. I would hazard a guess that Isaac was made to take part in the aborted attempts to make Christine's murder look like suicide. That's why the job wasn't finished. Isaac panicked and left his mother to it. Bevan had made a confession to Olivia Harkness the previous day. His need to fully confess was nearly his undoing. Are you with me, Inspector?'

'Yes, I am. This will all be in your statements, I take it? You can arrange with DS Forstall to meet with her for that purpose on your return to Bosworth Bishops if you would. The sooner the better.'

Peddyr opened his arms, inviting more from Webster. 'Well? Where is Austin Harkness?'

'I'll chase that up and get back to you. We were seeking to question him, given his suspected presence at the hall, but we must be diplomatic. Have no fear, Mr Quirk, the DCI is adamant that this investigation will be far-reaching.'

Peddyr sighed inwardly. He hoped for everyone's sake that the Chief Super was overseeing the whole intertwined set of crimes, because the media would soon be in a state of frenzy.

* * *

Sylvia had not fully recovered from the drama of Olivia Harkness's arrest, and as a result she failed to take possession of mobile phones, despite agreeing to guard Peddyr's motorbike gear and keep it warm while he and Connie went to see Bevan.

'Bevan, this is my husband Peddyr Quirk.'

Connie had been right when she said Bevan was terminally ill. It was plain to see his health was failing fast. The strain of the morning had also taken its toll. He was far from 'right as rain' as Webster had said.

The Quirks took a seat at his bedside and Connie resumed taking notes while Peddyr sought permission to make a voice recording. He was careful to note the date and time and full verbal consent from Bevan. 'And the camera in your room is recording us,' he added. 'We want you to feel safe and secure in the knowledge that we are here to help.'

Bevan gave a dismissive wave. 'I have to tell you this. You have to know. I buried the body because I was ordered to. Austin was in the house. He took the letter from me. He told me to bury her. It was then I knew all the things in the letter from the woman—'

'Christine Fowler,' Connie reminded him.

'Yes, that was the name. The letter from Christine Fowler was all true. I knew it was because he was so desperate to cover up the suicide. I knew it was his sister hanging from the tree.'

'You had chance to read the suicide note that she pushed through the letterbox. What did it say?' Peddyr asked.

'The letter said she was killing herself because of what he had done and because he was the reason she had her child taken away from her. All she wanted was to have her baby back.'

'She hung herself as a sort of punishment. Knowing that he would have to call the police and there would be questions asked,' Peddyr stated.

Bevan nodded slowly and deliberately. 'I'm certain of it.' He let out a weak sigh before adding, 'He didn't tell the police though. He covered it up and I helped him. We both cut the woman down, we both carried her across the lawn. He took the letter and burned it. I told this to Mrs Harkness on Sunday, and she said she would call the police.' As a single tear trickled down his left cheek he said, 'Now you can tell Olivia Harkness to come back and finish the bloody job. I'm done.'

49

A FEW WEEKS LATER

'The service was very fitting,' Monica said. 'They did Christine proud. All the pomp and ceremony with enough space for the family to grieve in their own ways. What her husband had to say was so heart-warming.'

Connie reflected on Desmond Fowler's words and couldn't disagree. 'She stood up for what she believed was right. You have to admire that about her. She wasn't going to let Mr H off the hook. And in a way, she achieved what she set out to do. This story won't disappear.'

Peddyr was away on another case and couldn't attend but Monica stepped in to accompany Connie to pay their respects to Christine Fowler's family. After the funeral service, she and Connie had decided to head off for coffee and cake at a local bookshop rather than head to the town hall for cucumber sandwiches and to mill about avoiding the Phwaa-Phwaa set. Bernard Kershaw's wife Deidre was sure to have been there and she was one to be avoided at all costs. 'Did you see the ghastly hat she was wearing at the church?' Connie asked, not expecting an answer. 'Can't abide that woman. Bernie is so much better off without her.'

The bookshop was an eccentric sort of place where readers were encouraged to browse, to have a drink and take time to chat with fellow bookworms. The two ladies found a quiet corner of the crime fiction section and talked in hushed tones, avoiding use of full names. Even if they were overheard, the listener would think they were discussing the plot of a whodunit.

'I thought young Miss C handled things remarkably well,' said Connie. 'What do you think she'll do with the information?'

Monica laughed. 'The moment I met that girl I was struck by her inquisitive nature. Add to that her strong moral compass and I would say she won't let this drop. Once the court cases and inquests are over, you mark my words, she'll let fly. She wants her mother to be remembered as the woman I met. The feisty, desperate mother who would try anything to find her child, even begging help from a brother she loathed and probably feared. No wonder she never set out to find him. Miss C was very much a wanted baby and, now she knows that, it's a good outcome.'

'She also knows what Mr H was guilty of as a child, and as an adult who rejected every plea for assistance, a man who has no remorse.' Connie sighed, feeling empathy for how Cara had taken this news, how she had wept and how she had vented her anger. 'I knew he'd get off the hook somehow. His wife did the necessary and he gets away with it.'

'Our friendly neighbourhood DS tells me the forensics from a certain pet cemetery near the river Ouse seem to support Bevan's statement as far as finding what they were expecting. If by some miracle they can find evidence to connect Mr H with burying the body, he will have to hope those barristers he's so fond of hiring will do a good job. Personally, I think they should throw the book at him. The big red book... "This is your Life Sentence".' She snorted at the irony of her own joke.

'But so far he hasn't been charged with a thing,' Connie said, throwing her hands up. 'Not enough proof he was even at the hall the night you-know-who was killed. The letters sent to us that were in her possession can't be used as evidence. There's nothing to back up that they are a true account of anything. And they've only got the words of a dying man to go on when it comes to who put the body with the pets. So frustrating. At least the fake V got what was coming to her. On remand, I hear. Good job.'

She looked across at Monica who seemed to be in a daydream. 'Does Miss C look much like her mother?' she asked.

Monica snapped out of her reverie, blinking. 'From what I can remember, yes she does. V was not much taller than you, lots of fine sandy coloured hair. Not ginger, more of a light blonde but not brassy. She wasn't in a good state when I met with her, mentally or physically, but if you could see past the bedraggled self-neglect then she was quite an attractive woman. And if you notice the gap between Miss C's front teeth, I'd say that is a family trait. Her mother had the same, and Mr H himself.'

Connie was amazed that neither she nor Peddyr had made that observation, but Monica had noticed. Clearly, the subject of the case study she had carried out all those years ago had stuck with her. Had bothered her. Now she too had an ending, one tinged with considerable sadness.

'I hear they've just released the body,' Monica said.

'That will please Miss C. She's going back to Yorkshire any day soon. She can't put it off much longer. This place is too full of bad memories for her, except for Lois of course.'

'Personally,' Monica went on, 'I think Mr H the Younger will get a much lighter sentence than his mother. And when he's sentenced, that starchy wife of his will be heading straight for the divorce lawyers, so he won't have much to look forward to when he is released. If what they say in the press is true, he was there but failed to stop his mother. They say he bottled it, left the hall, and crashed his car. He's nowhere near as despicable as the unhinged Mrs H Senior. She's going straight to jail, do not pass go, because she is as bad as her husband, if not worse. Fancy protecting him. Is the money, the prestige, the family name... so important you would kill to protect it?'

Connie finished the dregs of her coffee and reached for her handbag. 'It would appear so in her case. Those horses will have to manage without her. Anyway, it's time to go. I need to change out of these clothes, black is not my favourite colour. Besides, I have last minute wedding planning to do with Joe and Alleyn. March is nearly upon us.' She blew a kiss at Monica. 'Thanks for keeping me company. Stay in touch.'

Monica waved at her as she too gathered her belongings together. 'My pleasure. I will. There is bound to be news before too long.'

* * *

Cara hated goodbyes and she was having no luck in stemming the flow of tears as she gave Lois a final hug a month later. 'I'll be gone by the time you get home from school tomorrow, but Dan will take care of you. He has my approval and I'm thrilled you let him move in. I want an invite to the wedding and if you have children – name the little girl after me.'

Lois was in much the same emotional state and was sobbing loudly between words. 'Cara or Caroline, which would you prefer?' She held Cara tight and said, 'You already stayed much longer than you planned. I'm glad you did. I wanted to hear the end of the story.'

Lois had sat with Cara when Connie and Monica had visited three weeks previously to share with her what they knew of the real Vera Hudson, a woman who always went by the name Verity or simply V, but never Vera. The tears they both shed now were almost as torrential as the ones they experienced then.

The emotions had been tough to cope with, especially the searing grief when Cara was told that her real mother had died a year to the day after she was born. Anger was hard to contain when she realised that Verity had the chance of finding her baby taken from her by Austin Harkness to keep his dirty secret safe. Astonishment hit her like a blow to the head when she was told that in fact Christine Fowler had fought for Verity and never given up. Cara had been so close to knowing about her mother, so close to tapping into the truth through Christine. Worst of all, Verity had been wrongly labelled, wrongly accused of things she never did and ultimately her life had been ruined at the hands of her own brother. A tragedy in every sense.

Lois finally relented and let her go. 'What are you going to do? How are you going to rewrite the family history?'

'I am going to be brave,' Cara replied. 'I owe her that much. Her and Christine.'

They parted on the landing as they had done so many times before, but this occasion was more final. Visits to see each other would happen, but it wouldn't be the same.

Back in her flat, Cara made straight for the kitchen. 'A brew. A strong brew. Then we negotiate.' The budgies livened up at her words and they watched with interest as she settled into the office chair, phone to her ear. Most other belongings were packed in boxes, ready for the removal van to arrive first thing in the morning.

'Konrad? It's Cara. Don't speak, just listen. I will assist you in making the "best ever", potentially award-winning TV documentary about the Harkness family. These are my conditions. Number one, and no exceptions to this: a non-disclosure agreement about me as your source. Number two: as well as paying me a substantial amount for the information I'm about to tell you, you will make an equivalent payment to the mental health charity Rethink. And number three: you are to pay for a memorial service, a burial in a Scottish graveyard in Paisley, and a proper headstone.'

'Who for?'

'Verity Anne Hudson.'

'Right. One small problem... they will only release the body to a family member.' She heard him gulp. 'Are you talking about Austin Harkness? He'll never let me anywhere near... What's going on?'

'Konrad, listen carefully... They *have* released the body to a family member and it's certainly *not* Austin Harkness. The family member is the daughter of Verity and Ray Hudson. Her name is Caroline Hudson, and she needs you to tell the truth behind the lies.'

ABOUT THE AUTHOR

Alison Morgan lives in rural Bedfordshire UK with her engineer husband and bonkers dog. She spent several decades working on the front line of NHS Mental Health Services and latterly as a specialist nurse and clinical manager for a dedicated psychosis service across her home county. However, when a heart problem brought her career to a juddering halt, Alison needed to find a way of managing her own sanity. She took up writing. Her intention was to produce a set of clinical guidelines for student nurses but instead a story that had been lurking in her mind for some years came spewing forth onto the pages of what became her first novel.

Since then she has become an established crime writer, unable to stem the flow of ideas. From a writing shack at the top of her garden she creates stories with memorable characters, always with a sprinkling of humour, often drawing on years of experience in the world of psychiatry where the truth can be much stranger than fiction. To find out more about Alison please check her website **www.abmorgan.co.uk**.

Connie and Peddyr have recently joined the Twittersphere. To follow their daily antics you'll find them lurking on Twitter @TheQuirkyFiles.

ACKNOWLEDGMENTS

As always, I would like to say a special thank you to the 'book parents', Rebecca and Adrian, at Hobeck Books. Their dedication is beyond admirable. A special thanks to Jayne Mapp for being able to see inside my head and produce great Quirk Files covers for the series. The polishing of the book is down to Helen Gray, editor extraordinaire, who took the time to chat and get to know me.

And finally, a big thank you goes to the friends, readers, reviewers, and bloggers who help me to believe in myself. Yes, Donna Morfett, I do include you in all those categories!

THE QUIRK FILES BY A B MORGAN

OLD DOGS, OLD TRICKS: A QUIRK FILES NOVELLA

David Corcoran is dead. Did he die of natural causes, or was he murdered? His daughter seems to think there is more to his sudden death at the sleepy Blackthorne Lakes Retirement Village than a case of another day, another resident meets their maker. Enter Peddyr and Connie Quirk, newly formed PI husband-and-wife team, to 'act' as residents to see if they can sniff out the truth. Can they pull it off? Will Connie convince the Blackthorne golfing set that she's a real resident? Is there more to this story than simply old man dies happy?

To download your free copy of the prequel to the Quirk Files series, please go to the Hobeck Books website **www. hobeck.net**.

OVER HER DEAD BODY: THE QUIRK FILE BOOK ONE

A B MORGAN

OVER HER
DEAD
BODY

THE QUIRK FILES BOOK ONE

CAN GABBY'S
DEATH CHANGE
HER LIFE?

Gabby Dixon is dead. That's news to her...
Recently divorced and bereaved, Gabby Dixon is trying to start a new chapter in her life.

As her new life begins, it ends. On paper at least.
But Gabby is still very much alive. As a woman who likes to be in control, this situation is deeply unsettling.

She has two crucial questions: who would want her dead, and why?
Enter Peddyr and Connie Quirk. husband-and-wife private

investigators. Gabby needs their help to find out who is behind her sudden death.

The truth is a lot more sinister than a simple case of stolen identity.

Over Her Dead Body **is a 'what if' tale full of brilliantly drawn characters, quirky humour and dark plot twists**

Praise for Over Her Dead Body

'OMG WHAT A PAGE TURNER!! … I finally turned the last page at 2am.' Peggy
'This really is one of the best books I have ever read!' Pat
'A clever, clever read.' Livia
'A hope there are plans for this to be a series.' Dee
'excellent.' Billy
'A compelling read.' Kes
'Just couldn't put it down.' Lynn
'Couldn't put this down.' Janet

THROTTLED: THE QUIRK FILES BOOK TWO

Scott Fletcher is dead – his lifeless body in a pool of blood.

Sarah Holden's life is turned upside-down the day she is discovered with her fiancé's body next to the motorbike he'd been working on. She has blood on her hands, but the screams do not come.

If she didn't kill him, then who did?

The answer seems too easy. The likely culprit too obvious.

With a dead husband and now dead fiancé, is Sarah just unlucky in love?

Peddyr and Connie Quirk, husband-and-wife private investigators, are brought in to unravel the tangle, prove Sarah's innocence and find the true culprit. As they are about to discover, the truth is sometimes much more than skin deep.

Praise for Throttled

'Brilliant story you will love trying to figure it out. I love Connie, she is my hero!' Jan
'This series is just going to get better.' Terry
'Brilliant story.' Janet
'It's a top story, brilliant characters, and the Quirks. I could not ask for more!' Susan
'I can't wait for the next Quirk adventure.' Deb

HOBECK BOOKS – THE HOME OF GREAT STORIES

We hope you've enjoyed reading this novel by A B Morgan.

Hobeck Books offers a number of short stories and novellas, including the prequel to this series *Old Dogs, Old Tricks*, free for subscribers in the compilation *Crime Bites*.

- *Echo Rock* by Robert Daws
- *Old Dogs, Old Tricks* by AB Morgan

- *The Silence of the Rabbit* by Wendy Turbin
- *Never Mind the Baubles: An Anthology of Twisted Winter Tales* by the Hobeck Team (including many of the Hobeck authors and Hobeck's two publishers)
- *The Clarice Cliff Vase* by Linda Huber
- *Here She Lies* by Kerena Swan
- *The Macnab Principle* by R.D. Nixon
- *Fatal Beginnings* by Brian Price
- *A Defining Moment* by Lin Le Versha
- *Saviour* by Jennie Ensor

Also please visit the Hobeck Books website for details of our other superb authors and their books, and if you would like to get in touch, we would love to hear from you.

Hobeck Books also presents a weekly podcast, the Hobcast, where founders Adrian Hobart and Rebecca Collins discuss all things book related, key issues from each week, including the ups and downs of running a creative business. Each episode includes an interview with one of the people who make Hobeck possible: the editors, the authors, the cover designers. These are the people who help Hobeck bring great stories to life. Without them, Hobeck wouldn't exist. The Hobcast can be listened to from all the usual platforms but it can also be found on the Hobeck website: **www.hobeck.net/hobcast**.

OTHER HOBECK BOOKS TO EXPLORE

Swindled

'Definitely one you can't put down.' Nicki Williams

'What a great read this is.' C. White

'Page three hundred and eleven is reached before you can even blink!' Piers Rowlandson

'…will definitely takes your breath away…an absolute stunner of a thriller…' Surjit's Book Blog

'He's out there somewhere. He's taken everything from me, and … I hate him!'

Lottie
Beautiful, but a little spoilt, Lottie Thorogood leads a charmed life. Returning home from horse riding one day, she finds a

stranger, drinking tea in the family drawing room – a stranger who will change her life, forever.

Hannah

After a bad decision cut short her police career, Hannah Sandlin is desperate to make her mark as a private investigator. She knows she has the skills, but why won't anyone take her seriously? She's about to become embroiled in a mystery that will finally put those skills to the test and prove her doubters wrong. It will also bring her a friend for life.

Vincent

Vincent Rocchino has spent his life charming the ladies, fleecing them and fleeing when things turn sour. How long can he keep running before his past catches up with him?

Blood Loss

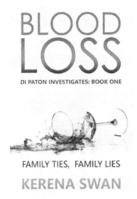

'…in the same league as Ian Rankin and L J Ross…' Graham Rolph

'My arms broke out in goose-bumps! Wow!' Susan Hampson, *Books From Dust Till Dawn*

Sarah
With one eye on the rear view mirror and the other on the road ahead, Sarah is desperate to get as far away from the remote Scottish cabin as she can without attracting attention. But being inconspicuous isn't easy with a black eye and clothes soaked in blood...
... and now the fuel tank is empty.

DI Paton
When a body is discovered in a remote cabin in Scotland, DI Paton feels a pang of guilt as he wonders if this is the career break he has been waiting for. But the victim is unidentifiable and the killer has left few clues.

Jenna
With the death of her father and her mother's failing health, Jenna accepts her future plans must change but nothing can prepare her for the trauma yet to come.

Fleeing south to rebuild her life Sarah uncovers long-hidden family secrets. Determined to get back what she believes is rightfully hers, Sarah thinks her future looks brighter. But Paton is still pursuing her...

... and he's getting closer.

ALSO BY A B MORGAN

A Justifiable Madness
Divine Poison
The Camera Lies
Stench
Death by Indulgence
The Bloodline Will